TRACEY JANE JACKSON

BOUND BY TEARS

Book #6 in the Cauld Ane Series

Sale of this book without a front cover may be unauthorized. If this book is coverless, it may have been reported to the publisher as "unsold or destroyed" and neither the author nor the publisher may have received payment for it.

Bound by Tears is a work of fiction. Names, characters, places, and incidents are the products of the author's imagination and are used fictitiously. Any resemblance to actual events, locales, or persons, living or dead, is entirely coincidental.

Cover Photo
Couple:
Tracey Jane Jackson

Landscape:
Jökulsárlón Glacial Lake
by
Ira Goldstein

Cover Art
Jackson Jackson

Cover Models
Gordon Avery
Jess Kirsch

2014 Tracey Jane Jackson
Copyright © 2014 by Tracey Jane Jackson
All rights reserved.

ISBN: 978-1501009112

Published in the United States

"Tracey Jane Jackson will enthrall you with her talent for vivid story-telling, and her gift for creating real characters that will make you ache and sigh!" *Julianne MacLean – USA Today Bestselling Author*

"I've followed Tracey Jane Jackson's Cauld Ane series from book one and am constantly impressed by the way her characters keep growing and developing. Her dialogue is realistic and witty and her fast-paced storylines keep the series progressing nicely. I've enjoyed each Bound book, but Bound by Dreams is my favorite so far. I can't wait to see what happens next!" *Amanda Washington – Author of the Perseverance Series and the Chronicles of the Broken Series*

"Sizzling and original!" *Leah Banicki – Historical Author*

Other books in the Cauld Ane Series

Bound by Blood
Cauld Ane #1

Bound by Fire
Cauld Ane #2

Bound by Secrets
Cauld Ane #3

Bound by Song
Cauld Ane #4

Bound by Dreams
Cauld Ane #5

Other books by Tracey Jane Jackson

The Bride Price
Civil War Brides Series, Book #1

The Bride Found
Civil War Brides Series, Book #2

The Bride Spy
Civil War Brides Series, Book #3

The Bride Ransom
Civil War Brides Series, Book #4

The Rebel Bride
Civil War Brides Series, Book #5

The Bride Star
Civil War Brides Series, Book #6

The Bride Pursued
Civil War Brides Series, Book #7

The Bride Accused
Civil War Brides Series, Book #8

The Brides United
Civil War Brides Series, Book #9

Acknowledgements

Ása Erlingsdóttir, thanks again for the Icelandic translations!

Gordon & Jess…thanks for your gorgeous faces!

Thanks to Ellen and Amanda for the edits and critiques…you guys are amazing!

For My Girls
Vandy, Caren Ann, and Kim – you guys are the greatest Street Team Leads on the planet!

For the Brihards & Cauldaniacs
Thanks to the hard working members of my Street Team! I wouldn't be here without you!

For Brady, Lulu & Kai
Love you guys!

PROLOGUE

**Portland, Oregon
Ten Years ago**

JESSKA SHANE RUSHED out of the last class of her last year of high school and ran smack dab into her boyfriend of nearly four years. Brady chuckled as he wrapped his arms around her and lifted her off her feet. "Hi beautiful."

Brady King was six feet tall with dark-blond hair, chocolate-brown eyes, and the epitome of a high school jock. Quarterback on the varsity team and top wrestler in his weight class, but also funny as hell, and a guy Jesska admired greatly. She'd met him at church when she was fourteen, but both sets of parents had made them wait until she was sixteen before they could officially date.

They'd spent a lot of time together over the two years they weren't "official," but Jesska tried to follow the rules, and Brady felt it was important to respect their parents. Sometimes that irritated the hell out of Jesska. She often wanted to sneak away to somewhere private whenever they could, but Brady would always talk her into doing what was right. She knew beyond a shadow of a doubt she was going to marry him, and she had a feeling he'd propose before they headed off to college.

"Can you believe we're done?" she asked, looping her arms around his neck and kissing him.

"None too soon," he said as he set her on her feet again. "I can't believe your parents are going to let you come to Paris with us."

"*Please*." She grinned. "I turn eighteen in a week, plus they're more worried I'm a prude. They kind of think you are too."

"A prude? Not true!" He flexed his left arm, his purity ring sitting proud on his finger. "Who said sexy couldn't be moral?"

Jesska laughed. "Yes, I can see your humility is working overtime."

"Hey guys."

They turned to see Brady's best friend Jason jogging toward them. Jesska gripped Brady's hand a little tighter. He glanced down at her with a frown, but she forced a smile and he focused back on Jason. "Hey, bud. You ready to lose at bowling?"

"You mean, am I ready to smoke you?"

Brady chuckled. "We'll see. I take it you're coming today?"

"Hell, yeah. I'm so over this dump…can't believe I have to do a class over summer or I won't graduate."

Jason Rogers had been Brady's best friend since middle school. A couple of years ago, Jason had started smoking pot and decorating his body with tattoos and piercings, but Brady stayed close, hoping he'd turn a corner. His parents had both died of cancer, so Jason was forced to live with his grandparents, which didn't seem to be going so well.

Jesska used to adore Jason, but lately he'd gotten weird, trying to corner her alone at school and touching her "accidentally." In general, he just creeped her out.

"We'll meet you there, bud," Brady said.

Jason glanced at Jesska, but didn't say anything as he nodded and strolled out the door toward the parking lot.

"Hey." Brady squeezed her hand. "What's going on with you?"

"What do you mean?"

"You get all squirrely around Jase now. Did something happen?"

"Nope." She shook her head and forced a smile. "Let's go, Bradykins. I'm starving."

Brady frowned, but he let it go. He always let it go, giving her space to tell him whatever she needed to tell him in her own time. Brady had driven this morning, so she tugged him out of the building and to his car. He opened the passenger door for her, but pulled her close before she climbed in, stroking her cheek as he smiled at her. "Do you know how much I love you?"

She nodded. "You tell me every day how much you love me, so I have some idea."

He leaned down and kissed her, and she found her hands sliding under his T-shirt and up his back. She didn't know if she could possibly ever love another human being as much as she did him. It was overwhelming at times.

"Get a room, losers!"

Jesska giggled, breaking the kiss and following the sound of her best friend's voice. "Jealous much?"

Amanda Winkler had long, dark-red hair, thick and curly, the kind most folks tried to achieve with hot rollers and curling irons. She and Jesska had been best friends since freshman year when they sat next to each other in biology. Amanda laid her hands over her heart and groaned. "I'm so, so jealous."

"Are you coming with us?" Brady asked.

"Not today." She held up her keys. "I have Marilyn."

Marilyn was Amanda's VW Rabbit that was held together with duck tape and a prayer.

Brady chuckled. "Nice."

"We'll see you over there," Jesska said.

"Sounds good." Amanda climbed into her car and took off, the VW backfiring its way out of the parking lot.

"It's getting worse," Brady observed.

Jesska laughed. "I don't get why she won't just sell it and get something that isn't destined to kill her one day."

"Me neither." Brady stepped back. "In you go."

Jesska climbed into her seat and secured her seatbelt while Brady walked to the driver's side. They took off toward the bowling alley on SE Morrison, which wasn't far from their high school in downtown Portland.

The majority of Lincoln High School's senior class squeezed into the large bowling alley, commandeering every lane available, although not everyone chose to bowl. Jesska gave Jason a wide berth, particularly because of the sidelong, creepy stares he managed to give her.

When Brady bowled another gutter ball, he shook his head good-naturedly and then frowned down at his phone.

"Everything okay?" Jesska asked.

"My sister's locked herself out of the house," he complained.

"Don't your parents have that spare key...the one under the rock in the backyard?"

"Oh, they have three. All of which she still has in her car, which she has also managed to lock herself out of. Either I go help her or she has to call Triple A." He shook his head. "I should make her call a tow truck."

"You're not far. Just go, babe."

"It's the principal of the thing."

Jesska laughed. "I get it. Carly's a little absentminded. Just go. I'll play your turns."

Brady smiled, leaning down to kiss her. "This is why I love you."

"Because I'm a better bowler than you?"

"Yes, exactly." He kissed her one more time and then left to help his sister.

Jesska bowled a strike and a spare with Brady's next turns and then nature called, so she turned to Amanda. "Hey, Winky. Play my turn if I'm not back in time, okay?"

"You got it," Amanda said.

Jesska finished up in the bathroom and took some time to fix her makeup. Stepping outside, she found Jason lurking.

"Hey," he said, and pushed away from the wall.

"Hi." She glanced around, her stomach churning to find them alone in the hallway. "Did you need something?"

"Um, yeah." Jason gave her a leering smile. "You."

He shoved her back into the bathroom and up against the wall, locking the door and pushing his thumb into her throat. "If you scream, I will press on this vein right here and make you pass out." He kissed her neck and she tried not to cry out.

"Stop, Jason. Don't do this," she whispered, hoping someone would bang on the door and interrupt him.

"Come on, Jess, you know you want this. I don't know why you're fighting it."

When he kissed her, she bit his lip and he yelped, but still managed to keep hold of her. He slapped her. "Bitch!"

She had shifted so she was in a better position, but he had her so tight, she didn't have any leverage. "No!" she screamed. He hit her again, but at least it meant he had to back up a bit. With all the strength she could muster, she kneed him in the groin and ran. She heard him yell obscenities as the bathroom door closed and she rushed back to the group.

"Jess, you okay?" Amanda asked. "Oh, my god, your lip is bleeding. What happened?"

Jesska laid her fingers over her swelling mouth. "Jason just attacked me."

Amanda glanced at something over her head. "Okay, Brady's back, let's go tell him." She wrapped an arm around Jesska and led her to Brady.

"Babe? What happened?" he asked, studying her face. "Come outside for a second where it's quiet."

She nodded and let him lead her out to the parking lot, bursting into tears as she slid into his arms.

"Oh, babes, tell me what happened," he said.

"Jason attacked me in the bathroom." She shook her head. "Shoved me into the ladies' room and locked the door."

"What the hell?" He stroked her back. "Is he still in there?"

She shrugged. "I don't know. I'm so sorry, Brady."

"Why are you apologizing?"

"Because I don't know if I did something to make him think—"

"Is this why you've been so weird around him lately?" He stroked her cheek.

She nodded. "He does stuff like rub against me, but then is all apologetic like he didn't do it on purpose, and I can't prove he's being a perv, but he's just so gross."

"Bastard."

"I'm sorry, Brady. I didn't want to tell you in case I was wrong. I didn't want to ruin your friendship."

"It's okay, babes. I'll take care of it," he said, his face forming a rather terrifying expression she'd never seen before. Anger and disgust twisted his normally smiling face into something she didn't like.

"Can we just go home?" she asked.

"No. I need to have a conversation with my good *friend*, Jason."

"Here? Now?"

"As good a time as any," Brady said with a nod.

"Make sure you do it around other people. I don't trust him not to hit you or something."

"I can handle myself, Jess."

"I'm not saying you can't." She grabbed his arm. "He's just so slimy."

Brady leaned down and kissed her gently. "Don't worry. I'll just end our friendship, tell him to stay the hell away from you, and we'll go to Paris. Okay?"

Jesska smiled. "Okay."

She followed him back inside and over to their group. Amanda raised an eyebrow in question as Brady dragged Jason aside, away from eavesdroppers, but still within sight.

"Is he going to kill Jason?" Amanda asked.

Jesska nodded. "I think he wants to."

"Maybe he'll leave you alone now. Good riddance, I say. I found your purse." Amanda handed it to Jesska. "It was in the hallway."

"Oh, thanks, Winky. I totally forgot about it."

"I hope Jason doesn't make a scene," Amanda said. "He should just leave."

"I know. But he'll probably be all weird…he's always weird."

Jesska watched as Brady and Jason argued in the middle of the bowling alley, but what happened next was so out of left field, she wasn't sure she could believe what she was seeing. When someone screamed, Jesska realized all too quickly, her world was about to come crashing down.

"Knife! He's got a knife!"

As Brady collapsed on the floor, Jason took off, to where, she didn't know and didn't care. All she cared about was getting to Brady. Falling beside him, she saw blood flowing from his chest. She pressed her hands against it to try and stop the bleeding. "Someone call 9-1-1!" she bellowed.

"I'm on it," Amanda said, her cell phone to her ear.

"Brady, come on Bradykins, open your eyes."

He blinked his eyes open with a grimace. "I didn't count on a knife," he rasped.

"I know," she said. "Try to stay awake, okay? Paramedics are coming."

"Hey, I love you."

She forced back tears. "I love you, too."

He coughed. "I can't breathe."

"Help's coming." She pressed harder on his wound.

He closed his eyes again, his breathing labored.

"Open your eyes!" she screamed. "Open your damn eyes."

He did, but they were glassy. "Tell my family I love 'em, okay?"

"No! No, I won't tell them anything. You're going to tell them," she sobbed. "You're going to be fine. We're going to get married and have lots and lots of babies." His arm dropped to his side and Jesska shook her head. "Brady King, you open your eyes right now! Right this minute!"

Gentle hands wrapped around her arms and tugged. "Jess, the ambulance is here."

She glanced up to find the EMTs wheeling a gurney in and opening their bags. "Miss, if you'll give us some room."

Jesska nodded, stumbling to her feet and into the arms of her friend. Once they had Brady loaded onto the stretcher, she tried to follow, but the paramedics wouldn't let her.

Amanda turned her around. "We need to call his parents. And yours. Jess! We need to call your parents."

Jesska nodded. "I'll get my purse."

"No, wait." Amanda pulled her back. "You're covered in blood."

"What?"

"Blood. You have blood on you. I'll get your phone, okay? Here come the police. We'll tell them what we know and then we'll get you cleaned up."

Jesska didn't fully understand everything Amanda was saying, but nodded her head and stayed where she was. She managed to give the police a statement, at least she thought she did, and then Amanda was guiding her to the bathroom and helping her wash her hands. She held out a bright green hoodie someone had retrieved from Marilyn, and Jesska stared at it, not sure why she needed it. Amanda helped Jesska remove her blood-soaked shirt and then, much like a mother did for a child, slid the hoodie over her head and guided her arms into the sleeves.

"Jess?"

"Hmm?"

"I called your parents." Amanda shoved Jesska's soiled clothing into a plastic bag and handed her her purse. "They said they'll meet you at the hospital, okay? Come on, I'll drive you."

Jesska nodded. "Yeah, okay."

She prayed the whole way to the hospital, truly believing that Brady would be fine. He'd come out of surgery a little battered and stitched up, and maybe they'd have to postpone Paris, but they'd just go a little later in the summer. Everything would be okay.

"We're almost there," Amanda said.

Jesska smiled. "Thanks for taking care of me, Winky."

"Always, buddy." Amanda glanced at her with a smile and then focused back on the road.

"Brady's going to be so mad."

"About?"

"Having to postpone Paris."

"Huh?"

"He'll probably need some time to recover," Jesska said. "Even as much of a badass as he is, I don't think he'll be able to go to Paris in two weeks."

"No, I wouldn't expect so," Amanda said.

Jesska pulled her compact out of her purse. "Why didn't you tell me how bad I looked?"

"Jess, it doesn't matter what you look like."

"I can't have Brady waking up and seeing *this*." Jesska didn't know if Amanda said anything, more interested in fixing her appearance for

Brady. Jesska focused on making herself look as perfect as possible. She wiped at a wrinkled on the borrowed hoodie, grabbed a wet towelette from her purse to try to get some of the blood off her jeans. Her need for everything in its place was on overdrive and anyone watching her would have understood why her siblings had taken to calling her "Messka." She hated disorder or dirt of any kind.

"We're here," Amanda said, and opened her door.

Jesska climbed out of the car, shoving her compact back in her purse as she followed Amanda into Emergency and to the nurses' desk. "We're looking for Brady King."

"Jess."

She turned to find her half-brother, Cameron, rushing toward her. Cameron Shane was tall, dark, and one of the nicest people on the planet. A musician by passion, but having graduated the police academy a few years earlier, he was working towards his detective's badge and played at church on the weekends to "always remember what was important." He was just about perfect in Jesska's mind. The epitome of the best big brother a girl could ever hope for. She'd always had a bit of hero worship toward him.

"Cam, what are you doing here?" she asked.

"I was close by, but Dad's on his way." He pulled her in for a hug. "What happened?"

"Brady and Jason were arguing and Jason stabbed him," Jesska said. She refused to feel anything beyond this bare fact. There was only one possible outcome. "I just need to know how long his recovery time is going to be and how soon they can throw Jason in jail." She looked up at him. "We're going to Paris."

"I know, sissy."

"Brady King? We're looking for Brady King." A woman's frantic voice broke through Jesska's haze.

"If you will just take a seat, ma'am, someone will be out to speak with you shortly," the nurse said.

"Mrs. King," Jesska called.

"Oh, Jess, honey. Do you know anything? What happened?"

Jesska relayed the story, trying to give accurate information.

Brady's mom fell into one of the seats, her face ashen as tears streamed down her cheeks. Brady's dad arrived within minutes, and Jesska found herself having to relay the story again. She started when Cameron wrapped an arm around her shoulders and forced her to sit down. "What are you doing?"

He gripped her chin gently. "You're in shock, Jess. This is going to hit you, and when it does, I want you sitting down."

Jesska's heart raced when a doctor approached Brady's parents, pulling a chair up to sit facing them. "We did everything we could."

"So, he's okay, right?" Jesska jumped in.

"I'm sorry. No. We couldn't save him."

"No," she whispered as Brady's mother melted down beside her. "No. Wait, doctor, can you try again? Jason only stabbed him twice. People survive that kind of thing all the time."

"The knife pierced the heart, unfortunately, and he bled out before he got here. There was nothing we could do. I'm sorry."

"No!" Jesska rasped. "No, no, no, no."

"Can we see him?" Mrs. King asked, reaching out to squeeze Jesska's hand.

The doctor nodded. "We're getting him cleaned up, and if you'd like to see him when we're done, then yes, you can."

Jesska stared at her brother, not sure what she was supposed to do. She felt like her body was on fire and there was a buzzing in her brain whenever she tried to think...put any of this into some form of order. It was like the walls were closing in on her and she was claustrophobic.

* * *

Cameron sat beside his sister, watching her as the shock wore off. Her body started to shake and as she rocked back and forth in her seat, she kept saying Brady's name over and over again. He glanced up at her best friend. "Amanda, would you please ask the nurse for a bucket or something?"

Amanda nodded and rushed to the nurses' desk. She returned with a plastic container and Cameron slid it onto Jesska's lap just before she threw up.

"How did you know?" Amanda asked.

"It happens often with shock," Cameron said. "I've seen it before."

The doctor returned to take Brady's parents back to see him, but knelt before Jesska first.

He took her pulse and called for someone to bring her a blanket. "I think we should sedate you."

She shook her head. "No. I want to see Brady."

"I can't let you do that, I'm afraid. Only immediate family."

"But..." She burst into tears. "I want to see him. Please, can I see him?"

"Jess, I think it would be harder on you if you see him like this," Cameron said. "You want to remember him alive and well, right? He'd want to protect you from those types of memories."

"Shut up, Cameron! You don't know anything. I want to see him." She stared at Mrs. King. "Please can I go with you? *Please*."

"Sweetheart, you're not eighteen yet," Mr. King said, his wife obviously unable to answer. "But if your parents say it's all right, then I have no problem with you seeing him, okay?"

Jesska nodded, falling against Cameron before throwing up again. A nurse brought a clean bucket, removing the soiled one. The Kings went back with the doctor, and Jesska completely broke down. She sobbed uncontrollably and her body shook, despite the blanket. Cameron planned to talk to his father about getting her some heavy-duty sedatives to get her through a few days.

Their father arrived not long after Brady's parents left the emergency room. He sat down beside Jesska. "Is he okay?"

Cameron shook his head.

"They said he died, Daddy," Jesska mumbled. "But I don't believe them. I want to see him."

"I don't think that would be a good idea."

"Mr. King said I could see him," she said. "He said if you said it was okay, I could see him."

"Shhh, sweetheart," their father whispered. "People are starting to stare."

She forced herself to her feet and waved her hands around. "I don't give a rat's ass if people are starting to stare at me! I want to see him! I have to see him!"

Cameron stood, retrieving the dropped bucket from the floor and pulling his sister into his arms. "Okay, Jess. It's okay."

"I want to see him."

Cameron caught his father's eye and raised an eyebrow. His father shrugged, frowning, but gave him a reluctant nod.

"I'll go with you, okay?" Cameron offered.

Jesska nodded into his chest. "Yes. Okay."

"Sit with Dad for a minute and I'll go talk to the nurse."

She sat beside her father and Cameron made his way to the desk. "Hi. My sister would like to see Brady King. She's been given permission by our father and Mr. King."

"I'll call back there and see what I can do."

"I appreciate that," Cameron said, and headed back to his sister.

A few minutes later, Jesska's name was called and Cameron took her hand and led her through the automatic doors. She shuffled behind the nurse, and Cameron wondered if this was such a good idea.

* * *

As Jesska followed the woman down the hallway, she felt like she was in some kind of alternate universe. Her emotions swung from calm to panic every few seconds, mostly because she still didn't believe that the love of her life was dead. Everyone had it wrong.

The nurse led her into a brightly lit room. Brady was lying face up, a sheet covering his lower body, his perfectly formed chest exposed, the blood that she remembered seeping through his clothing no longer visible. Just an open wound.

"He's so pale," she whispered. Cameron took her hand, but she pulled away and stepped toward Brady. She ran her hand up one of his chiseled arms, unprepared for how cold he felt. Laying her palm against his chest, she leaned down and kissed his cheek. "Wake up now, Bradykins. I think the joke has gone far enough. It's not really funny anymore."

He didn't respond, and Jesska stared at him. Only, it wasn't him. Everything that was Brady was gone. His essence, his energy, *he* was gone. She allowed the sadness to wash over her. She was going to feel this. All of it. She laid her cheek on his chest and let her tears fall.

"Jess?" Cameron said, gently. "I think we should go."

"Just one more minute," she begged as she kissed Brady's chest, then his face again. "I love you, Brady King. I will love you always. You are it for me. I will never love anyone else. I will carry you with me forever and ever and ever." With one last gentle kiss on his lips, she let Cameron lead her out of the room and then out of the hospital.

The next few days were filled with people, some Jesska knew, others she didn't. Jason had been captured and was being held without bond until trial. The prosecutor would try him on first-degree murder, even though it wasn't clear yet if his actions had been premeditated.

The night before Jesska's graduation commencement, Brady's parents arrived and asked to speak with her alone. She led them into the living room and sat facing them by the fire. Mrs. King looked exhausted and very, very sad.

"We have a few things for you, honey," Mr. King said. "Things that Brady would have wanted you to have."

"Okay."

Mr. King took the paper bag he'd brought with him and set it on the floor. He pulled out a smaller gift bag and handed it to her. "I know he'd want you to have his purity ring. It's probably far too big for you, so we bought you a chain in case you ever want to wear it."

"Oh. Thank you," she said, pulling the ring from the bag. It matched hers perfectly. They'd bought them together as an outward sign of their commitment to their faith and each other. She kissed it and held it against her chest.

"I have some photos in here that I know he'd want you to have. I made sure to scan them so we'd have copies, but thought you might like the printed versions. I would be happy to e-mail you the scanned versions as well."

Jesska nodded. "Yes, please. Thank you."

Mr. King then pulled out a small blue box and handed it to her. With shaking hands, Jesska took the gift and opened it. Inside sat a white-gold engagement ring with a diamond that was small, but perfect.

"He was going to propose to you at the top of the Eiffel Tower. He'd talked to your dad and had gotten permission…we had it all planned." He reached out and squeezed her hand. "If you want to wear it, you can, sweetheart, but if you don't, we understand that too."

Jesska swallowed, trying to force back the tears.

"We'll leave you to go through these other things alone. They were very special to Brady, and I know you'll need some time."

Jesska nodded, tears streaming freely down her face. Mr. King rose to his feet, helping his wife out of her seat, and Jesska walked them to the door. Before they left, Mrs. King wrapped her arms around Jesska. "You will forever be welcome in our family. Don't ever feel you have to call ahead or tiptoe around us. We love you as a daughter, and that will never change."

"Thank you," Jesska managed to squeak out. Brady's mother released her and stepped outside, her husband following after he'd hugged Jesska.

She closed the door behind them and dropped her forehead against the door.

"Jess?"

She faced her brother and wiped her tears. Cameron hadn't left her side since *that* day. He'd even gone so far as to pack a bag and move into the guest bedroom. "You okay?" he asked.

She shook her head, sobs welling up in her that she didn't think would ever stop.

Cameron pulled her against his chest. "Oh, Messka, it's going to be okay."

"No it won't. It'll never be okay," she cried, and pulled away from him. "It's my fault."

"What do you mean?"

"If I'd just kept my mouth shut, they wouldn't have argued, and Jason wouldn't have killed him." She dragged her nails up her arm, relishing the pain. "If I'd just said nothing, he'd be here with me. We'd be planning our trip and then getting married. It should have been me that died. Not him."

"What can I do?" he asked, his eyes searching hers. He was always wanting to fix things.

"Just leave me alone. Please. I just need to be alone." She grabbed the bag that Mr. King had brought and ran upstairs to her room, slamming the door behind her and collapsing on her bed in a puddle of tears. She opened the little blue box and stared at the engagement ring before lifting it out of the satin and sliding it on her finger. The ring clinked as it touched her purity ring, and it fit perfectly. Of course it did. Brady knew her better than anyone, and did everything right all the time.

With a determination she didn't really feel, Jesska forced herself to sit up. She gently poured the contents of the paper bag onto the middle of the bed. She sorted everything into chronological order. Her OCD tendencies were the only thing helping her to cope at the moment.

She smiled, running her finger over the face of the little teddy bear holding a heart that she'd given Brady on their first Valentine's Day. She remembered being so nervous. She'd never given a boy anything before, and she wasn't even sure he liked her. But he'd surprised her with roses and, when their parents weren't looking, he'd kissed her. It had been her first kiss ever and the first of many to come between them. She laid her fingers against her lips as the memories flooded her mind.

Jesska touched every item on her bed, committing the emotions to memory. Every picture tore at her heart more and more, but she forced herself to look at them, even though she thought she might die of sadness. A knock at her door sounded but she ignored it. It came again, and she scowled. "Go away."

Her brother pushed open the door. "I brought you something to eat."

"I'm not hungry."

Cameron set the tray on her desk and sat in her chair. "Jess, you have to eat. Megan and Sophia are downstairs, and Megan's threatening to come up here and force-feed you."

"Why?"

"Because you haven't eaten in two days!" Megan pointed out as she forced herself inside.

"I thought you were downstairs," Jesska grumbled. Her siblings were everywhere.

"I was. But now you're going to eat."

"I'm not hungry," she insisted.

"Well, you have to eat," Megan said gently as she pushed into Jesska's room. Megan was in her forties, but barely looked thirty. Jesska thought she could have modeled, but law was Megan's passion. That and her daughter, Sophia.

"I would just puke it up," Jesska muttered.

"Cam, give us a minute, okay?" Megan said.

Cameron nodded, rising to his feet and walking out the door, pulling it closed behind him. Megan sat on the edge of the mattress and slid Jesska's hair away from her face. "Did Brady's parents give you this stuff?"

Jesska nodded.

Megan grasped her hand, staring at the ring. "Oh, Jessie, it's beautiful. He did well, didn't he?"

Jesska took in a quick breath and nodded. "Did you know, too?"

Megan nodded with a smile. "Dad told us the other night."

"He was going to propose in Paris. I would have said yes."

"I know you would have, honey." Megan grabbed the plate from the tray and set it in front of Jesska. "I would like to know about everything on your bed, but I want you to tell me all the stories while you eat, okay?"

"I can't, Megan."

"Yes, you can." She held up the teddy bear. "What's this from?"

"It's from our first—"

"Eat," Megan demanded.

Jesska rolled her eyes and bit into a chip. She grabbed another one as Megan held up something else that interested her. Megan didn't stop asking questions until Jesska went to reach for a chip and her plate was empty. She'd polished off the sandwich, chips, even the pickle, without even realizing it.

"You did it," Megan said, and took her plate from her.

Jesska took the water she offered and took a swig before nodding. "I guess I did, huh?"

"How do you feel now?"

"My headache's better."

"I bet it is," Megan said. "Tomorrow's the big day."

"I'm not going."

"Do you think Brady would have wanted that?"

"Don't pretend to know what my fiancé would have wanted, Megan."

"Honey, he wasn't your fiancé."

"Shut up, Megan. He *was*! In my heart he was and he would have been in a matter of days." Jesska dissolved into tears.

Megan raised her hands in surrender. "Okay, honey, I'm sorry."

Jesska sighed. "No, *I'm* sorry. Everything is just so…I don't know…pointless."

Megan smiled. "The school is doing a tribute to Brady at graduation tomorrow, and I know that you'll regret it if you don't go. You might not think you will right now, but you will one day. I loved Brady. We all did. And I do think he wouldn't want you holed up in this house forever. He'd want you to go on. He'd hate to think you missed your ceremony because of him. He loved you, honey, and he would have wanted the best for you."

"Well the best would have been for him not to die, Megan! I can't live without him."

"I know it feels like that right now," Megan placated. "But unless you're planning to do something to do yourself in, you will find a way to move on, honey, I promise."

"Like anything I try wouldn't be interrupted by the hovering Shanes," Jesska complained.

Megan gasped. "Is that…are you wanting to do something?"

"No, Megan," Jesska said in irritation. "Don't worry, I won't kill myself. At least not quickly."

Her sister grasped her hands. "Look at me." When Jesska met her eyes, Megan smiled. "If you ever feel like everything's hopeless, you call me, okay? Anytime, any hour, any day."

Jesska nodded.

"I'm serious, Jessie."

"I get it," she grumbled.

"Promise."

"I promise," Jesska said.

Megan squeezed Jesska's hands and then stood. "Think about tomorrow, okay? We'll all be there to support you. You won't be alone. Dad said he canceled the after party, so you can just be with us."

Jesska nodded. "I'll think about it."

"That's all I ask." Megan gathered up the dishes and left the room.

For the most part, Jesska was left alone the rest of the evening. Cameron checked on her several times, but she guessed it was probably because Megan had told everyone to be on high alert.

Jesska did take a couple of her sedatives, something she'd been trying not to do, but the last two nights had been filled with horrific nightmares. If she did wake up and want to go to her graduation event, then she'd need to be rested. After emerging from her room just long enough to bid her family good night, she headed to bed, holding the tiny Valentine's bear close to her as she drifted into a drug-induced sleep.

* * *

Awakening the next day, Jesska made the choice to put on a brave face and join her class for commencement ceremonies. Her family oohed and ahhed as she walked into the family room in her red graduation cap and gown.

There was a lightness in the air during the ceremony, something Jesska thought she'd never experience again. Guilt welled up within seconds, and she stamped down her brief bit of levity. She was alive. He was dead. She had no right to be happy, even if it was for a second.

She shut herself down during the tribute, shut down even further when they called Brady's name and his father accepted his diploma on his behalf. She bit the inside of her cheek, trying to stay focused enough to hear her name. She felt a tap on her shoulder and then Amanda nudged her forward when her name sounded.

"Jesska Shane," the principle said again.

Jesska lifted the ring attached to the chain around her neck and kissed it. "I love you, Bradykins," she whispered as she walked on stage, took her diploma, and shook the principal's hand. She heard her family hooting over the crowd, but she refused to allow herself to feel their joy. She forced a smile and headed to the opposite side of the stage.

This is for you, Brady. Everything I do from now on will be for you.

* * *

The day she and Brady were scheduled to go to Paris arrived with a rare summer rainstorm. Jesska couldn't get out of bed. Her sadness so overwhelming, she could barely open her eyes. Her parents had been arguing for close to a week about "what to do with Jesska," and at this point, she didn't care if she never opened her eyes again, she just wanted out of her life.

Feeling overwhelming guilt, she slid out of bed and walked on aching legs to her bathroom. She hadn't realized just how much inactivity caused pain in a person's extremities. She opened her medicine cabinet and swore.

"Where the hell are you?" she grumbled as she went through every drawer, every cabinet, every crevice she could think of without luck. She sat on the toilet lid and dropped her face in her hands. Her parents had found it…damn it!

They'd found *it*. She had two more in her purse. She rushed to her bedroom and dumped the contents of her bag on her bed. The little blue box containing her relief landed on the duvet and fell upright like her saving grace. It had once held an engagement ring; now it held the peace she so desperately craved. She grabbed for it and locked her bedroom door before rushing back to her bathroom. Prying open the box, she carefully pulled out the razor blade and held it between her teeth. She had several wounds already healing on her arms and legs, evidence of her ongoing punishment. She deserved this. She was the reason Brady was dead. She'd killed the love of her life. If she'd just kept her mouth shut, he wouldn't have tried to defend her honor. For now, she should hurt physically as much as she hurt emotionally.

Sliding her pajamas and undies off, she settled herself in the tub in an effort not to get blood on the tile, and set her foot on the spout. With a deep breath, she ran the blade down her inner thigh, whimpering at the pain, but soon feeling the emotional high and relief as it covered her.

I'm so sorry, Bradykins.

She closed her eyes and slipped into bliss.

A scream pulled her from her haze, and she blinked open her eyes to find her mother pressing on her leg. "Ow. Mom, what are you doing?"

"I thought you found them all, Chip!" her mother bellowed.

"I thought I did too," her father said as he walked into the bathroom.

"Dad, get out! I'm naked."

"You should have thought about that when you tried to kill yourself," he snapped.

Jesska glanced down at the tub streaked with blood and her mother holding a towel against her leg, the cotton now soaked red. She shivered, suddenly freezing. "What's going on?"

"I need another towel," her mother said.

"She's in here," Jesska heard Megan say. She tried to stand when two paramedics pushed into the bathroom.

"What's going on?" Jesska screamed.

"You're going to the hospital," her mother said as she tried to keep the towel on Jesska's leg.

"No! I'm fine. I don't need to go to the hospital. I just need you to leave me alone."

"Ma'am, if you'll give us some space," the young woman said, "I'll take over putting pressure on her wound."

"I'm fine." Jesska couldn't stand, partly from the blood in the tub making everything slippery and partly because her legs were shaking so bad, they couldn't hold her weight.

The older man took her wrist to check her pulse, but she yanked it from him. "No! Go away," she screamed. "Get away from me."

"Ma'am, if she's eighteen, we can't force her to do anything," he said.

"She's not eighteen for two days," her mother said. "I want her to get help. Whatever you need to do."

"Shut up, Mom!" Jesska screamed. "Leave me alone!"

She screamed one more time as the needle went into her arm, and then there was nothing but black.

* * *

Jesska smacked her lips together, her mouth uncomfortably dry as she forced herself to open her eyes. Her head pounded, but when she moved to rub her temples, she realized she was stuck. Raising her head, she found her arms and legs in restraints.

"What the hell?" she grumbled, trying to make sense of her surroundings. A hospital maybe? "Hello? Help! Can someone help me?" she yelled. No one came, so she continued to call out.

A nurse walked into her room and gave her a gentle smile. "Hi there, hon. How are you feeling?"

"Why am I tied up? Where am I?"

The nurse checked her pulse. "You must be confused, huh? You're in the hospital. Your parents have you on a seventy-two-hour hold. A doctor will be in to speak with you shortly. Is there anything I can get you?"

"Well, I'm dying of thirst, and I have to pee."

"I'll get you some water and a bed pan."

"What? You can't be serious. Why can't I use the bathroom?"

"Because you tried to kill yourself."

"No. I didn't," she insisted. "I just cut a little too deep."

The nurse smiled again…that condescending, calm-the-beast smile. "Well, that cut nearly killed you, sweetie, so until the doctor can speak with you, I have to keep the restraints on. Are you hungry? I can bring you some pudding if you like."

Jesska shook her head, tears slipping down her face. She wanted to rage. She wanted to tell the nurse where she could shove her pudding, but this woman was part of the key to the outside, and she wasn't going to jeopardize her release.

The nurse patted her arm. "I'll be right back."

Jesska stared at the ceiling. The tiles evenly placed except one. The one wonky tile drew her attention mostly because it annoyed the crap out of her. Within minutes the nurse returned with a tray, followed by an older man in a white coat. Doctor, or loony bin attendant? She wasn't sure.

The nurse raised Jesska's bed so she was sitting up and then helped her with the straw so she could drink. Water had never tasted so good.

"I'm Dr. North," the older man said. "I thought we could talk a bit and see how you're feeling."

"Is today Wednesday?"

"Tuesday," he said.

"So, if tomorrow's Wednesday, then you can only keep me here today, right?"

The doctor checked her chart. "That's correct. You turn eighteen tomorrow."

Jesska squeezed her eyes shut. "Get the paperwork ready, Doc, 'cause I'm out of here at midnight."

"Unless I deem you're a danger to yourself or others."

"I'm good. No desire to hurt myself or anyone else." *That you'll hear about, anyway.*

"Well, let's just have a chat and we'll see how you're feeling, okay?" The doctor pulled up a chair and typed something into the computer. "Why did you try to kill yourself?"

"I didn't," she stressed. The doctor raised an eyebrow and Jesska took a deep breath. "I really didn't. I just cut a little too deep."

"And why do you cut yourself?"

"You're the shrink." She squeezed her eyes shut. "You tell me."

"This won't work if you don't tell me how you feel," he pointed out.

"My fiancé was murdered in front of me. Yesterday we were supposed to go to Paris. I feel a butt-load of guilt. I'd imagine that's why I cut myself."

The doctor smiled. "Now we're getting somewhere."

Jesska sighed and suffered through the next hour of probing questions. Her one saving grace was that the doctor ordered her restraints removed and she was able to take care of her own personal business and feed herself when it was time for dinner. She checked herself out the next morning, against medical advice, and then headed home. After packing a bag, she left her parents' home and checked into a hotel, using money from a trust fund she received from her grandmother. She had enough to look for and set herself up in her own place. She vowed never to return to her parents' home and didn't even look back as she drove away.

CHAPTER ONE

Present Day

JESSKA HEARD THE doorbell peal through her little duplex and, after checking the peephole, pulled open the door. "Well, hi there, Winky."

Amanda giggled. "You can't call me that anymore, you know."

"You might have married Marc Miller, but you'll always be my Winky." Jesska grinned. "Come in. Where's Kiana?"

Amanda's four-year-old was the cutest, and busiest, little girl on the planet.

"She's with Marc. Daddy-daughter bonding time," Amanda said, and took off her coat before holding up a bottle of Jesska's favorite wine. "I thought you and I could drink a little and find out who Manny sends home this week."

"You know I love it when you just pop over," Jesska droned.

"No, I know you hate it, but since you've been dodging my phone calls for almost a week now, I figured desperate measures and all that."

"I haven't been dodging you."

Amanda pointed at her. "So, you have no idea what today is."

"What do you mean?"

"You're wearing his sweatshirt, babe."

Today was the tenth anniversary of Brady's death, and Jesska had been inconsolable most of the day, as she was every anniversary. Her friends and family knew to leave her alone... except for Amanda, who inserted herself whenever possible.

Jesska huffed. "Fine. Okay. I'd hoped to be by myself, but if you insist on joining my pity party, you better get comfortable. You're just lucky you brought the wine—you'd never have gotten in without it."

Amanda handed her the bottle. "It's *Bachelor* night. We can watch it together in real time."

"I was thinking I might just watch it, drink some wine, and take a bath."

"Yeah, your obsession with tubby time's a little weird."

"You're just jealous."

Amanda sighed. "You're right. I never have time to relax like that anymore. Plus, I don't have a kickass claw-foot tub at my disposal."

Jesska laughed. "Is it weird I chose my house based on the tub?"

"Oh, babe, you surpassed weird about a lot of different things a while ago." Amanda grinned, flopped onto the couch. "Come on. Which lady will it be this week, hmm? Enquiring minds want to know."

"I think 'lady' is generous. Especially when talking about that Rosa chick."

"Yes, probably." Amanda giggled. "Got ice cream?"

"Do I have ice cream?" Jesska snorted. "This ain't my first rodeo."

Amanda cued up *The Bachelor* while Jesska prepared bowls of ice cream and poured wine. Manuel Garcia was the new bachelor and the epitome of tall, dark, and handsome. He was the Latino dream, with his chiseled body and beautiful face, complete with dimples that Amanda and Jesska were convinced he used as weapons. Manny was the most popular bachelor in six seasons, and the women were horrible. All but a couple of them, anyway.

By the time the show ended, and Jesska and Amanda had discussed Manny's date with Alana, one of the ladies both Jesska and Amanda liked, they'd gone through an entire carton of ice cream and a bottle and a half of wine. Jesska had even broken down and grabbed a box of tissues.

"I should have had that," Jesska complained.

"The chance to vie for a guy's love and devotion against twenty-four other psycho women?"

"I'm not psycho."

"Oh, right, sorry. Twenty-four psycho women and *you*."

Jesska snorted. "Do *not* tell me you didn't think Alana's date was über romantic. Manny was adorable. And Brady did stuff like that all the time. I should have had that."

"I know, buddy," Amanda agreed. "But maybe there's someone else out there for you. Maybe God has a bigger plan."

Jesska bit back an insult. It wasn't Amanda's fault she still believed in some old man in the sky who liked to devastate young women by killing off the people they loved. It also didn't matter that even though Amanda had graduated with a degree in rocket science and had just quit her job at NASA, Jesska always thought she was very, very pretty, but lacked a little in the brains department. She was far too loving and trusting to be a genius. But outside of Amanda's paltry street smarts and her religious views, Jesska adored her.

"I see you're trying to reconcile my looks with my brains again."

"Don't talk to me like you know me," Jesska retorted.

Amanda laughed as she checked her phone. "Marc's wondering what time I'm going to be home."

Jesska smiled. "How much have you had to drink? I'm not sure you should drive."

"I had two glasses, lady. You drank the rest."

"Shut up."

"Serious." Amanda rose to her feet and stretched.

"So you're okay to drive?"

"I'm great to drive. My directive has been achieved."

"Which was?"

"Keeping you distracted for a few hours."

Jesska sighed, realizing she felt quite a bit better after girl time and a good cry. "Again, Winky, I'd appreciate it if you didn't talk to me like you know me."

Amanda laughed. "Too late. Will you go straight to bed, or do you need me to stay and sing you a wuwwaby until you fall asweep?"

"Suck it, Winky," Jesska joked as she rose to her feet. "I wish I could say you're annoyingly mommy-ish now that you're actually a mom, but that trait started long ago."

"Guilty." Amanda grabbed her purse and coat. "Oh, would you be able to watch Kiana on Wednesday night?"

"Totally. It's my turn to drive for the carpool, so I can pick her up after I drop off Kim, if you like."

"You're a life saver!" Amanda exclaimed. "Marc and I need a date night and he has tickets to a movie preview."

"Ooh, fun. Which one?"

"Okay, don't laugh."

Jesska laughed.

Amanda raised an eyebrow. "I said don't laugh."

"Which makes me want to do it all the more."

"That's true. My bad," Amanda conceded. "Anyway, his high school buddy did this documentary on Portland and its history, and he's premiering it for family and a couple of close friends. Marc was invited."

"That's actually really cool," Jesska said.

"I hope so. If it sucks, Marc and I'll just make out in the back row." Amanda grinned. "Anyway, thanks again. I'll text you when I get home."

"Sounds good. Hey, thanks, Winky. Seriously."

"Love you."

"Love you too." Jesska hugged Amanda and watched her walk to her car before closing and locking the door. She was exceedingly grateful to her best friend as she fell asleep relatively quickly.

* * *

Thursday morning Jesska sat in her boss's office and went over the proxy filings in front of her. An executive assistant for a high-powered human resources benefits guru, she was still trying to figure out what she wanted out of life. For now, however, she sat staring at the verbiage only people far smarter than she understood swimming before her.

Or it could be that babysitting her surrogate niece had worn her out. Kiana loved coming to Auntie Jess's house, and made Amanda pack a small suitcase with all manner of outfits for them to play dress-up. Jesska was convinced Kiana would one day be a writer…her storytelling unmatched by most adults.

For now, however, Jesska was required to pull the relevant information from the documents for her boss by noon, and her eyes were starting to cross with the tedium of it all. She hated her job most days, but she lived with it because she needed the money. And, if she was being honest, she pretty much hated her life as well. Why should her job be any different?

"Aha," she breathed, locating the company information she needed. Maybe she *was* starting to understand some of this gibberish after all. She highlighted her findings, made a neat pile for her boss to go through, and headed back to her own desk.

"Hey, Jess." Her coworker, Kim, peeked over the partition. "Ready for lunch?"

Jesska nodded. "Yep. Just let me check my e-mail, and then I'll be all set."

Kim sat back down at her desk and Jesska opened her e-mail just as her phone rang. Without taking her eyes from the screen, she answered it. "This is Jess."

"Ah, Jessie Shane?"

Only Megan called her "Jessie."

"Yes, this is Jessie." She took a second to check the caller ID, but it didn't give any helpful information.

An older woman's voice said, "Miss Shane, your sister and niece have been in a motor vehicle accident, and you're in her phone as an emergency contact."

"What happened? Are they okay?" Jesska stood and grabbed her purse.

"That's all I can tell you right now. I'm sorry."

"Okay, where are they? I'll be right there."

"Legacy Emanuel. ICU."

"Ah, thanks," she said, and hung up the phone. "Kim, my sister and niece have been hurt. I have to go."

"Is she okay?" Kim asked, popping her head over the cubicle again.

Jesska grabbed her jacket. "I have no idea. Can you let Tim know? I'll call as soon as I know anything."

She rushed down to her car and sped out of the parking garage a little faster than she probably should have, hitting Naito Parkway and heading to the freeway. "Call Dad," she ordered her hands-free system. The call went to voice mail, so Jesska left a message and tried her mother. "Call Mom."

No luck there either, so she left a message just as she arrived at the hospital entrance. She sent up a silent prayer to the traffic gods and hunted for a parking space.

CHAPTER TWO

Bíldudalur, Iceland

KASPAR BALDURSSON WAVED his hand, catching the book that came flying from the top shelf, and sat in one of the library chairs facing the large bay window in his home. He didn't really know why he'd grabbed the book; he doubted he'd be able to focus enough to read it anyway.

He stared out the large bay window at the great expanse of snow covering the ground. Winter lasted much longer in his remote corner of the world, which suited him just fine. He'd lived in the tiny fishing village for longer than most people could fathom, and he wouldn't live anywhere else.

A knock at the door brought his youngest brother, Gunnar. Their middle brother, Ari, had disappeared, and no one had heard from him for more than a week. Not wholly unusual, but for whatever reason, this time Kaspar was worried.

"Any news?" he asked, and laid the book on the table next to the chair, standing to face his brother.

Gunnar shook his head. "Nothing. He's just gone."

"And he's not at his apartment?"

"His man said Ari hasn't been there for several days."

Kaspar sighed. "Well, he can't just be gone, Gunnar. Still, it's not like he hasn't done this before. He heads out somewhere, sees a shiny object and follows it, but usually we're able to reach him."

Ari was notoriously easy to distract, and with unlimited money from his sometimes creative business dealings, he could afford to do whatever he liked. He didn't answer to anyone, which occasionally meant he'd disappear for a while, remembering too late to let his brothers know where he was.

Gunnar chuckled. "I suppose that's true."

"Have you looked into these allegations against him?"

"That he refused to pay some kind of extortion money?" Gunnar snorted. "You're not seriously going to listen to some woman who's angry that he won't give her money, are you? Whatever she has to say will be a lie. Just another way to get his money."

"Are you sure that's it? Have you looked into her claims?" he asked again.

"No, I haven't looked into them."

"Well, I have."

"Why, Kaspar? The allegations are unfounded. She's a gold digger."

"She hasn't asked for anything. Not one *aurar,*" Kaspar countered.

"She will. They always do."

"What do you mean, they always do?" Kaspar leaned forward in an attempt to intimidate Gunnar. His brother pressed his lips into a thin line. "Gunnar."

Gunnar crossed his arms. "This is not the first woman who has demanded money not to 'out' the actions of our brother."

"What?" Kaspar frowned. "This has happened before? When?"

"Ages ago, brother." Gunnar waved his hand dismissively. "It's not even worth mentioning."

Kaspar dragged his hands down his face. "Why have you kept this from me?"

Gunnar chuckled and then grew serious again. "Kaspar, you're never here. At least, not in the sense of what the people expect. You sit on your gilded throne, where you hear nothing, and you think everything's fine."

"Are you saying I'm out of touch?"

"A bit, yes," Gunnar said. "But no more than you usually are."

Kaspar swore. His brother was right. He'd been out of sorts for a long time. "I apologize."

"You don't need to," Gunnar insisted. "This is what I'm trying to say. We have it handled."

"I don't think you do," Kaspar challenged.

Gunnar shook his head. "Fine. If you think you can do better, what is your proposal?"

"I'm going to come with you into town tomorrow and speak with the woman personally."

"Does that mean you're coming down from the gilded throne?"

Kaspar shook his head. "Look, I understand that I've been a little hands-off lately, but I will endeavor to make changes to rectify that. Will that suffice?"

Gunnar bowed low. "Yes, Your Majesty."

Kaspar flicked his hand, sending a book flying toward his brother's head. Gunnar was obviously ready for the assault, and he stepped aside before being hit.

"I'll be ready to go at nine. I'll be sure the woman is available."

"Thank you," Kaspar said, and effectively dismissed his brother.

CHAPTER THREE

JESSKA RUSHED INTO the hospital and straight to the ICU. Memories flooded her heart and mind as she made her way to the all-too-familiar section of the hospital. She arrived to chaos. Her father paced the floor and her mother had her phone to her ear, so Jesska made her way to her father.

"Any updates?" she asked.

"No," he said, giving her a quick hug. "We don't even know what happened."

Jesska felt the energy in the room change and turned to see her half-brother rush into the waiting area.

"What happened?" Cameron demanded.

"We don't know, Son," their father said.

A nurse walked into the waiting area. "Cameron Shane?"

"That's me," Cameron said.

"Your sister is asking for you."

"Can we see her?" Jesska asked.

The nurse shook her head. "Right now, Megan has asked to speak with Cameron alone. But you'll be able to talk to her shortly."

Cameron squeezed Jesska's hand and followed the nurse through the automatic doors. Jesska frowned and turned back to her parents. Her father held his hand out to her and grimaced, although Jesska was sure he was trying to smile. "Why just Cam?"

"I don't know, honey," he said.

She grabbed for the ring around her neck, as she often did when feeling anxious. Brady would help her. He always did.

Her mother finally got off her phone and joined the family. Cameron didn't return for close to an hour. By the time he walked through the automatic doors again, Jesska had bitten her fingernails down to their nubs. She'd even managed to draw blood. She rushed him, her parents close behind. "Is she okay? Can we see her? How's Sophia?"

Cameron reached for her hand. "Sophia's in surgery. We'll be able to see her when she's in recovery. The prognosis is good, though."

"What about Megan, can we see her?"

Cameron nodded. "Yes, in just a bit. The nurse will come find you. I have to go."

"What?" Jesska snapped. "Where?"

He squeezed her chin gently. "You are always so inquisitive."

She tugged her face away. "And you're always so vague."

Cameron smiled. "I love you, Messka." He pulled their father aside, spoke to him briefly, and was out the door before Jesska could object.

"Shane family?" a woman's voice called out.

"Yes," Jesska said, as she faced the nurse.

"You can see Megan now."

Jesska followed the nurse, leading her parents down the hall and into a private room. She noticed a uniformed officer standing outside the door and frowned when he insisted on checking their IDs. On the one hand, she was grateful they were a diligent hospital, but on the other hand, she didn't want to waste time being vetted by some hired badge. She wanted to see her sister.

"Go on in, miss," the officer said, and Jesska pushed open the door.

She bit her lip as she rushed to her sister's side. Megan looked so small in the giant bed. Her arm and head were wrapped with bandages and she had an IV set up above her. Jesska watched the liquid dripping slowly through the tubing.

"Hey, Jessie," Megan rasped. "Do you know anything about Sophia?"

"All I know is that she's in surgery." Jesska gently linked her fingers with Megan's and kissed her cheek. "What happened?"

"Can you find a doctor, please? I need to know about Sophia."

"I'll take care of that," their father said, and left the room.

"Tell me what happened," Jesska said.

"A car spun out of control and hit us, pushing us into the median divide." She raised her broken arm. "This happened when I was trying to get Sophia loose. Her seatbelt jammed and another car bumped us. I was in the worst position, I guess. I have to have a CT done on my arm and leg to see if I need surgery."

"How's your head?" Jesska asked.

"I got a nasty scalp laceration and a bit of a bump, but they think I'm okay. They're watching for concussion." Megan closed her eyes for a few seconds.

"Are you in pain?"

"A little." Megan pushed herself up when their father walked back into the room. "Any news on Soph?"

"She's almost out of surgery," he said. "A doctor will be here soon to fill you in."

Megan sat back. "Okay."

Jesska said. "How are you so calm?"

"Oh, sissy, I'm not. Although I'm on some pretty heavy pain meds. I'm trying to hold it together so I don't freak you guys out more than necessary."

"Well, freak out," Jesska ordered. "It's what we're here for."

Megan nodded, glancing toward their father. "Dad, can I talk to you about something?"

"Of course, honey."

"Privately, please?" Megan said.

"What? Seriously?" Jesska ground out. "What's going on? Cam's acting all weird and secretive, now you are? What aren't you telling us?"

"Jessie," Megan said with a sigh.

"No, Megan. What's going on?" Jesska forced back tears, her fingers reaching for Brady's ring at her throat. "You're not telling me something. It's bad enough you could have been killed today, but now I feel like you're keeping something from me that maybe I should know."

"Have a seat," Megan said, and Jesska sat in the chair beside her. "I got a call from an ADA down at the Multnomah Courthouse. Jason's attorney has discovered some legal technicality in his case, so they are going to release him."

"What? No, that can't be right."

Megan nodded. "The DA has promised he's going to retry him, but for some reason, they can't keep him in prison. Cameron went to the courthouse to find out what's going on and why Jason's being let out instead of being held until the new trial can be set. He's got access to more information than I do."

"Do the Kings know?"

"I would think they would," her father said. "They're on the victim's contact list, so someone would have called them."

"I should go over there tonight."

"Do you think that's wise?" Megan asked.

"Why wouldn't it be?"

"No reason," their father said, sending Megan a look Jesska couldn't quite decipher.

A nurse entered the room and smiled. "Miss Bailey, I'm here to take you down to radiology."

"Have you heard anything about my daughter, Sophia?" Megan asked.

"She's still in surgery. But don't worry, your X-rays will be quick. You'll be back before you know it."

Megan nodded and the nurse unlocked the brakes on her bed and wheeled her out of the room. Jesska sat by the window to wait for her to return.

Her father sat next to her, taking her hand. "How are you, honey? We haven't seen you in a few weeks."

Jesska forced a smile. "I know, Dad. I've been busy."

"But not so busy you can't have dinner with the Kings every night."

She pulled her hand from his. "It's not every night."

"Well, it's certainly a hell of a lot more time than you're spending with us."

"Dad, don't start, okay?"

He frowned. "At some point you have to move on."

Jesska stood, trying to gain some distance. "I have moved on."

"You know what I mean."

"Yeah, I do. And you lost the right to tell me what to do ten years ago."

"I'm still your father, Jess," he said, sadly.

"Well, for the last time, let me spell it out for you. I know you want me to find some nice church guy and settle down. But what you fail to see is that I had my one true love, and God took him away from me."

"He doesn't need to go to church, honey. He just needs to treat you right."

"Well, I'm not interested in anyone...or church," she stressed.

"But church used to be so important to you."

"And now it's not." She crossed her arms. "At least I'm not going the way of Mom."

He frowned. "You know your mom's sensitive."

"Maybe she wouldn't be so sensitive if she stopped drinking four bottles of wine a day," she snapped.

"I'd rather you didn't speak about your mother that way." He sighed.

"Look, I don't want to fight. I just miss you. We all miss you."

She forced down her guilt, grabbing again for Brady's ring around her neck. "Maybe I can clear something in my schedule next week and come over for dinner."

"That would be really appreciated," her father said.

She stared out the window as they sat in tense silence. When her sister returned, Jesska tried not to yell in celebration. Now her father could turn his worry onto Megan instead of Jesska. The nurse got Megan settled in her bed, gave her another dose of meds, and then went to find out what was going on with Sophia.

"How are you feeling?" Jesska asked.

"Worried," Megan admitted.

Their father took her hand. "She'll be fine."

Expecting the nurse, Jesska was surprised when a handsome young doctor entered Megan's room. Tall with dark hair and hazel eyes. He looked more akin to a model than a doctor.

"I'm Dr. Washington," he said, and shook everyone's hand. "I wanted to give you an update on Sophia."

Megan sat up a little further. "Is she okay?"

"She's great," he said. "We expected there to be some internal bleeding, which there was, but we were able to get it under control quickly. All of her X-rays and the MRI are clear, so she's in recovery right now. She has a small incision on her abdomen from our exploration, but I don't think that will give her much of a problem. We'll keep her for a couple of days, and then she should be able to go home."

"When can I see her?" Megan asked.

"I can take you now, if you like. We can also put her in here with you when she wakes up."

"Yes, that would be great," Megan said.

"Can we come, too?" Jesska asked.

"No, I'm afraid just Mom this time. But you'll be able to see her in a couple of hours."

"You should go home, Jessie. Or back to work. I'll call you if anything changes, okay?"

"Are you sure?" she asked.

Megan nodded. "Definitely. There's no point in you sitting around here. We're fine. A little banged up, but fine. Why don't you come back tonight?"

"Okay, I will." Jesska leaned down to kiss her cheek. "I love you. Kiss Soph for me, okay?"

"I will."

Her father pulled her in for an awkward hug, kissing the crown of her head. "Let me know about next week, okay?"

Jesska nodded and headed out to her car. She found herself grabbing for Brady's ring as she walked through the all-too-familiar halls of the hospital, her stomach roiling as memories flooded her. She sped up, almost to a run, and escaped the halls of death.

Arriving at her car, she slid inside and laid her head on the steering wheel. She couldn't stop the tears. Didn't even try. She still missed Brady, even after all this time, and she was convinced nothing would ever change.

Her phone rang. She considered ignoring it, but Cameron's name came up, so she answered. "Hi, Cam."

"Hey. You okay?"

"Yep," she said, and wiped her cheeks. "What's up?"

"They're letting Jason out."

"Megan told me." She sighed. "When?"

"He'll be out on Friday."

"What? Really? Why so soon?"

"I don't know the details, unfortunately. But he'll have to wear an ankle bracelet and he'll be on house arrest."

"Is he going back to his grandparents'?"

"No, they died about five years ago."

She bit her lip. "So he's lost everyone, then."

"Yeah."

"Good," she said.

"Jess," Cameron said with a sigh.

"What?"

"You and I need to have a talk, I think."

"Nope. I'm good."

"Tonight. I'll pick you up around seven."

"I'm having dinner with my in-laws," she countered.

"Eight then. I'll come to their place and you can follow me home."

"Why? There's no point."

"What's that? You're break-ing...hel-lo..."

The call disconnected and Jesska dropped her head back onto the steering wheel. She could text him and tell him not to bother, but it would be futile effort. He'd be there at eight whether she wanted him to be or not.

After fixing her makeup, she left the parking lot and headed back to work. Might as well be at the only place the demons didn't taunt her.

* * *

Jesska arrived at the Kings' home just before dinner. She'd been eating dinner with them three or four nights a week since *that* thing had happened, and she loved how close she felt to Brady when she was there. Before they had boxed up all of his personal items, she'd go into his room and lie down on his bed just to smell him.

She didn't knock—she didn't need to—but she did call out as she walked through the door. "I'm here."

"Hi, Jess," Carly said. Brady's sister was the spitting image of him. A beautiful woman, with dark-blonde hair and a height that rivaled most men. She'd recently gotten engaged after a failed first marriage, and the family was preparing for the wedding.

"Hi, Carly. Where's Jude?"

"He's working late. He'll be her in about an hour."

"Did you hear?" Jesska asked.

"About that bastard getting out? Yes. Mom and Dad are in the kitchen. Come on in."

Jesska followed Carly back to the kitchen and welcomed the hug that Brady's mom, Leslie, offered.

"Have you heard about Jason, honey?" she asked.

Jesska nodded. "Yeah. Do you have any details?"

"Not yet," Brady's dad said. "Your brother said he'd let us know what he found out."

Jesska rolled her eyes. "You know, for a worship pastor, that man can get some serious shi—I mean, stuff, done outside the church."

"Yes, he can."

"What can I do to help?" she asked.

"If you and Carly could set the table, that would be great," Leslie said.

Jesska spent the next two hours laughing without feeling happy, answering questions about her life that really didn't mean a whole hell of a lot at the moment, and using diversion tactics in an effort to take the focus off of her. She didn't know why Brady's parents had started in with the twenty questions about her love life all of a sudden, but chalked it up to Jason's impending release and the trigger that it probably pulled.

Cameron arrived at 7:59, much to Jesska's irritation. He was never late. Ever. After saying goodnight to the Kings and Jude, who'd arrive an hour before, Jesska agreed to follow Cameron to his loft in the Pearl.

She spent her drive time plotting revenge for her brother's nosiness. Laxative brownies were currently at the top of the list.

She followed him into the underground parking garage and parked in his extra space. Maybe if she just sat in the car, he'd forget about her and she could sneak out.

Her car door opened and she groaned. "*Cam.*"

"Come on. Time for a 'come to Jesus' meetin'," Cameron said, and held out his hand.

Jesska slid out of her car and locked it. "Can we just have a bottle of wine and call it good?"

Cameron chuckled, stepping into the elevator and hitting the button for the twelfth floor. She followed him into his gorgeous three-bedroom apartment overlooking the Willamette...one that he could never have afforded on a worship pastor's salary, but what Cameron did outside of the church was sufficiently vague, highly confidential, and incredibly lucrative.

She dropped her purse on the granite island and slid her shoes off. Cameron's place was her home away from home, and if she were being honest, she didn't really want to go back to her tiny little duplex alone anyway.

Cameron poured her a glass of Merlot and she took it to the windows overlooking the Steel Bridge. "So, what do you want me to say, Cam? Do you need a rundown of my life?"

"Not at all. I just want to see where you're at. We haven't talked in a while, and I miss my sister." He smiled. "What's new?"

Jesska rolled her eyes. "Nothing, really. I work eighty hours a week, I go home to my charming little duplex in a converted bungalow, I try not to drink several bottles of wine, and then I fall into bed, *greatly* looking forward to the morning so I can do it all again."

Cameron sat on the sofa and patted his hand on the cushion beside him. "Have a seat."

"Oh, my *god*, Cam. Are we really doing this?"

He smiled gently. "We're really doing this."

Jesska flopped onto the couch, managing not to spill her wine, and twisted her body so her back was against the armrest and she was facing her brother. "Grill away."

"Why haven't you gone back to church?"

She shrugged. "I don't like church."

"That's not the reason," he challenged.

"Well then, it's because God sucks."

"No, He doesn't."

She forced back tears. "Yes, He does."

Cameron squeezed her knee. "What happened was awful, Jess. No one's saying it wasn't...isn't even still, but you're turning away from the only one who can comfort you."

"Says the man who's all godly and shit. Tell ya what, Cam. When your fiancée is murdered in front of you, we can have this conversation, but you know nothing about pain and losing the only person you've ever loved." She pointed to the ceiling. "*He* did that. *He* could have saved Brady, but He didn't."

Cameron tilted his head and nodded. "What you're feeling is all normal, Jess, but it's been over ten years, and you need to let it go."

"Screw you, Cameron."

"I'm not saying you need to forget. I'm just saying you need to forgive him... *them,* Jason *and* Brady, and then forgive yourself."

"Why do I have to forgive Brady? All he did was die and leave me to live in the world without him...oh." She wrinkled her nose. "Stop counseling me, Cameron. It's annoying."

He smiled and grasped her hand. "None of this was either of your faults."

"I never said it was our fault."

Cameron pulled her arm forward and slid her sleeve up.

"Stop it!" Jesska tried to pull her arm back, the evidence of her non-dealt-with pain etched in the scars.

Cameron tightened his hold. "*This* has to stop."

"These are old," she said as she shoved her sleeve back down her arm. "I'm fine. I haven't cut myself in a long time."

Cameron raised an eyebrow. "Really?"

"Really."

He gripped her chin gently. Something he'd done since she was little so he could look into her soul. "Messka."

"What?" She couldn't stop the tears.

Twice in one day, damn it. Crying jags were not on the approved list of reactions, but they seemed to come anyway, and at the most inopportune times. She needed to rein in her emotions.

Cameron sighed, taking the wine from her hand and setting it on the coffee table before pulling her into his arms. "Tell me."

"Day before yesterday."

"Where?"

"On my thigh," she confessed. She always told Cameron the truth, eventually.

Cameron stroked her hair, praying quietly for peace and acceptance as he promised her he'd always take care of her. She sobbed into his chest until she was sure she didn't have any salt or water left in her body. After a few minutes of blissful silence, she pulled away from him.

Cameron gave her a gentle smile. "What are we going to do when you meet someone who captivates your heart, little sister?"

She snorted, grabbing for the tissue box next to the sofa. "I'm never getting married, so you can just shove that idea where the sun don't shine."

"Will you make me a promise?"

She picked up her wine. "No."

Cameron chuckled. "Then tell me...now that we've talked a bit...how do you feel?"

"Better...jerk."

He nodded. "I had a feeling you needed to cry. So, make me a promise."

"Still no."

He pulled a card out of his pocket and handed it to her. "Call my guy."

"Again with this shrink crap, Cameron?" she snapped as she glared at the embossed cardstock.

"It works."

"It doesn't work and I'm no longer a minor, so you have no power to put me in the psych ward without my consent...again." Jesska handed the card back to him, but he refused to take it.

"First, that was not me," he said with a sigh. "Second, Dad and Denise just wanted to keep you alive."

"By putting me in restraints and keeping me drugged up for almost two days?"

He pinched the bridge of his nose. "They were desperate, Jess. You cut yourself so deep, you passed out. You could have died if Denise hadn't found you."

"Whatever. Mom overreacted." She sipped her wine. "Besides, talking about my problems isn't going to make them go away."

"Neither is cutting the hell out of your skin!"

She shrugged again, forcing down the shame.

Cameron took a deep breath. "If you don't want to talk to someone, come to church with me."

"Hell, no."

"I'm not leading worship this weekend. Come with me."

"No."

"I'll pick you up for the Saturday service. We can do dinner after."

Jesska kicked his leg. "I'm busy on Saturday night."

"With Merlot or Pinot?"

"I don't know, maybe both."

"Jess, just how much are you drinking?" he asked.

"Don't worry, Cam. I'm not going the way of my mother. I cap myself at a bottle or two of wine a night. If I'm really upset, I use the heroin."

"Not funny, Messka."

"Not even a lot a bit?"

"Where did you get your warped sense of humor?" he asked.

"Television. Where else?"

Cameron rolled his eyes. "Five thirty."

"Why do you go to a church in the 'Couve? It's so far away! Why not go to Graceland right here in town?"

Graceland was the church that Jesska attended with Brady, and was one of the largest churches in the Pacific Northwest.

"Even better," he said. "You'd probably feel better with your friends around anyway. Perfect. Graceland it is. I'll pick you up at ten on Sunday. We can do lunch instead."

"I really can't this weekend, Cam. Seriously. I promised Amanda I'd help with Kiana. Marc's out of town."

"Then next weekend."

Jesska groaned in irritation. His manipulation was unmatched. "I hate you so much right now."

Cameron laughed. "You hate me because I'm right. Let's pop some corn and watch a movie."

"Only if we can find one where the sister murders her brother *really* slowly."

He rose to his feet. "I take back any references to you being normal."

She laughed and followed him into the kitchen.

CHAPTER FOUR

KASPAR'S DRIVER OPENED the door for him, and he joined his brother in the back of the large SUV. He had a lot to do today and, although Gunnar felt it would have been more convenient for the woman to come to them, Kaspar was a stickler for his privacy and no one came to his home unless invited. "Where are we meeting her?" he asked.

"Vegamót," Gunnar said, and raised a hand, cutting off Kaspar's objection. "There isn't really anywhere else."

Kaspar sighed. "No, I don't suppose there is."

Bíldudalur was a tiny little fishing village on the coast of one of Iceland's Westfjords, Arnarfjörður. It had one tiny little eatery, slash general store, Vegamót. Kaspar wished there was another option, something bigger, some place they wouldn't be noticed.

Kaspar's grandfather was one of the original Norsemen who emigrated at the end of the ninth century. It was the perfect place to hide what they were and control the information they could provide to the new world. No one expected they were anything other than human. They'd settled in Bíldudalur and the town flourished until the twentieth century, when the fishing industry declined. Only a few families remained faithful to the village and stayed on. For the most part, the Kalt Einn didn't interact with humans, but on rare occasions such as this one, it was necessary to meet in town.

Their driver pulled up to the small restaurant and the shop owner smiled, his friendly demeanor a little off-putting for Kaspar. He was wary of people who were overly friendly…they usually wanted something from him.

"Wipe that look off your face, brother," Gunnar warned.

Kaspar tried to do as his brother said as he followed Gunnar to the back of the building. A feminine gasp pulled him from his thoughts, and he looked up to see a tiny woman huddling under the eaves for shelter from the blinding sun. She curtsied, blushing bright red. "Sire. I was not expecting you."

At least she was Kalt Einn. "You were not very forthcoming when my man spoke with you last week," Kaspar accused.

"I-I— ," she stammered.

Gunnar gave him a look of "I told you so" and crossed his arms. "I want you to tell the king what you told me."

Kaspar noticed her hands shaking and tried to give her a reassuring smile. "You are safe. No harm will come to you."

"I am resigned to my fate, Your Majesty."

"What do you mean?" he asked.

"They will find me and kill me. Nothing you do or anyone else does can change that. But you need to know before they find me."

Kaspar frowned. "What do I need to know?"

"The prince…Ari, he had a human woman. He kept her, and she bore him three daughters."

"What do you mean, he had a human woman?" Kaspar asked.

"I don't know all the details of their relationship. I just know that they lived together and she gave birth to his daughters. The first two babies were taken from her. I don't know where or by whom. But when she had the third, she hid and then managed to disappear completely."

"Why are you telling me this?"

"Because they are looking for the three girls."

Kaspar's irritation rose. "Who are *they*?"

"We don't know." She sighed. "We have been trying to find out, but haven't had any luck. Your nieces are the Trifecta, my lord. Fire, ice, and earth. Do you know how powerful they would be together? Ari found the first two in Scotland, but he hasn't located the third. There are rumors that she's in America. All they have is a first name of the mother. Megan. They called the daughter Ása, but there is no trace of her, so it is possible she changed her baby's name."

"Was she Ari's mate?" Kaspar asked.

The woman shrugged. "Like I said, I don't know the particulars. I met Megan just before she left."

"Do you want money?"

"No!" she snapped, and scowled. "You're not listening to me. They are after them. The two older girls are mated to Cauld Ane's, but the youngest is not safe. She has no protection. I think your brother has been captured and held by the Cauld Ane who are mated to your nieces. Not that Ari did anything to protect sweet Megan," she said in disgust. "You are the only one who can save her."

"How am I to save her?" he asked.

She handed him a flash drive. "Everything is on here. Please, Your Majesty. Her name is Megan Shane. She confided in me before she ran. Please help her. She is such an amazing young woman and your brother...well, he took advantage."

"How did he take advantage?" Kaspar pressed.

"She loved him. Truly loved him, but she was young, and he wasn't always kind to her."

"My brother would never harm a woman."

She squared her shoulders. "Perhaps not physically, sire, but he hurt her deeply when he pulled away from her."

"How so?"

"From what I understand, they were both deeply in love until she reached *ár mökunar*. That's when she was able to get out from under his suggestion and ran. He has been looking for all four of them ever since then. He's obsessed with them. And I believe he hates the woman now."

Kaspar closed his hand around the drive and slipped it into his pocket. "Your name."

"My name isn't important. In fact, it's better you don't know it."

Kaspar frowned again, annoyed by her subordination.

The woman smiled. "The answers you seek are on that drive."

"I can offer you protection," he said.

"I know you believe that, sire, but you can't."

Kaspar felt irritation rise. "Are you underestimating my power?"

"No, Sire, never. But if you try to protect me, that will lead them to you, and I could never take the chance that you might be harmed."

Kaspar pulled out his phone and fired off a text, glancing at her as he typed. "You'll take the protection I'm offering you."

She shook her head, but when he scowled at her, she bowed her head. "Thank you, Your Majesty."

Within minutes, one of his guards arrived and ushered the woman into his car. Kaspar told him to take her somewhere he wouldn't know about and then led his brother back to their awaiting SUV.

"What do you think?" Gunnar asked.

"I don't know just yet," he admitted. "But it's disconcerting."

"If the Cauld Ane have our brother, what are we going to do?"

"I don't know, Gunnar. But if they have him, then they now know we are still here. We have spent all this time erasing any evidence of our existence and, with one stupid move by Ari, all of that work is undone." He rubbed his forehead. "I will figure it out, but it might take some time."

He rode the rest of the way home in silence, his brother engrossed in his phone. Arriving at his compound obscured by the small mountain next to the sea, Kaspar waited for his driver to open the door and then headed into his house. He called his secretary on the way to his office and removed his jacket, laying it over a chair.

Camilla arrived a few minutes later, knocking on his open door and waiting for him to acknowledge her.

"Come," he said.

"I have that number for you, Sire."

He handed her his phone so she could enter the phone numbers he required. After she gave it back to him, she left, closing the door behind her. Kaspar sat in his chair and made a call while he opened his laptop.

"Gunnach."

"*Góðan dag, læknir Gunnach. Ég skil að þú ert bróðir minn í vörslu.*" (Good afternoon, Doctor Gunnach. I understand you have my brother in custody.)

"*Og þú ert?*" (And you are?)

"Kaspar Baldersson."

A sigh sounded through the phone and Kaspar waited for Kade to respond. "So, it's true."

When Kade's father had escaped Iceland and the wrath of Kaspar's father, the agreement was that none in the new generation of Cauld Ane would know about the Kalt Einn. In order for Kade's father to keep his head, he had to agree to the terms of secrecy, sail for Scotland, and never return to Iceland.

"It's true," Kaspar said, answering in English. "Do you have my brother?"

"Aye," Kade said.

"The details, please?"

"From what I understand, Ari was looking for his daughters. He found two of them. We allowed him to explain, and he attempted to dose us with Red Fang. He will not give us any other information. We will not release him."

Kaspar pinched the bridge of his nose. "He found my nieces?"

"Aye."

"Their names?"

"Not going to happen," Kade said.

"What of the third?"

"You know the story, I see."

"I know some of the story," Kasper admitted. "However, none of it came from my brother."

"I am not willing to put my people in danger. There will be a trial, and he will be sentenced."

"I understand," Kaspar said. "But I'll not allow you to work within the laws your father made."

"You knew my father?"

"Já."

"My father did not... shall we say, handle things fairly. I am not him."

"That's good to hear," Kaspar said. "Will you allow me to see my brother?"

"Could I stop you?" Kade challenged.

"No, but I'm giving you the courtesy of asking."

"Aye, you can see him. But only with me."

"I understand. I will have my secretary make the arrangements."

"All right," Kade said. "I'll wait for the details."

Kaspar hung up, tapping his phone with a finger. Ari had always been troubled, but if he did in fact hurt this Megan woman, physically *or* emotionally, Kaspar was going to have to do something about that. He fired off directions to Camilla and then went about investigating what was on the flash drive.

* * *

Kaspar sat in his chair on the plane and stared out the window as they took off. His visit with his brother had not gone as well as he'd hoped, but he'd agreed with Kade that Ari needed to be kept in Edinburgh until they could sort out the truth. Kaspar wasn't convinced Ari was telling him the whole story, and he couldn't believe he was heading Stateside again. More than anything, he couldn't believe he was nervous. He didn't get nervous, but something on that continent unsettled him.

His cell phone buzzed and he answered it. "Hi, Gunnar."

"What's the matter?" Gunnar asked.

"Nothing, brother."

"I can feel your distress."

"I know." He sighed. "I feel a little unsettled is all."

"Your mate perhaps?"

Kaspar shook his head. "It can't be. We have no people there."

"What if she's human?"

Kaspar swore.

Gunnar laughed. "Right, we don't mate with humans. It's why the Cauld Ane were banished, etcetera, etcetera."

One of many reasons, Kaspar thought. "We're taking off."

"I'll see you in a few days. Safe travels."

"Thanks." Kaspar hung up and turned back to the window, effectively shutting his brother's words out. At least Portland was cold and wet. If he had to return to the States, he was glad it was in the winter. If he was right and his niece was there, then he could bring her home where she belonged and Ari could finally get out of Scotland. The deal with Kade Gunnach didn't leave much room for grace where his brother was concerned. Even Kaspar had to admit if one of the Cauld Ane did to him what Ari had done to them, Kaspar would have reacted the same way. He didn't know what the hell his brother was thinking, dosing the entire royal family with Red Fang. He rubbed his chin in thought. Things were going to change.

Arriving at the private airstrip in Portland after an all night flight, Kaspar exited the plane and climbed straight into a hired car. Austri, his head security guard and driver, and Jóvin, his second in command, bowed as he approached. Jóvin climbed into the passenger side and Austri held the door for Kaspar.

"Welcome, Your Majesty," Austri said.

"Austri. Thank you for being on time."

Austri nodded and closed the door. Kaspar was traveling lighter than usual, with only two bodyguards for him and two for Gunnar, who would arrive the next day. He also traveled with his secretary and his valet, both who had gone a day before him to prepare everything for his arrival.

The cars Camilla had chosen to pick him up in once again proved her salary was well-earned. Where she found a Bentley in Portland, he didn't know, but if anyone could, she could. He hoped the hotel would be just as appropriate. Kaspar watched the scenery fly by, pleasantly surprised by how beautiful Portland was. His driver maneuvered through the city traffic, expertly dodging cyclists and pedestrians. The other drivers were a bit more of a challenge. With the rain, it was a bit chaotic.

Camilla met the party at the entrance to the Hotel Monaco and smiled as Kaspar climbed from the car. "Sire," she said.

He nodded. "Camilla."

"We have the top two floors of the hotel. You and His Highness will be on the top floor, we will be on the floor below."

"Excellent," he said, and followed her inside.

They took the elevator to the top floor, and Camilla opened the door to his suite. He stepped inside, happy with the size and décor. It was a lovely room, with a private bedroom, comfortable enough to stay for an extended period of time if he were forced to.

"Well done, Camilla."

"Thank you, Your Majesty."

He didn't miss her blush as she lowered her head. He knew his compliments were few and far between, but he'd assumed she didn't need them. She'd been in his employ for close to fifty years, but with the delighted expression on her face...one he didn't see very often...he realized he should probably tell her more often when she was doing a good job.

"Dinner is in an hour, if that is acceptable to you. I have hired a chef who comes highly recommended, and he will be at your disposal for as long as you need him."

"Very good."

"Jens will be here with your bags momentarily," she continued. "Is there anything you need, currently?"

"No, Camilla, thank you."

"I'll leave you now," she said.

Kaspar nodded and headed straight to the shower, confident his people would take care of everything. Jens would unpack and then assist Kaspar with his clothing when he was finished.

As the water washed over his body, Kaspar felt deep sadness cover him. The pain was so heart-wrenching, he couldn't stifle a gasp. He realized quickly something was wrong with his mate. She must be here somewhere, but he was at a loss as to where. He'd searched for his kind...there'd been no trace.

It took a few minutes, but the sadness passed, and Kaspar climbed out of the shower. He wouldn't have much time to rest before he began his search. Kade Gunnach had offered one of his human security men and Kaspar accepted his assistance, however, reluctantly.

Interacting with humans was not something he'd ever thought to do, but it was becoming more and more evident that if he didn't rely on this Dalton Moore's assistance, he'd get nowhere in America.

Stepping out of the bathroom and into the bedroom, he found clothing laid out for him. Jeans and a T-shirt. Not his normal choices, but when in Rome… He dressed quickly and ran his fingers through his damp hair before heading into the living room.

He grabbed his phone from the bureau and found a text from Camilla informing him that Dalton Moore awaited him in one of the rooms downstairs. He left the suite, and with a slight nod to Austri standing sentry outside his room, he led the way to the elevator and waited while the security guard took care of the rest.

Kaspar felt panic race through him, and it took him a second to realize it wasn't his own. He was going to have to find his mate quickly, because he didn't know how much more of this he could take.

As only he could do as a mate, he did his best to calm them both, and followed Austri down the hall and to the room they'd set up for meetings. It was much like his own, perhaps a little smaller. A tall, dark-haired man was speaking with Camilla, and Kaspar didn't miss her blush, frowning at the exchange.

When Camilla caught Kaspar's eye, she stepped away from the man and gave Kaspar a slight curtsy. "Your Majesty, this is Dalton Moore, and here is his information." She handed him a folder and stepped away, taking her place near the door.

Moore held his hand out and Kaspar shook it before he motioned to the sofa. "Have a seat."

"Why do I feel like this is some kind of an interrogation?" Moore said in a thick southern American accent.

Kaspar continued to read his credentials without looking at him. "Because it is."

"Did Kade not give you my information?"

"Not the information I require."

Moore chuckled without mirth and rose to his feet again. "Well, you feel free to call me when you decide what to do. I'm sure your assistant has my number."

Kaspar was so surprised that the human walked out the door without permission, he didn't react right away. "Skíta," he hissed, and turned to Camilla. "Fáðu hann aftur hingað." (Get him back here.)

Camilla rushed out the door, returning without Moore, and Kaspar scowled. "*Hvar er hann?*"

Her face crumbled. "*Hann sagði að hann myndi hringja í þig seinna.*" (He said he would call you later.)

"*Fjandinn. Sendu Austri inn.*" (Damn it. Send Austri in.)

CHAPTER FIVE

CAMERON FELT HIS phone buzz and pulled it from his pocket, surprised to see Dalton Moore's name on the screen. "Hey, Dalt."

"Hey, you got time for a beer?"

"You're still here?"

"Actually, I returned to Scotland, but was asked to come back here. Long story. Just had to spend five minutes I'll never get back with one of the most entitled pricks alive."

Cameron laughed. "Ah, sure. Where do you want to meet?"

"Rock Bottom?"

"I'll see you in twenty."

"'Bye."

Cameron hung up and grabbed his jacket. The day was wet, so he decided to take the car instead of his bike. As he drove to the brewery, he contemplated why Dalton might be back in town. Dalton's new responsibilities in Scotland were vague, even to Cameron, who had worked with him when they were both part of the FBI. Cameron had left the bureau three years ago to pursue private interests; however, his private interests didn't mean he was out of touch.

Cameron still went after some of the worst of the worst, only secretly, and for a lot more money than the FBI offered. He also had control now over which assignments he took, and he made sure he gave himself time off in between jobs. His responsibilities at church were an outlet to remind him why he was on the earth and give him important moments to recharge. Arriving at Rock Bottom Brewery, he parked on the street and headed into the restaurant.

Dalton joined him a few minutes later, and they headed into the bar. A small stage was set up in the corner, but the band wouldn't play for another few hours. Maybe he should start playing out more. Shake off some of the live gig rust...

"So, what's up?" Cameron asked.

Dalton sipped his beer and then sighed. "My sister's husband—"

"Your brother-in-law—"

"Only when I claim him." Dalton smirked. "Anyway, my sister's husband has asked me to find out what I can about a person or persons who might be up to something nefarious. They're looking for something, and that "something" just so happens to involve Megan."

Cameron went on high alert. "*My* Megan?"

Dalton nodded. "She's connected to this somehow, I'm just not sure of the details yet."

"Does your brother-in-law know about me?"

Dalton shook his head. "He doesn't even know you exist...in the capacity you exist, anyway. He only knows you as her brother. But they are looking for Megan and I need to find out why."

"Who are 'they'?"

"My family."

"Your family's looking for Megan?"

"No. But my family is involved," Dalton said. "This whole thing is actually about her daughter."

"Sophia? What about her?"

"Her father's looking for her."

"What do you mean? Megan said he was dead."

"Well, he's not," Dalton informed him.

"I knew it," he said with a sigh. "My sister's the worst liar ever."

"She said he was dead and you knew he wasn't, but just dropped it?"

"Hell, no," Cameron said. "I just couldn't ever find him. Megan wouldn't give me a name and his DNA isn't in any system. At least the DNA of whoever Sophia's father is. Believe me, I called in favors to try and find him."

"No, it wouldn't be," Dalton said without elaborating. "But now you don't have to look for him. His brother's looking for *her*."

"Hold up. Sophia's uncle is looking for her."

"Yep. He's the entitled prick I was referring to. Some Icelandic royalty or something."

"Of course he is. Trust my sister to get herself mixed up with someone with money and means." Cameron ran his hands through his hair. "What do you need from me?"

"Nothing right now. I'll meet with this guy tomorrow or the next day and let you know."

"Damn it, Dalton. That's not really an answer."

Dalton shrugged. "I don't have an answer for you. But I know I don't have to tell you what you'll need to do until this is sorted out."

"You mean, remove all my guns from their hiding places and move my family into a compound of some kind?"

"Sure, if that floats your boat." Dalton smiled. "We have it under some control from our end. Just keep an eye on Megan and Sophia so I can focus on finding out who these people are. I don't know if they're in danger, but someone's really interested in finding them, so best to be on the safe side."

"That goes without saying. You do your thing, Dalton, and don't worry about my family."

"Thanks. I promise I won't keep you in the dark."

"I appreciate that." Cameron sipped his beer. "What do you suggest I do about Megan?"

"You can talk to her. Try to get her side of things. These people have a lot of money…more money than you and I will ever see in a lifetime… which gives them power. I have yet to determine whether or not this man, Kaspar, will abuse that power."

"Kaspar. Is he the father or the uncle?"

"The uncle."

"Damn it," Cameron whispered. "What the hell did my sister get herself into?"

"Only she can tell you that."

"And she will," Cameron said. "Are you getting any down time this trip?"

"I have to deal with this guy and then maybe I'll have a little," Dalton said. He pulled out his cell phone and shook his head. "Speak of the devil at hand." He answered the call. "Dalton Moore."

Cameron watched him as he tried to figure out what to do with Megan. His sister wasn't naïve…at least she wasn't anymore, and he was sure she knew he'd done some digging on Sophia's father. But he had a feeling she had no idea just how far he had gone to find out the truth. Since no one knew he was head negotiator for the FBI's kidnap and ransom division, she couldn't possibly know how much information was at his fingertips. His family believed he'd left the FBI years ago and had gone into the private sector. He made sure they continued to think that for their own safety. Over the years, he'd exhausted every avenue when it came to finding Sophia's father, including involving Interpol and Iceland's police, but he still came up empty. Whoever this man was, he either had reach, or was off the grid.

"Hey, I've gotta go," Dalton said, and dropped a twenty on the table.

"No problem." Cameron stood and followed him outside. After shaking Dalton's hand, he made his way to his car and headed home. He called Megan on the way home.

His sister answered immediately. "Hi, Cam."

"Well, hi there." Cameron smiled. "How are you feeling?"

"You mean, since the last time you called me? About five minutes ago?"

"Feel up to a visit?" he asked, ignoring her sarcasm.

She sighed. "Probably not."

"I'm about twenty minutes away."

"Jessie's here," Megan said.

Cameron frowned. "This can't wait."

"Great," she droned.

Cameron hung up and headed to his father's home in the West Hills.

* * *

Jesska sat next to her niece on the overstuffed sofa in her parents' family room. She hated this house. Hated everything it represented. But Megan and Sophia were staying there to recuperate, so she was there to visit. Hopefully, they'd be back in their own home soon, especially considering they were healing faster than anyone expected.

"Cam's on his way," Megan said as she returned from taking the call in her room.

"Everything okay?" Jesska asked.

"Who knows?"

Jesska giggled. "Which one of us is in trouble?"

"That would be me," Megan said.

"Why is Uncle Cam so…um…intense?" Sophia asked.

"He used to have to deal with some serious criminals when he was with the FBI, Soph," Megan said. "He's probably seen things we will never have to and he wants to keep it that way."

Sophia rolled her eyes. "My nurse thought he was super hot."

"What?" Jesska asked. "She talked to you about him? How unprofessional."

Sophia chuckled. "No, she thought I was still asleep. She was talking to one of the other nurses. 'Oooh, did you see that Cameron guy? Wasn't he hot?' Stuff like that."

"Yeah, all my friends have adored him as far back as I can remember," Jesska admitted. "But he was even more intense back then, and *way* more of a pain in the ass."

Megan laughed, and sat down in the chair by the fireplace. "But we love him anyway."

Jesska grinned. "That we do."

"Anyone hungry?" Megan asked.

Jesska jumped to her feet. "You rest. I can make us something."

"I'm fine, Jessie."

"Which I totally don't get. How is that even possible? It's only been a day since you got home."

"Miracle, I guess."

"I guess so," Jesska murmured.

"Which means I go back to school tomorrow, right?" Sophia chimed in.

"I don't know," Megan said as she headed to the kitchen off the family room.

"Mom, I'm fine. Even the doctor said so."

Megan turned to her and frowned. "If you wake up tomorrow without pain, I'll think about it."

Sophia jumped to her feet, rushing to kiss her mother. "Thank you, Mummykins. I'm going to call Bree." She took off up the stairs, dialing as she went.

Jesska grabbed for Brady's ring. Sophia's nickname for her mother brought memories back of her beloved Bradykins.

"Megan?" Cameron called from the foyer, and Jesska heard the front door close.

"Can I hide?" Megan asked.

"Probably not," Jesska said.

"Back here, Cam."

Cameron strolled into the room, slipping his keys into his pocket. "Hey, Jess."

"Hi. How are you?" she asked in a sing-song voice.

He grinned. "I'm good. How are you?"

"Curious."

"Of course you are." He turned to Megan. "Where's Soph?"

"Upstairs," Megan said.

"Cool. Let's talk, huh?"

"About what?" Jesska asked.

Cameron raised an eyebrow.

She rose to her feet. "Fine. I'll go find Sophia."

"Thanks, sissy."

"One day, you will tell me what's going on, so help me God." She pointed a finger to Cameron and then Megan. "Your little pow-wows are really beginning to piss me off."

"Love you," Cameron and Megan said in stereo as Jesska walked slowly up the stairs.

She knew they waited until she was out of hearing distance before they started to talk...and the reason she knew that was because she could no longer hear them.

* * *

The next morning, Jesska woke up with the hangover from hell and called in sick. It was only the second sick day she'd taken in three years, but she still felt guilty about taking a day off of work because she'd drunk too much the night before. And alone. She'd eaten an entire carton of Ben & Jerry's and a bottle and a half of red wine. She was officially pathetic, and admittedly, maybe a bit more like her mother than she was willing to admit.

After napping most of the morning away, she forced herself out of bed, grabbing a beer and making herself a sandwich. A little hair of the dog and food helped take the edge off, and she felt well enough to take a shower...but that's about when her day went to crap, starting with the phone call.

"Hi, Megan."

"Hey. Can you do me a huge favor?"

Jesska squeezed her eyes shut, knowing she was going to regret her answer. "Of course."

"Sophia's at school and having some stomach pain, and I'm stuck in court. Can you pick her up? I'd ask Cam, but I can't get a hold of him. You can just drop her home, so you don't have to take too much of your lunch hour."

"Yep, no problem. I actually took a sick day."

"You did? Are you okay?" Megan asked.

"Yeah, just felt a little off this morning. I feel great now." Jesska grabbed her keys and purse and locked up her duplex. "Let Sophia know I'll be there in a few."

"Thanks, Jessie. Love you."

"Love you too."

Jesska jumped in her car and took off to her alma mater. She had a moment of panic as the memories flooded her heart again, but just as quickly, she calmed and actually didn't feel like puking this time around. Returning to the school had always been difficult, and she'd avoided it as much as possible. She must be making progress.

"*Or*...maybe I'm forgetting," she mumbled, as she parked and took a minute to envision Brady's face. She kissed his ring and then slid out of her car and walked inside. Now that the school was considered a closed campus, there was only one way in, which meant she had to pass the glass box that held a tribute to Brady. Not just because of his horrific death, but because no one had managed to beat his wrestling record. Even ten years later. She held her hand against the side of her face like a blinder so she could pass it without seeing his face, and headed to the office.

"I'm here to pick up Sophia Bailey."

The receptionist nodded and picked up her phone. "I'll call her."

"Thanks."

"Jesska Shane is that you?"

Jesska glanced behind her to see her old English teacher walk into the office. She had to be in her late fifties by now. "Oh, hi, Mrs. Acker."

"I hardly recognized you with that black hair."

Jesska felt her cheeks heat. "Oh, right. I haven't been blonde in a long time. How are you?"

She smiled. "I'm doing well, honey. How about you?"

"Not bad."

"Are you visiting your niece?"

Jesska nodded. "I'm picking her up, actually. She's not feeling well, and my sister's stuck in court."

"Yes, I heard about her accident. I'm surprised she's here so soon afterwards."

"You know us Shanes," Jesska said. "We are all about surprising people."

"That you are, dear. Update me on you. Have you met a nice man and settled down yet?"

Jesska forced down her irritation. "No, ma'am. I doubt that will ever happen."

"Oh, honey, you need to get back to living. Brady was a wonderful young man, and he wouldn't have wanted you to be alone."

Thank you so much for the unsolicited and wholly unwanted advice, Jesska thought to herself. What she said was, "Thanks for your concern."

Mrs. Acker pulled her in for a motherly hug. "Don't be a stranger."

"I'll try my best."

The older woman left the office just as Sophia hobbled inside. "Hi Jess."

"Hey, babe." Jesska wrapped an arm around her shoulders. "You don't look so hot."

The receptionist opened the swinging door for her so she could join Jesska. "Yeah, I got hit in the stomach with a ball."

"Why the hell were you in phys ed?" Jesska demanded.

"I wasn't. I was walking to class and some idiot had it in the hallway. A different idiot smacked it out of his hands and it hit me. I'm okay. It just stings a bit."

Jesska pulled Sophia's shirt up to look. "There's no blood."

"No, I told you. I'm fine. Just got a bit winded."

"Okay, we'll get you home and we can watch a movie, okay?" Jesska signed her out.

"Sounds great," Sophia said.

Jesska led her into the hallway and towards the parking lot, the empty halls eerier than she remembered. She felt the air in the building shift, and she was drawn to a tall man striding purposefully toward her. She stalled, her heart racing as he approached. He had to be the best looking man she'd ever seen, and that thought sent her reeling. He had blond hair and wide shoulders and as he drew closer, she could see deep green eyes that stared through her…all the way to her soul. His skin was like porcelain, other than a day's growth over his chin. He looked to be her age or younger, but carried himself with the confidence of a man who'd lived life and probably ruled it, too.

For a brief second, he glanced at Jesska, and surprise covered his face. He then focused on Sophia. "Ása," he said.

Jesska gently pushed Sophia past him.

"Wait. Ása," he repeated.

"I think you have me confused with someone else," Sophia said.

"I might agree with you if you didn't look just like your papa."

"What?" Jesska's heart raced again. Something wasn't right. "Who *are* you?"

* * *

Kaspar stared at the beautiful young woman standing in front of his niece, protecting her even though she'd never have a chance against him. Black, shoulder-length hair with a tinge of red at the ends, big hazel eyes, and a tiny little diamond circle sitting proudly in the crease of her button nose, she was a little taller than most humans, however, still a good six inches shorter that him. His mate. He shook his head and took a moment to process the fact that she was the one. He didn't know how it was even possible, but a human had just wrapped herself around his heart, and he didn't even know her name.

"How did you get in here?" she asked.

"Your name, *elskan*," he said.

"Excuse me?" she snapped.

He wondered if he'd said it wrong in English. "What is your name?"

"None of your business." She turned to his niece. "Sophia, I need you to disappear. Understand?"

"Wait," he ordered.

Ása...or Sophia as his mate had called her, froze to the spot, but this woman was unaffected by him.

"You are in pain," Kaspar noted, and laid his hand on Ása, healing her.

"Don't touch her," his mate demanded as she grabbed Ása's arm, pulling her away from Kaspar. "Soph, you need to go," she said, obviously not understanding that Ása physically wouldn't be able to move until Kaspar released her.

"She can't," Kaspar said.

"Why?" The raven-haired beauty focused on him and frowned. "What did you do?"

"Your name."

She crossed her arms. "What did you do to my niece?"

"Tell me your name."

"What did you do to my niece?" she repeated, irritation and fear pouring off her.

He sighed and released his niece, who took off after a minute of stunned confusion. Kaspar couldn't stand the fear emanating from his mate. The last thing he wanted was for her to be frightened of him. "Will you tell me your name?"

She squared her shoulders. "It's Jesska."

"Jesska." He smiled. "A beautiful name."

"Thank you, I think." She bit her lip. "But I'm going to leave now, because you're frightening me."

He noticed she clasped something attached to a chain around her neck. "I apologize. I don't mean to frighten you."

He stepped forward and she didn't retreat, so he reached out and touched the hand that was at her throat. He felt her sadness, and when she dropped her hand, he saw a ring around a chain.

"What the hell are you doing here?" a voice bellowed.

Jesska turned toward the angry voice with a gasp. Dalton Moore rushed toward them, and Kaspar scowled as the man stepped between him and his mate, facing her. "Jesska, are you all right? Did he hurt you?"

Jesska shook her head. "How do you know my name?" she whispered.

"I'm Dalton Moore. I'm a friend of Cameron's."

"Oh," she squeaked. "I have to go."

"Yes. Go," Moore said.

Before she could move, rage filled Kaspar and he slammed Moore against the brick wall. Jesska screamed in fright.

"I have Red Fang on my hands, dumbass," Moore said. "Let me go or your ass will be on the floor."

Kaspar didn't have a chance to respond as a security guard ran toward them. "Hey. What's going on?"

Kaspar stepped back, noticing Jesska tugging on her necklace again. Moore diffused the situation quickly, using his FBI credentials to appease the security guard. Kaspar could see Jesska wanted to run, but for some reason, she didn't. He stepped closer to her. She stepped aside and then turned on her heel and bolted out of the school so fast, Kaspar wondered if he'd have been able to stop her.

"Come on," Moore demanded. "You need to leave."

"What are you doing here?"

"Making sure you don't do something stupid. Apparently, I'm too late." Moore studied him and then scowled. "Damn it. Is she...?"

"Is she what?" Kaspar asked.

"Is she your mate?" he whispered.

Kaspar was blindsided.

Moore chuckled without humor. "You didn't see that coming, huh?"

"How do you know?"

"You have a file an inch thick on me," Moore pointed out. "You tell me."

"I know you were FBI before working for Gunnach Pharmaceuticals."

"And Kade's mated to my sister."

This time Kaspar swore.

"You cannot interfere," Moore said. "You do this my way, or they will disappear again, including Jesska, and you will never be able to find them."

Kaspar moved toward him again, angry that Moore didn't appear concerned at all.

"Red Fang, buddy," he said, and held up his hands. "Please, give me a reason."

"*Einn daginn mun ég drepa þig í svefni,*" Kaspar said, seething. (One day I will kill you in your sleep.)

"And you're an entitled prick," Moore retorted.

Kaspar shook his head. "You haven't learned to speak Icelandic, apparently."

"Only a word or two, but I figure you just insulted me, and I've wanted to say that to you for two days." Moore started toward the door. "Coming?"

Kaspar followed him out of the school, albeit at a distance.

CHAPTER SIX

JESSKA WALKED OUTSIDE to find Sophia in her car, idling at the curb. "What *are* you doing, Sophia?"

"I'm the getaway driver," she said.

"Melodramatic much? Scooch. I'm driving," she said, and forced Sophia from the driver's seat into the passenger side. Securing her seatbelt, Jesska took off toward Cameron's house. She didn't know what was going on, but she knew enough to get to the safest place on earth.

"Who *was* that, Auntie?" Sophia asked.

"I don't know, babe. Call Cam, okay?"

"On it." Sophia grabbed her phone and called Cameron. While Sophia filled him in on what just happened, Jesska drove the back streets to his apartment, entering the code for access to the parking lot, relieved to find his extra space free.

Jesska's phone rang just as she locked her car. "Hey, Cam."

"Okay, what the hell's going on. Really?" Cameron demanded.

"I met your friend, Dalton," she said, trying to keep the fear from her voice for Sophia's benefit.

"Damn it. Are you okay?"

"Yep."

"Did he say why he was there? Was anyone else with him?"

"No and not *with* him per se."

"These vague answers are because Sophia's with you, right?" he deduced.

"Yep," she said.

"Okay. You're at my place, right?"

"Yep."

"Okay. Let yourself in and then lock the door. No one comes in but me or Megan, got it?"

"Yep," she said, a forced a smile toward Sophia.

"Dalton's ex-FBI, Jess. And honestly, I'm not entirely sure how 'ex' he is. Someone has been looking for Megan and Sophia, but I don't know all the details, so it's important you hear me on that."

"Yep, got it," she said again.

"Okay. I'll be there soon. 'Bye."

"See ya."

"Is everything okay?" Sophia asked.

"Everything's going to be fine." Jesska tugged Sophia into the elevator and then walked quickly to Cameron's door, nearly dropping her spare key when she tried to put it in the lock. She took a deep breath and turned the lock, pushing Sophia inside before her and locking the door before entering the code for the alarm. "How about I make us something to eat and we'll watch a movie."

"I have to study," Sophia said, dropping her backpack on Cameron's sofa.

"Did anyone ever tell you you're an overachiever?"

Sophia giggled. "Not today."

"Why don't you use Cam's office? It'll be quieter in there."

"Good idea," Sophia said, picking up her bag and heading down the hall.

Jesska lowered herself onto the sofa and dropped her face in her hands. Now that the adrenaline was beginning to wear off, she started to shake. Who was that man and why was she drawn to him? She rubbed Brady's ring and felt guilt settle over her. Whoever he was, she needed to make sure she never saw him again. For a brief time, she'd forgotten about Brady, and that was unacceptable. This man was entirely too good-looking and when he touched her, she felt like she knew him, but worse than that, she felt like he knew *her*.

She shook her head, her thoughts turning to him again. He had eyes so green, they reminded her of emeralds, and when he looked at her, his face softened, and she felt her breath catch. She'd itched to reach out and touch the day's growth of stubble that covered his strong jaw. She groaned, shaking her head again.

"You okay?" Sophia called.

"No, I'm an idiot," she mumbled.

"Auntie? Are you okay?" Sophia asked again.

"Yep, I'm fine," she called back, and stood to head down the hall. Arriving at the office, she pushed open the door and leaned against the doorjamb. "Are you hungry or is your stomach still sore?"

Sophia looked up from Cameron's desk. "I feel totally fine. No pain, no nothing. And yes, I'm starving."

Jesska smiled. "I'll find us something to eat."

Sophia nodded, placing an earbud in her ear and going back to her book while Jesska headed to the kitchen to raid her brother's pantry. Her thoughts turned to the mysterious man again and she reached for Brady's ring. "I won't forget, Bradykins."

She focused on making sandwiches, grateful Cameron kept fresh bread and every fixing imaginable. Hearing the locks turn in the door, she grabbed a knife and stepped out from behind the kitchen island, positioning herself between the office where Sophia studied, and whoever was coming in. She sighed when her brother walked inside.

"Jess," he warned. "What were you planning on doing with that?"

"I don't know." She frowned at the knife. "I was going to defend Sophia, I guess?"

"Put the knife down, Jess," Cameron said. "You could end up being the cautionary tale of what happens when you bring a knife to a gun fight."

"You have your gun?"

"I always have my gun."

Jesska set the knife on the island and watched as Cameron locked up the apartment again. "Do you want a sandwich?" she asked.

"Sure. Where's Soph?"

"In your office, studying."

"I'll go say hi and then you and I can talk, sound good?"

"Yep. Here, take this to her." Jesska handed him a sandwich and a bottled water.

He returned and they sat side-by-side at the island to eat. Jesska couldn't stop her knee from bouncing as she chewed.

Cameron set his hand on her leg and shook his head with a smile. "What do you want to know?"

"Everything. Who was that guy? Why is he looking for Megan and Sophia? Why did he call her Ása? Does he have the wrong person? If not, then what does he want with them?" *Why am I so freaking attracted to him?* That question, she kept to herself.

"He is Sophia's uncle, we're still not sure, and in answer to your third question, again, we're not sure."

Jesska let out a frustrated sigh. "Useless."

Cameron chuckled. "I know."

"Let's discuss what you do know."

Cameron nodded as he chewed.

Jesska took a swig of water and then asked, "Why didn't Megan tell us about this uncle person and that he might come looking for them?"

Cameron shook his head. "I don't think she knew about him. I don't know all the details, but when Megan got back to the States, she changed Sophia's name, took on Mom's maiden name, and filled me in on what she said she could. I don't know all the details. I think she's a little surprised it's taken this long for these people to come looking for her. I think she expected it to happen a while ago."

"This guy that Megan ran off to Iceland with, what happened to him?"

"No idea," Cameron admitted. "Megan's on her way from court, so she'll hopefully be able to fill us in."

"Are they in danger?"

"I don't think so, Messka. I think Kaspar's just looking for answers."

"Kaspar? That's the uncle?"

Cameron nodded.

Jesska tried to stamp down her dreamy reaction. Sexy man, sexy name, sexy everything. Yep, she was in big, big trouble. Shaking off her thoughts, she carried her plate to the sink and finished the dishes.

* * *

Megan arrived almost an hour later, rushing in to see Sophia before sitting down with Cameron and Jesska. Jesska frowned. Her sister was frazzled. Megan didn't *get* frazzled.

"Sophia filled me in on everything, including this man putting his hand on her," Megan said. "Which is not okay. No one touches my girl."

"He was helping her, I think," Jesska rushed to say. She had no idea why she had the sudden need to defend him.

"No one touches her, period."

"Yes, of course."

"Did he say what he wanted?" Megan asked.

Jesska shook her head. "Not in so many words. He called her Ása and said he was her uncle."

"Crap."

"Dalton told me to let me know someone's looking for you and Sophia," Cameron said.

"And you didn't think that would be something I should know?" Megan ground out.

"I wanted more information before I worried you."

"You are a total pain in the ass, Cameron," she said. "Stop trying to protect everyone."

"No," he countered.

"What do you know?"

"Not much, Megan," Cameron admitted. "Just that someone is looking for you."

Megan swore.

"Do we get the story now?" Jesska asked.

Megan nodded, flopping onto Cameron's sofa facing the large picture window. "I guess it's time, huh?"

"Does Sophia know anything?" Cameron asked.

"I haven't really told her much, although she's smart, so she might have figured out more than I'm guessing," Megan admitted. "That being said, however, she's never really asked about her father. There were questions when she was little, but I just told her that her daddy couldn't live with us. I've been putting her off for more than ten years." She frowned. "I don't know why Ari's suddenly made this an issue. Where the hell has he been for the last sixteen years?"

"Wait," Jesska said. "I thought he was dead."

"She lied," Cameron said.

"I had to." Megan rolled her eyes. "Not that you believed me, apparently."

"No, I didn't believe you," he said. "But when I couldn't find any information out about the guy, I assumed you'd left him and changed your names so he couldn't find you."

"You looked for him?"

"Hell, yes, I looked for him. What kind of bastard just lets his woman walk out the door with his baby daughter and not scour the earth looking for her?"

Megan nodded. "I get it. But, I'm not mad that he didn't come looking for us back then, I'm just confused about why he is now."

"Was he that horrible?" Jesska asked.

"No. He was wonderful."

"What? Seriously?" Cameron asked. "Why did you leave, then?"

"It's complicated," she said.

"Megan," Cameron warned.

"Look, I was young and stupid. Obviously. I would have followed him anywhere. But all of a sudden, things between us changed, and it frightened me. We'd been to hell and back, but he was different. I had to leave. He was just…so…intense. I can't explain it."

Cameron studied her.

"What?" she asked.

"What do you consider to hell and back? What aren't you telling us?"

"*Cam.*"

"Tell us, Megan."

"Sophia has two sisters." Megan's eyes filled with tears. "I gave birth to them several years before her."

"What?" Jesska squeaked. "You had more babies?"

Megan nodded, reaching for the tissues.

"Where are they?" Cameron demanded.

"I don't know. I had two really difficult deliveries and lost a lot of blood with each of them. I was hospitalized for a week with the first and four days with the second. With the first one, when I woke up, Ari was in a rage and the baby was gone. He'd taken precautions with the second, but she disappeared as well right after I gave birth."

"Where?" Cameron demanded.

"I don't *know*," Megan said. "For a while, I forgot. Literally forgot I had ever been pregnant before." She shook her head. "Somehow Ari was able to protect us this time, I don't know how, but Sophia was in my arms when I woke up. I was really out of it, because I'd lost a dangerous amount of blood again. But soon after I had her, he changed. I remember it really well, because it was on my twenty-fifth birthday, which he managed to ruin spectacularly." She shuddered. "I had to leave him, but it took me three tries before I succeeded. A lovely woman helped me get out of Iceland, and then I managed to get home."

"I still don't quite understand why you had to leave him," Jesska said. "Was he abusive?"

Megan shook her head, closing her eyes for a second. "No. He was just…different. I can't explain it." She groaned. "I'm a coward. I know I am, but I was too frightened by what I was feeling to stay. And then to remember my babies and not know where they were, I just couldn't function. If Ari, with all his money and influence, couldn't find them, we were screwed. But I knew that Sophia and I could disappear without a trace. I just needed to find a way to keep her safe."

Jesska reached out and squeezed her hand.

"Who is this man looking for us?" Megan asked.

"Ari is it?" Cameron asked. "Your ex?"

Megan nodded.

"It's Ari's brother. Kaspar. He's some kind of royalty."

"I knew about the royalty part, but Ari would never introduce me to any of his family. I only knew he had a couple of brothers who lived in some isolated place in Iceland. Ari and I lived in a ridiculously opulent apartment in Reykjavík, and he'd occasionally leave me for a weekend or a few days to visit with them, but would never take me." Megan wiped her eyes again. "I think he was ashamed of me. I was just a normal girl, without a royal connection and therefore, unworthy to meet them."

"What an entitled jerk," Jesska said.

"What do we do now, Cam? What does your friend say about the whole thing? Do I have to see Kaspar?" Megan asked.

"You don't have to do anything you don't want to do," Cameron promised. "I think he wants some answers, which I will be happy to provide. I do think you should stay here for a couple of days, though. Just to be safe. He won't be able to get to you here. Can Sophia get her assignments from her teachers and work from here?"

Megan nodded. "I don't have court for a week, so I can work from here too. Perks of working for yourself, I guess."

Jesska rubbed her temples. Her hangover was catching up with her, and she just wanted to go home and sleep. "I think I'm going to take off. I didn't sleep much last night, so I need to get an early night if I'm going to be able to function tomorrow."

"Are you feeling okay?" Megan asked in concern.

"Yes. I'm fine, sissy. Just tired." Jesska rose to her feet and stretched. "I'll say good night to Soph and then get out of your hair. Do you want me to run by your place and pick up anything?"

"I can do that," Megan said.

"Let's wait a bit, huh?" Cameron countered. "I can pick up anything you need later tonight."

"Really?" Jesska challenged. "You're going to grab tampons and undies and the like?"

Cameron groaned, his face bright red.

Jesska and Megan giggled.

"I'll be happy to grab whatever you need," Jesska said. "Just give me a list."

"Thanks, Jessie," Megan said. "I'll write it while you say good night to Sophia."

Jesska hugged her niece and then grabbed her purse and keys and the list from Megan. "I'll run by your place now and then Cam can pick the stuff up from me later. Sound good?"

"Perfect."

Megan hugged her and then Cameron did the same, and Jesska headed to her car.

CHAPTER SEVEN

JESSKA PULLED UP to Megan's home on Alberta and parked on the street. She loved her sister's little house that suited her and Sophia perfectly. It might be small, but Megan owned it, and had worked hard to afford it after paying for law school. Letting herself inside, Jesska didn't have any warning before the energy shifted in the room and she realized she wasn't alone. Spinning back toward the front door, she let out a squeak to find Kaspar filling the frame, blocking the light from the porch.

"What the hell do *you* want?" she demanded.

"I don't mean to frighten you, little one."

"Says the man standing inside my sister's doorway, uninvited and threatening."

"I apologize." He stepped outside and smiled. "I'm now not in the doorway."

"Smartass," she said, and tried to close the door, but he laid his palm against it, and his strength far outweighed hers.

"I'm not here to hurt you, elskan. I am looking for my niece."

"She's not here."

"Where is she?"

"None of your business," she said.

Anger flashed in his eyes, and Jesska tried not to panic.

"I'm sorry, elskan." He reached out and ran a finger down her cheek, and she immediately felt calmer, much to her amazement. "I will not hurt you. I would never hurt you."

She believed him. To her core, she knew he'd protect her with his life. She just didn't know how or why she knew that. She took a deep breath. "Maybe that's true, but I don't know you, and the fact that you're stalking my niece makes me question your intentions."

"Will you allow me to explain?" he asked. "I will tell you everything I know if you'll just let me."

Jesska stared up at him for several seconds. "Fine. I'll give you five minutes, but not inside. This isn't my home, and I don't feel comfortable inviting you in."

"On the porch, then."

Jesska paused for a second before stepping outside, locking the door behind her, and sitting in one of the porch chairs.

Kaspar sat in the other and stared out to the street. "My brother has made a few unfortunate choices of late—"

Jesska snorted. "A few?"

"Já. More than a few, eh?" Kaspar sighed.

"Já," she mimicked. "What's his deal with my sister anyway? She obviously left him for a reason."

Kaspar cocked his head. "What do you know of their story?"

"Probably less than you."

"I doubt that," he admitted. "Did she tell you how they met?"

"All I know is that Megan met him at some party, and ran off with him to Iceland. She came home when Sophia was one, but she never talked about your brother, and I never asked. I was only ten when they got back." Jesska stared out to the street. "As I got older, I just assumed something bad had happened and respected Megan's privacy enough not to ask her about it. She told us he died, and I remember thinking it was weird that she changed their last name to Bailey, but I was too young to really understand the reason behind it. I've only recently learned a few of the details around her story with your brother, so I'm sure it's cloudy memories anyway."

"I understand why she did it now." Kaspar grimaced. "I just wish I'd known about it at the time."

"Why?"

"Because I could have helped. I could have protected them."

"From what?" Jesska demanded.

"From everything. Right now, we are unclear as to exactly what is going on, but if I'd known about Megan, I would have insisted she come to my residence during her pregnancies. It's the safest place in Iceland, perhaps in the world."

"What did your brother tell you?" Jesska asked.

"Not much," he said. "I'm still ignorant of the entire truth, because Ari's afraid. Of what, I'm also not entirely clear about. All I know is that

I have three nieces that no one in our family but he knew anything about until recently, and that someone wants these girls...for what purpose, I don't know."

Jesska frowned. "You don't seem to know much, do you? Do you know why our nieces are in demand, so to speak?"

"They are special."

Jesska pushed out of her chair and paced the small porch. "Special, how, exactly?"

"That you're not ready to hear yet."

"What? Why not?" she asked, leaning against the railing.

"There are things that you can't believe, elskan, and until you're open to believing, you won't."

"What does elskan mean? Why do you keep saying that?"

He chuckled. "Something else you're not ready to hear."

She pulled out her cell phone. "I'll look it up then."

Kaspar cocked his head and gave her a snarky smile, so she found an Icelandic translation site and typed in the word. She gasped. "Um, no. Did I spell it wrong? E-L-S-K-A-N, right?"

He nodded.

She stepped away from the railing and made her way to the front door again. "I am nobody's sweetheart or baby," she snapped, and unlocked her sister's door.

Before she could open it, he took her hand gently and turned her to face him. "As I said, elskan, you are not ready to hear it."

She felt the heat creep up her neck and dropped her gaze from his. "Stop calling me that."

Kaspar smiled, raising her palm to his lips. As he pressed his lips to the middle of her hand, he frowned, pushing her sleeve up her arm. "What the hell is this?"

She tried to yank her hand from his, but he held firm. "Let me go."

"Who did this to you?" he demanded.

"Nobody. Let me go."

"Jesska, who did this to you?" he repeated, his eyes searching hers.

She shook her head, forcing back tears. "No one did it *to* me. I did it to myself."

"Why?" She shook her head again, but he lifted her chin gently and stroked her cheek. "Why, elskan?"

She bit her lip. "It helps."

"It helps what?"

"The guilt...and the pain."

He sighed, kissing one of her scars gently and pulling her into his arms. She squeezed her eyes shut. She could hear the steady beat of his heart when she pressed her cheek against his chest. She felt like she was home. Like she was supposed to be there, standing on her sister's porch in the twilight, in the arms of the best-looking man she'd ever seen. She didn't know how or understand why, but Kaspar was someone she could trust with her life. But even more importantly, she could trust him with her heart. She slid her arms up his back, reveling in the warmth of his body as he held her.

When he pulled away and leaned down to kiss her, hesitating millimeters from her lips, asking without words if it was okay, she answered by closing the distance between them, and then she was truly lost.

She whimpered as emotions flooded her. Guilt, anger, sadness, despair...her heart ran the gamut as he deepened the kiss and seemed to wipe away the negative feelings with each passing second. Her grief was replaced with desire and then joy before he broke the kiss, stroking her cheek as they both tried to catch their breath.

"How did you do that?" she asked.

"We are connected, elskan. I will always protect you...even from your own feelings."

She hissed, pushing away from him. "Is that what your brother did to Megan?"

"Elskan."

He reached for her again, but she shook her head. "No. Don't touch me. If you can do to me what he did to her, then that means I have no control."

"That's not true, sweetheart," he countered. "You have all the control."

"*She* didn't."

"Why do you think she was able to leave him?" he challenged.

"I don't know." Jesska dragged her hands down her face, shaking her head. "She told me he was able to stop her twice before she finally escaped."

"I don't believe that is accurate, little one. If what I think is true, then he would not have been able to stop her."

"What does that *mean*?" she snapped. Before he could answer, she raised her hand. "No, don't bother answering. I have a lot to do. Please leave."

She pushed open the door and stepped inside, locking it behind her and leaning against it in an effort to catch her breath.

CHAPTER EIGHT

KASPAR LET HER retreat. He knew that if he pushed her, she'd only run...or hurt herself again. He needed some answers of his own before he could accurately explain anything to her. He returned to the car, Austri opened the door and Kaspar climbed inside. Once Austri slid into the driver's seat, Kaspar said, "Wait and see if she comes out soon. If she does, follow her."

Austri nodded and Kaspar raised the partition glass, pulling out his phone and dialing Kade Gunnach.

"Gunnach."

"I need to speak with my brother."

Kade sighed, but didn't respond.

"The calls are recorded, Kade. There's no reason to stop this."

"You're becoming a pain in my arse, that's a good enough reason. Why do you need to speak with him?"

"That I can't tell you," Kaspar said.

"As you so eloquently pointed out, I will have every chance to listen to your conversation while and after it takes place, so you might as well tell me now."

"My brother should answer my questions before you are aware of what they are."

Kade sighed again, but Kaspar knew he understood. Whether he'd allow another conversation was the question.

"I'll patch you through. But I'll be listening."

"I don't doubt it."

The line went quiet for a few seconds before Ari's voice sounded over the wire. "Kaz?"

"How are you?"

"Fine, Kaspar. *Fannstu þá?*" (Did you find them?)

"Já."

"*Hvar eru þeir?*" (Where are they?)

"*Öruggir.*" (Safe.)

"*Segðu mér,*" Ari demanded. (Tell me.)

"*Nei, ég er með spurningu áður en ég segi þér eitthvað.*" (No. I have a question before I tell you anything.)

"*Hvað?*" (What?)

"*Er þessi kona maki þinn?*" (Is this woman your mate?)

"*Við bindumst ekki með mönnum.*" (We don't mate with humans.)

"*Við erum alin upp við þá trú, en ég þarf að vita, er hún maki þinn?*" Kaspar asked again. (That is what we are raised to believe, but I need to know, is she your mate?)

"Já," Ari admitted.

"Then why didn't you bind her?"

"Because I thought I was wrong."

"Were you afraid of what might happen if you bound a human?"

"I suppose. When she reached ár mökunar, I knew she felt what I felt and, God help me, I was going to bind her despite our laws, consequences be damned, but before I could, she was gone."

"Skít," Kaspar snapped.

"You've really found her?" Ari asked again.

"I have found your daughter. I have yet to see Megan."

"Is she happy? My beautiful Ása?"

"I believe so, brother."

"Who does she look like?" Ari asked. "I bet she's as beautiful as her mama."

"She actually looks just like you."

"I wish I could see her. Just one last time." Ari sighed. "Find Megan, Kaz. Please. I can't die without knowing she's safe."

"You're not going to die, Ari."

"You don't know that, brother. I have no idea what Kade Gunnach is capable of."

"We'll cross that bridge when we come to it," Kaspar said.

"You must promise me you'll protect her."

Kaspar pinched the bridge of his nose. "What the hell is going on, Ari? The truth. Why did you not tell me?"

"I don't know why. I thought I'd lose her if I did, I suppose."

Kaspar decided to pose a calculated question, knowing he was being recorded, but also aware that Ari didn't. "Why did you threaten the Gunnach family? Why did you try to hurt them?"

"I had no intention of harming anyone. I knew I would never find Ása without my other girls, but I misjudged their mates' powers...or how far they'd go to protect them."

"Which makes you an idiot," Kaspar snapped.

"Já. This is new territory for us, brother. I have no excuse."

Kaspar glanced up as the car pulled away from the curb. Jesska must be leaving, and he hoped she'd lead him to her sister. "I have to go. I'll try to contact you when I know more."

"Protect her, Kaz. *Please.*"

"I will," he promised, and hung up.

* * *

The next day, Jesska had planned to have dinner at Cameron's, something the siblings tried to do a couple of times a month. As she drove further into the city, she glanced into the rearview mirror and then behind her...then in her side mirrors, a strange feeling of being watched covering her again. She didn't see anyone following her. At least, nothing seemed out of the ordinary to her as she maneuvered the busy Portland streets. "There is something seriously wrong with you, Jess," she grumbled out loud.

She'd dropped the things off for Megan and Sophia the night before and ended up hanging out at Cameron's until far later than expected. After the strange run-in with Kaspar, she'd needed her family, and they'd stayed up until the wee hours talking about the strange events that were happening. Unfortunately, none of them had been able to come to any conclusions about what any of them meant.

Arriving at her brother's building, she entered the code for the garage and waited for the gate to open, drove inside, and parked in his space. She climbed out of the car and glanced around. No one had followed her. She was just going batty. Popping the trunk, she locked her car, grabbed the wine bag, and then headed to the elevator.

Instead of letting herself in, she knocked, unprepared for what happened when Cameron opened the door. Kaspar pushed past her into the apartment, and then all hell broke loose. Jesska couldn't stop a scream as Cameron, obviously anticipating the attack, pulled his gun from his holster and aimed it at Kaspar's heart. Jesska found herself jumping in front of Kaspar and holding her hands out to her brother. Kasper sidestepped her, and she had to move again.

Cameron aimed the gun away from her, taking a second to close and lock the front door. "Move, Jess."

"No," she said. "I don't want you to hurt him."

"I want to see my niece," Kaspar demanded, and settled his hand on Jesska's lower back, moving out from behind her again.

"She's not here," Cameron said.

"Then I'll wait."

"Like hell you will," Cameron snapped.

Jesska faced Kaspar. "What are you doing here? I'm assuming you followed me?"

"Followed, no...waited for you to show up, yes," Kaspar said.

"He stalked you?"

"Cam," she snapped, glancing over her shoulder. "Shhh."

Cameron swore and Jesska turned to face him.

"Will you please put the gun down?" she insisted.

"No," Cameron said.

She frowned and faced Kaspar again. "You need to leave."

Kaspar shook his head. "I need answers, and I can't get those answers until I speak with your sister."

"This isn't the way to get them."

"I disagree." He cocked his head and smiled. "I think it's the perfect way."

"You can't hurt them," she begged.

"Elskan." Kaspar frowned, taking her hand and squeezing it. "Haven't you figured out I have no intention of harming anyone? I just need some answers."

"Do you know this guy, Jess?" Cameron asked...actually it was more of a demand than a question.

She tugged her hand from Kaspar's and faced her brother. "No. Not really."

Cameron stepped toward them. "Then why are you letting him touch you?"

"I don't really have a choice," she grumbled.

"He's forcing you?" Cameron bellowed, and aimed the gun at Kaspar's head.

"No!" Jesska insisted, stepping in front of him again. And again, Kaspar shifted, much to Jesska's irritation.

"Stop getting between him and the gun, Jess," Cameron warned.

"I'm not going to let you shoot him, Cam." Jesska glanced at Kaspar. "And you need to quit moving. He won't shoot me to get to you."

Kaspar shook his head. "And I won't allow you into the fray, so listen to your brother, please."

The click of the locks drew focus to the door and Megan and Sophia walked in. Megan caught sight of Kaspar and shoved Sophia back outside, telling her to run.

Kaspar was faster than Jesska would have ever guessed, and grabbed Sophia before she even stepped back over the threshold. Megan screamed and clawed at him to let her daughter go, but Kaspar managed to pull them both inside, past the doorway, albeit gently.

Jesska tried to stay between Kaspar and her brother's gun, even though she knew Cam would never shoot him in front of Sophia, so she relaxed a bit.

"I'm not going to hurt you," Kaspar insisted.

Sophia looked panicked, tears flowing down her cheeks. "Please, let me go," she pleaded.

Kaspar released her immediately, and Jesska realized he was telling the truth. He really didn't want to hurt anyone. He also released Megan, but watched her closely.

Jesska studied him warily. What did he want? She desperately wanted to know his intentions with her family...and with her.

Once Sophia was released, Megan calmed, pulling her daughter behind her and facing Kaspar. "What do you want? What does *he* want?"

"Perhaps Sophia should go to her room and we'll talk," Cameron suggested.

"Probably a good idea," Kaspar agreed.

"Mom?" Sophia squeaked.

"It's okay, honey. I'll come see you in a bit. Everything's okay."

"Wait," Kaspar said, closing the distance between them.

Megan stepped between them and Kaspar let her.

"I'm very sorry if I frightened you, child," he said. "I would never hurt you intentionally."

Sophia looked up at him and then her mother. Her mother nodded, and without a word, Sophia took off toward Cameron's spare room.

Before any more conversation could happen, someone pounded on Cameron's front door. "What now?" he snapped, opening the door to a fuming Dalton Moore.

The man stalked inside and headed straight for Kaspar, who quickly moved out of his way. "I told you I'd handle this," Dalton snapped.

Jesska stared at Kaspar. He looked genuinely concerned when Dalton got anywhere near him.

"Stop moving, you entitled bastard," Dalton demanded.

Kaspar shook his head. "I don't want you within reach of me."

Jesska frowned.

Dalton raised his hands, but didn't step away. "Then come with me."

"I require answers first."

"Actually, so do I," Megan said.

All eyes were on her as she crossed her arms and stared Kaspar down.

"I'll answer anything I can," Kaspar promised.

"Your decision, Megan," Cameron said.

"I will dispose of him if you want me to," Dalton added.

"No!" Jesska snapped, and couldn't stop a horrified expression as she stared at Dalton. He looked like he would enjoy "disposing" of Kaspar, given half the chance.

"It's okay, elskan," Kaspar assured her.

"I want answers, but I'd like them without eavesdropping," Megan said.

"Are you sure?" Cameron asked.

Megan nodded.

Cameron waved a hand toward the hallway. "You can use my office."

Megan motioned for Kaspar to follow her, and he gave Dalton a wide berth as he slipped past him. He paused to squeeze Jesska's hand. "Are you all right?"

She nodded, and he released her to follow Megan.

* * *

Kaspar walked inside the room and was instantly impressed with the office space. It had floor-to-ceiling windows that made him feel like he was standing at the top of the world, and the size itself was bigger than most double bedrooms in Iceland. The view was incomparable as the sun set over the water.

Megan closed the door behind him, and motioned to the chair facing the large mahogany desk. He sat down after she took Cameron's chair. "Why are you here?" she asked, her voice shaking. "You cannot take Sophia from me. I won't allow it."

"Sister," Kaspar said with a frown. "I have no intention of taking her from you. Did my brother make you believe that I would?"

Megan shrugged. "He never discussed you. I only found out through his staff that he had family and that you were royalty."

"What about when he came to visit me?"

"He left me behind."

"Obviously," Kaspar said. "But did he tell you where he was going?"

"No. He said it was business. I usually found out after the fact that he had visited his family."

Kaspar could see that Ari's deception had wounded Megan and, with the sheen of tears she tried to blink away, he could see it still did. "Tell me what you want to know," he said.

"What are you?" Megan asked.

"Excuse me?"

She cleared her throat. "What are you? I have been away from Ari long enough that I have figured out you're not what you seem. He was able to wipe my pregnancies from memory and replace them with entirely different ones. He could make me believe anything he said. It took me until I was here before I started to put the fragmented pieces of my mind back together."

"And from that, you believe that I would hurt you or Sophia?"

Megan stared at him for several tense seconds before shaking her head and rising to her feet. She made her way to the windows and stared out at the water. "I don't think Ari would ever allow us to be hurt."

Kaspar relaxed. "What do you remember?"

She faced him, crossing her arms. "I remember almost everything now. What I can't figure out is if what I'm remembering is accurate or not."

"Which parts?"

"Him. What we felt for each other."

"What did you feel for him?"

"I loved him. More than I had ever loved anyone…and probably ever will."

"Then why did you leave?" he asked.

"We weren't safe."

"From him?"

Megan shrugged. "I don't know anymore. At the time I thought he was the threat, but the longer I've been away, the less I believe that. Someone stole our babies. There was a woman…an old woman, who said that Ari had given them away. At the time, I was angry, horrified, inconsolable, everything you would imagine a mother to feel when she's lost her children. But Ari would hold me, and I realize now that he could manipulate my memories and emotions, and he made me forget I'd had any other kids."

"I think he did that to protect you," Kaspar said.

"I do too," she admitted. "When I had Sophia, Ari made sure she was never out of his sight. Her birth was the hardest on me, and I was in and out of consciousness."

Kaspar looked at Megan with a new respect. Giving birth to a Kalt Einn baby would have wreaked havoc on her human body, and the fact she did it three times meant she was stronger than anyone probably would have given her credit for.

"I had a wonderful nurse who said Ari didn't sleep for four days while I was unstable. He sat by my bed, one hand on me and one on her...we'd originally called her Ása. I woke up to find him in bed with me, her in between us."

"Then why did you leave him?"

"Because we really weren't safe. The nurse, the one who came to the house, said that people were looking for us, and if I didn't want to lose my baby, I had to leave."

Kaspar raised an eyebrow. "What was the nurse's name?"

Megan squeezed her eyes shut as if trying to remember. "Clara, I think."

"Did she say who these people were?"

"No." She sighed. "And to be fair, I didn't ask. I was tired, I had an almost one year-old, and I felt like I was going crazy. Maybe I felt like I was going crazy because I was tired. I don't know."

"Why did you feel crazy?"

"Ari changed. I guess I did too, but he was frustrated all the time. He'd snap at me and the staff, I'd hear him yelling at his valet, security guy, constantly. Honestly, I'm surprised Dreki stuck around. When we were alone, we were constantly bickering, and I could hear him in my mind. Speaking to me. I thought I was hearing voices. He also wouldn't marry me. Said that he couldn't." She blinked back tears. "God help me, but I was so in love with that man, I stayed. By the time I finally left, the only person he seemed to cherish was Ása."

Kaspar sighed. "Well, that's not even the least bit true."

"You don't think?"

"No, Megan, I don't. I'm sorry you felt that way...sorry he made you feel that way, but he loved you. He still loves you. We are bound by tradition and lore, and we are trying to break free from the archaic laws, but we find it difficult at times."

"You mean the ones that say you can't marry someone who isn't royalty?"

"You asked what we are. I will tell you the truth. I mean the laws that say we cannot be bound to anyone human."

Megan sucked in a great gulp of air, coughing as she choked. Kaspar rushed to her and did his best to calm her, but they weren't family yet—not until Ari bound her, so he wasn't able to do much to help.

The door slammed open, and Cameron had his gun ready again.

"What the hell are you doing, Cameron?" Megan demanded as she finally brought her coughing under control.

"Are you all right?" her brother asked.

"Yes, I'm fine. I just swallowed wrong. Why the hell do you have your gun out? God, Cameron, you'd think you're some drug lord protecting your product. Put. It. Away."

Kaspar noticed Jesska hovering in the background and made his way to her while Megan continued to chastise Cameron.

"What's going on?" she asked.

"We're just trying to sort all of this out, elskan."

She wrinkled her nose as she frowned up at him. "Don't call me that."

"Hey." He smiled and squeezed her arm. "Are you okay?" She nodded and he lifted her palm to his lips. "When this discussion is all over, will you allow me to take you to dinner?"

Jesska bit her lip. "No."

"I don't typically take no for an answer," he said.

Jesska glanced at her sister, still in a heated exchanged with Cameron, and then back at him. "Well, now's your chance to get used to it."

He smiled again. "We'll see."

Megan shoved Cameron past them and then turned to Jesska. "Out, please."

Jesska bit her lip again, and it took every bit of self-control for Kaspar not to pry it from her teeth and kiss her. He squeezed her hand and nodded, which elicited another frown from her, but she did step outside and close the door.

Megan turned the lock and headed back to the desk. "Where were we?"

"What did you hear?"

"That you're not human," she whispered.

"It's true."

"I don't understand."

Kaspar stared out at the water. "I know you don't, and I think Ari should be telling you this, but I also think it's something you've suspected for a while. Am I right?"

Megan nodded. "I think so. There were too many weird things happening for it to be normal. Is this why he was acting so strange?"

"Yes." Kaspar sat down again and indicated for Megan to do the same. "You have to understand that when we turn twenty-five, we reach what we call ár mökunar, which means that when we find our…ah, the person we are going to be with forever, we don't wait around. We bind them and move on with our lives. When Ari met you, he knew you were his mate, but he couldn't do anything until you reached ár mökunar as well. As a human, you were forbidden to him, but he would never have been able to accept that, so he tried to make it work."

"Well then, why are you here and not him?"

"He's ...ah... *hann er í fangelsi.*"

"He's in jail?" she squeaked.

"You speak Icelandic?"

"I lived there for a long time. Of course I picked up the language," she said in frustration. "Don't change the subject."

"Sorry."

"Why is he in jail?"

"Because he's an idiot."

"What did he do?" she asked.

"He found your other daughters and dosed their families with Red Fang; however, it didn't work. He was caught and is now in Edinburgh."

"*Scot*land?"

Kaspar nodded.

"He found our babies?" she rasped.

"Já. They are mat—ah, married and living there."

"What are they like? Were they happy growing up? Are they happy now? Do they know what happened?"

"I don't know, Megan. I'm sorry."

"I have to go there," she said, and pulled her phone out of her pocket. "Crap. It's dead. I need my laptop."

"Wait," Kaspar said. "We can't go anywhere until we sort this out. I don't know that you would be allowed to see him anyway."

"But I can see *them*, right?"

"I don't know," he admitted. "I need to know who took your girls first. Ari doesn't know, and I'm concerned that if you're not under my protection and your brother's, that something will happen."

She blinked back tears. "You're probably right. This just sucks."

"I agree."

Megan crossed her arms. "You said Ari dosed the family with something. What is Red Fang?"

"It's a native flower than can render us paralyzed."

She dropped her head in her hands and groaned. "Why would he do that?"

"I can't answer that."

"Is he reachable?"

Kaspar shrugged. "I can't answer that either."

"What do you mean? How do you know he's in Edinburgh if he's not reachable?"

Kaspar rubbed his forehead. "Whether or not a phone call can be put through is at the mercy of the Cauld Ane leader. He isn't happy with my brother, and quite frankly, I don't blame him. Ari threatened Kade's whole family."

Megan blinked back tears again.

"*Hvað, systir?*" (What, sister?)

"I just wonder what would have happened if I'd never left. I should have stayed and worked it out."

"You couldn't have known, Megan. Don't beat yourself off."

Megan giggled. "Up. Don't beat yourself up. The other means something entirely different."

Kaspar smiled. "I'll try to remember that."

"Could we please try to get a call through?" she asked. "I feel like I need to make a few things right."

"Of course," he said, pulling out his cell phone. "Before we do that, though, I have a question about your relationship to Jesska."

"She's my sister."

"By blood?" he asked.

"Well, no. Her father...our father...adopted me when he married my mother. It's complicated. My biological father died soon after my mother became pregnant with me, and she met my "dad" when I was about three months old. I was one when they married and they had Cam, then my mother died and he remarried. Jesska is theirs together...it's very complicated." Megan raised an eyebrow. "Why?"

"Curious," he said, and dialed Kade's number.

"Bloody hell, Kaspar. Again?" Kade snapped.

"Good morning to you," Kaspar retorted.

"Aye, 'tis morning, and bloody early. What do you want?"

"I have someone who would like to speak with Ari. Will you arrange it?"

"Who?"

"That I can't elaborate on," he said, glancing at Megan, who frowned.

Kade swore. "Because you're an arse, or because this person is standing in front of you?"

Kaspar scowled. "You'll watch your tone."

"No. I won't arrange it," Kade said, and hung up.

Megan settled her hands on the edge of the desk. "Did you have to be so rude?"

Kaspar scowled. "Me? He needs to understand who he's speaking with."

She held out her hand. "Give me your phone."

"*Nei.*"

"Give me the damn phone, Kaspar. I will get my phone call, or I'm getting on a freaking plane and demanding to see him."

Kaspar dialed Kade's number again and handed the phone to her reluctantly.

"Great," Megan snapped. "Voice mail." She left a message and then handed the phone back to Kaspar. "Your ego and rudeness might mean I don't get to talk to him, which is totally unacceptable. You get more flies with honey, Kaspar. Try to remember that next time."

He slid his phone into his pocket without comment.

"I'm going to check on Sophia," she said. "I will tell my brother and his friend not to kill you. Although, maiming is still an option in my book." She yanked open the door and stalked out of the room.

CHAPTER NINE

IRRITATION CRAWLED THROUGH Kaspar as he walked back to the living room in search of Jesska. Dalton Moore stood by the window, his phone to his ear, but he ended the call as Kaspar walked in.

"Where's Jesska?"

Moore crossed his arms. "She left."

"Where did she go?"

"I have no idea." Moore smiled. "But she did say something about getting the hell away from you."

Kaspar's irritation was quickly replaced with anger. Never in his life had he been surrounded by people uninterested in doing his bidding. He stared at Moore. "Where did Jesska go?"

Moore's eyes glassed over and he said flatly, "Home."

"And where is home?"

Moore rattled off Jesska's address and Kaspar smiled. The man must not have Red Fang anywhere on his person, or Kaspar wouldn't have been able to put him under suggestion. This fact had possibilities, and the desire to hit the lawman was almost overwhelming...but not enough to keep him from Jesska.

He left Cameron's apartment and headed toward the elevator. He heard a bellow from inside the apartment as Moore was released from Kaspar's suggestion. Kaspar couldn't help another satisfied smile as he slipped from the building and into the awaiting car. He gave Austri Jesska's address and sat back to figure out how to proceed.

Pulling up to Jesska's home, he scowled. She appeared to be leaving. When she caught sight of his car, she said something he assumed was a curse, before slipping back inside. Moore must have called her to tell her

Kaspar was on his way. He pushed out of the car before Austri could open the door for him, and headed to the front door. He knocked, but although he could hear her breathing behind the door, she didn't speak.

He dropped his forehead to the cool wood. "Elskan, open the door."

"No."

"Please, sweetheart. I just want to talk."

"About what?" she asked.

"I thought you might want to know what your sister and I discussed."

A few seconds passed and he heard shuffling, but not much else.

"Jesska?"

"You can tell me through the door."

He smiled. "No, that's not the deal."

"I didn't make any deal with you."

"What are you afraid of?" he challenged.

"Oh, I don't know. You brainwashing me into believing something I don't?"

Despite her snarky tone, he couldn't help but smile. "I can't do that, elskan."

"*Stop* calling me that!" she snapped.

He took a deep breath. "Were you going somewhere?"

"No...when?"

"Just now when you walked to your car and then went back inside."

"Oh, right. Um...yes. I was going to a friend's house."

He frowned. "Did Dalton Moore call you?"

"Why would Dalton Moore call me?" The innocence in her voice was forced.

"Jesska."

"What?"

"Did Dalton Moore call you and tell you I was coming?"

"That's not really any of your business," she said. "Now, go away."

"Please Jesska. Open the door and I'll explain everything and answer any questions you might have."

It took several more minutes before he heard the locks turn and the door opened. She peeked through the crack. "You have three minutes."

He smiled. "Would you like to speak out here?"

"No. It's freezing out there." She stepped back, opening the door wider. "You can come in. But not for long."

He stepped inside, the heat hitting him like a wave, and he stepped back out. "I can't come in, sweetheart."

"Why not?"

"Because it's too hot."

She glanced behind her. "It's only seventy-two."

"I can't come in unless it's below sixty-eight. I'm sorry."

"Good *lord*, you really are entitled," she complained. "Give me a second. I'll turn down the heat." She stepped over to the thermostat and adjusted it.

Kaspar watched her the graceful, elegant way that she moved, something he wished he could film and watch over and over. She was stunning.

"What?" she asked as she closed the distance between them.

"You're beautiful."

"Oh," she whispered, crossing her arms, her need to protect herself emanating from her. "Thank you. I changed the thermostat to sixty-seven. Figured I'd give you that extra degree."

He almost chuckled at her snarky tone. He could tell she was desperately trying to push him away. What she didn't understand was that he wasn't going anywhere.

"Are you coming in or what?"

He nodded. "In a minute."

"Well, I'm freezing." She rolled her eyes and moved to close the door.

He placed his hand on the flimsy wood and raised an eyebrow. She huffed and crossed her arms again. Smiling, he stepped inside, kicking the door closed behind him. As he studied her, she bit her lip, sliding her hands into her pockets and shifting from foot to foot. Kaspar reached out and pried her lip from her teeth, running his thumb along her mouth. She let out a small gasp, confirming she wasn't as immune to him as she'd like him to think.

Because he couldn't resist, he leaned down and covered her mouth with his.

Þú verður mín að eilífu. (You are my forever mate.)

The bond between them was strengthening, and as he thought the ancient words, he felt her shiver. She pushed against his chest, lowering her head to break the kiss. "What...what is going on with me?"

"We are destined, elskan."

She looked up at him. "I don't understand."

"I know," he said, and smiled. "I'm happy to explain everything to you, but you are a person who has to experience things. Words don't really help."

"Don't act like you know me," she said, wrinkling her nose.

"But I do know you."

"I just met you. You *don't* know me."

He chose not to point out that she was still in his arms and was now running her hand across his chest. "Which part of my statement is wrong?"

She shook her head. "*Not* the point, Kaspar. You're probably doing something to my mind to make me believe you."

He cupped her cheeks and frowned. "Listen to me. I can't do that. Literally. Not just 'won't,' but 'can't.'"

"How would I know the difference?"

Kaspar took a deep, steadying breath. "Why don't I tell you about my brother and your sister and let you decide what you think?"

"Okay." She stepped away from him. "But no touching. I can't think straight when you're touching me."

He raised his hands in surrender. "As you wish."

"I'm going to grab my hoodie," she said. "Do you want some wine?"

"I'd love some. Thank you."

She stared at him again for a few seconds before nodding. "I'll be right back."

Kaspar glanced around her front room. It was small, but it had a fireplace against the west wall, and a large window looking out on the street, and she could obviously decorate. Tasteful, if not smaller-scale furniture was artfully positioned to take advantage of the view and the warmth. After taking a few photos, he folded his large frame into one of the chairs by the window and checked his phone messages while he waited for her.

"I hope you like red," she called. "It's all I drink."

"Red's perfect," he called back.

He managed to reply to a few texts before she returned with two glasses of wine. He stood and took one from her, smiling at the oversized sweatshirt she wore that had obviously seen better days.

"What?" she asked.

"I was admiring your hoodie."

She blushed and grabbed for the chain around her neck, rubbing the ring attached to it. "It's my favorite," she said, and sat on the sofa facing him.

He took his seat again and sipped his wine, surprised it was good. "Excellent wine."

Jesska smiled and nodded. "I might not make much money, but I just can't buy bad wine."

"What do you do?"

"I'm an executive administrative assistant for a human resources and benefits company." She sighed. "It's my fallback, I guess."

"Your fallback?"

"I had planned to go to college. I'd even thought about being a paramedic or a nurse or something noble like that. But life has a way of beating the shit out of you and leaving you to die on the side of the road."

Kaspar widened his eyes. "Is that why you...?" He nodded to her arm, her scars peeking out from one her sleeves.

"I guess," she rasped as she pulled the sleeve down to her wrist again.

"Will you tell me why you hurt yourself, elskan?"

She shook her head, rubbing the ring again. "What did my sister say?"

He thought about pressing her, but knew she'd only push back if he did, so he let it go...for now. "She's still in love with my brother."

Jesska rolled her eyes. "Well, anyone with a brain could figure that out."

"Oh?"

"When Megan dislikes someone, she tends to shout it from the rooftops, tell all her friends, strangers, the mailman. But with him, she never mentioned him. Ever. And I remember at the beginning, she cried a *lot*. But she never ever said a bad word about him. We didn't even know his name. I figured something really bad had to have happened and that maybe it wasn't her choice to leave, but then time passed and I grew up...and other stuff distracted me, so I never thought to ask." She squeezed her eyes shut. "How does your brother feel about her?"

"He adores her." He sighed. "It's complicated."

"Which means?"

"I'll explain in a minute, but first, will you tell me why you keep tugging on that chain?"

"No reason." She dropped her hand into her lap. "Tell me what happened."

"The easy answer is that your sister and my brother fell in love and had three children together, but the complicated part is the first two were stolen from them."

"Yes, Megan told me. She's a wreck. What I can't quite figure out is why they would want to take them."

Kaspar shrugged. "We are very rich, very important people, sweetheart. We have enemies."

"And humble," she retorted as she tucked her feet under her bottom.

He sighed, setting his wine on an end table. "Look, I'm simply stating fact. We are the royal family of our people and we have enemies. I can't change what I was born into."

"No, I guess you can't," she conceded.

He rose to his feet and made his way to her, sitting on the sofa beside her. "Why do you keep tugging on that necklace?"

She lowered her hand again, shaking her head. He noticed a small diamond ring on her left hand and frowned. "Who gave you this?"

"No one."

"Are you engaged?"

"No. Not that it's any of your business," she said.

He forced himself to stay calm. "Tell me."

"I can't," she whispered, and shifted to face him.

Kaspar took her wine from her and set it on the floor, linking his fingers with hers. "Tell me."

Jesska licked her lips. "It was Brady's."

"Who's Brady?"

"He *was* my fiancé."

Rage flooded him, and she squeaked as she yanked her hands from his and jumped from her seat. She grabbed the necklace again and pressed it against her chest. "Why are you so angry?" she asked. "More importantly, how is it I *know* you're so angry?"

"Sorry," he rushed to say. "I won't hurt you. Just give me a second."

Silent tears slipped down her face as he worked to control his jealousy. He desperately wanted to comfort her, but wouldn't dare in his current state. When he felt he could openly hear her story, he tried to approach her, but she held her hand out. "Don't."

"Elskan, I won't hurt you."

"I don't believe you."

"I know." He took a deep breath and slipped his hands into his pockets. "Go ahead and tell me your story from there. I won't move. Who's Brady?"

"He was my high school sweetheart. We were planning a life together, but then he was murdered by his best friend. Stabbed in front of me. This ring was his purity ring." She held up her left hand, the same ring on her finger. "It matches mine. And this is the engagement ring he was going to propose to me with. And this,"—she tugged on her sweatshirt— "was his."

"When did this happen?"

"A little over ten years ago." She covered her face with her hands, sobbing now.

Kaspar couldn't keep his promise to give her distance as he wrapped his arms around her and pulled her close. "I'm sorry, sweetheart."

"The worst part is that Jason has been released. His lawyer found some technicality and because of overcrowding, they're letting him live in some halfway house until they can schedule a new trial."

"Jason? He's the one who killed Brady?"

She nodded into his chest. "They told Cam that Jason would be on house arrest, but he should have been given the death penalty! He shouldn't be allowed to live when Brady's gone."

"Shhh," he whispered as he rubbed her back. "It's okay."

She took a ragged breath. "You make me feel safe."

"You *are* safe, elskan. I will never let anyone hurt you."

Jesska slipped her hands under his shirt and stroked his back. Within seconds, she had pulled his shirt from his body and started to pepper kisses across his bare chest. Kaspar was so surprised by her assault, he couldn't react right away. He could just feel, but that was dangerous, because she was too naïve to understand what was happening, and far too vulnerable to handle it.

Kaspar lifted her chin, wincing when her lips left his body. This was the hardest thing he'd ever done…stopping what was so natural to him. "Jesska, wait."

* * *

Jesska blinked and then her face reddened. "Oh my…oh, sorry. What the hell is wrong with me?" She stared at Kaspar, his chest like granite, and her body drawn to him in a way it never had been to anyone else. She found herself reaching for him again, his stomach contracting at her touch. "Sorry."

He smiled. "If you keep doing that, I'm going to bind you here and now."

She looked at him and then stared at his chest again.

"Jesska?"

"Hmm?" she said distractedly, glancing up at him again.

"I'm going to bind you."

"I don't know what that means."

"I know, which is why I need my shirt back," he said.

"Huh?"

He chuckled and held out his hand. "My shirt."

She realized she was holding his clothing and handed it back to him quickly. "Oh, sorry. Right."

He slipped it over his head, and disappointment flooded Jesska. "Am I doing this because you're making me?"

"*No*, Jesska," he said again, irritation rising. "I can't make you do anything you don't want to do."

"Don't get all snappy with me! Your brother did it to my sister, so why wouldn't I assume you could do it to me?"

He took her hand, kissing her palm. "I apologize for biting you."

She tried not to giggle, but failed. "Snappy, not biting. It's an expression."

"Well, I'm sorry for that too." He smiled. "The reason my brother could use manipulation on your sister was because she had not reached ár mökunar."

"Ár mökunar?"

"Mating year. When we, the Kalt Einn, turn twenty-five, our gifts come into focus and our partners are shown to us if they are close. He knew your sister was his mate, but he would not have been able to make their union permanent until she reached twenty-five. When she did, she was no longer subject to his manipulation, because she now had all the power."

"I don't understand. What gifts? What's mating year?" She shuddered. "It sounds horrid. What aren't you telling me?"

"When we reach the age of twenty-five, we know our gifts. Some of us will get inklings earlier of what they are, but for the most part, we come fully into our abilities then."

"Like witchcraft?"

"No, baby. Nothing like that." He flicked his wrist, and the wine bottle levitated from the table and poured wine into each glass.

Jesska jumped out of her seat. "What the hell did you do?"

Kaspar reached for her at the same time as he lowered the wine bottle back to the table. "You have nothing to fear, elskan."

She felt her heart calm at his touch and she blinked a few times, not entirely sure she could believe what she was seeing. "How is that not witchcraft?"

"Because, one, I'm not a practitioner of Wicca." He shook his head. "Not really willing to let my soul burn in hell in order to practice witchcraft, sweetheart."

"Well, I suppose there's that," she said. "What else can you do?"

"Let's ease you into that, eh?"

"Oh, because making the wine fly around the room is so easy to accept."

"You have a point." Kaspar laughed. "I bring all of this up to say that since you are twenty-seven—"

"How do you know how old I am?"

"I just do. Because you're past the age of ár mökunar, it means you have all the power here, sweetheart. I can't make you do anything you don't want to do, and I'm at your mercy."

She licked her lips and smiled. "Oh, *really*?"

"If you keep doing that, Jesska, I will bind you here and now."

"Doing what?"

He ran a thumb across her lower lip. "Drawing focus to your very kissable mouth."

She shivered at his touch. "Maybe you should explain to me what binding is, exactly."

"Before I do, may I ask a favor?"

She nodded.

"Would you feel comfortable putting on something other than Brady's hoodie?"

"You're not jealous, are you?"

"Extremely so," he admitted.

She stared up at him. She could tell he was battling his emotions and if she was being honest, she'd worn Brady's sweatshirt as an armor of sorts. There was a pull towards Kaspar that she hadn't expected. It was strong, and she found herself not wanting to fight it. She smiled. "I will go find something else."

"Thank you," he said, and leaned down to kiss her again.

Jesska slid her hands into his hair, sighing against his lips. "Good lord, you can kiss."

He chuckled. "As can you."

"I'll change quickly." She forced herself to walk away from him, even though she could probably spend the rest of her life kissing him if given half the chance. Once in her bedroom, she couldn't quite decide what to wear. For the first time in a long time, she cared about what she looked like.

She took a few minutes to run a brush through her hair and clean her teeth, then found her Portland State hoodie and pulled it on. Even though it was a reminder of what she gave up, it fit her perfectly and the color suited her. Most importantly, however, it was warm.

She made her way back to the living room, smiling when Kaspar stood as she entered the room. The old world charm of him was endearing.

Jesska smiled and held her arms out. "Better?"

Kaspar grinned. "You're beautiful."

"Thank you." She bit her lip. "Will you explain what binding is now?"

He nodded as she sat back on the sofa, and he returned to the chair facing her, settling his arms on his knees. "When we, the Kalt Einn, find our forever mate, there is a private ceremony, words are spoken, vows are made, and then we are joined physically, completing the ritual. It's a bond that can never be broken."

"Isn't that what everyone hopes for? An unbroken bond?"

Kaspar smiled. "In the case of the Kalt Einn, sweetheart, it's literal."

"Why?"

"Because we aren't human."

"Wait, what?" She gasped and then let out a nervous giggle. "Sorry, I thought I just heard you say you're not human."

Kaspar stood and waved toward the sofa. "May I?"

She blinked up at him, not sure if she wanted him to sit next to her or not. "You can't make me do anything, right?"

"No. You are fully you."

"Okay, then."

He sat beside her and linked his fingers with hers. "I want you to know that I'm telling you the truth."

She nodded, her heart calming at his touch. "Are you really not human?"

"Já. I was born in 1014. My clan emigrated from Norway to Iceland about thirty years before my birth."

"Wait," she said. "You're a thousand years old?"

"In about four weeks, yes."

"Well, we must have a party," she retorted.

Kaspar smiled as he ran his thumb over her knuckles. "Take a deep breath, elskan."

She closed her eyes and did as he suggested, feeling his sincerity as she opened herself to him. She shivered. She'd never felt so cherished in all her life. She knew that this man, a man she'd just met, would go to the ends of the earth to protect her. How she knew, she had no clue, but she felt it in her bones.

When his lips covered hers, she sighed, her eyes still closed as she leaned into the kiss. She looped her arms around his neck and slid her fingers into his hair. He broke the kiss, but kept her close as he stroked her hair. "Are you hungry?"

She nodded.

"I'll take you to dinner, hmm?"

"I'd like that." Jesska glanced up at him. "I'll just change quickly."

"You don't need to change, elskan."

She pulled away from him. "I am not going out in public with you looking like *that* and me looking like *this*."

Kaspar smiled. "You are beautiful."

Jesska wrinkled her nose. "That would make you blind, then. I won't be long."

Kaspar laughed and Jesska ran to her room to change. She removed her hoodie and pulled her see-through, silver sweater over the black camisole she wore. She pulled on black leather knee-high boots over her jeans and pulled her hair into a ponytail, which instantly made her look less like a homeless person and more like she'd put some effort in. A spritz of perfume and she headed back to the living room.

Kaspar smiled and Jesska's heart raced. He looked as though he'd missed her and was happy to see her, even though she'd only been out of his presence for ten minutes. She still wasn't entirely sure how much she was going to ask, and if she *did* ask, how much he would answer, but he was certainly pretty, and right now, she didn't care how much she knew as long as she could just look at him for a little while.

"Wow," he said.

"Is this okay?"

He leaned down to kiss her cheek. "Stunning, sweetheart."

"You did say virtually the same thing when I was in a hoodie, so I'm not entirely sure your judgment is sound."

Kaspar laughed. "The truth is that I'd find you beautiful regardless of what you wear."

"Charmer."

Her phone rang and she grabbed it, seeing Cameron's name come up. "Hey, Cam."

"You okay?" he asked.

"Yeah, why?"

"Dalton thought Kaspar might be on his way to you."

"Um, yeah." She glanced at Kaspar. "He's here."

"I'll be right there," Cameron said.

"No, Cam. It's fine."

"It's not fine if the man's harassing you, Jess," Cameron ground out.

"He's not."

"Jess."

"Cameron. I'm fine. He's fine. It's all freakin' fine," she snapped.

She heard him sigh. "You call me if it starts to not be fine. Got it?"

"Yes."

"Love you."

"Love you too," she said, and hung up.

"Everything all right?" Kaspar asked.

"Yes." She forced a smile. "My brother's just being overprotective."

He smiled. "Where would you like to go for dinner?"

"Ooh, my choice, huh?" He nodded and she smiled. "If we can get in, how about Portland City Grill. Great food, amazing views, and excellent service."

"Lead the way, beautiful."

Jesska grabbed her coat and purse, locked up her duplex, and followed Kaspar to the car. Austri held the door and she climbed in first, securing her seatbelt. Kaspar joined her and linked his fingers with hers as Austri pulled away from the curb and headed to Big Pink.

Arriving at the restaurant, Austri headed to the bar. Kaspar held Jesska's chair for her, then sat across from her and ordered a bottle of wine.

"So, do you have a kryptonite phobia or anything like that?" she asked, once the server had left.

"What do you mean?"

"For your super powers," she whispered. "Is there anything that will bring you down?"

Kaspar chuckled. "You're adorable, you know that?"

"Thank you... I think." She grinned. "Are you avoiding my question?"

"Why would I do that?"

"Oh, I don't know. Maybe you're worried I'm Delilah to your Samson?"

He laughed and reached across the table to squeeze her hand. "Are you saying you want me to grow my hair?"

"Oooh, now that's an idea," she joked.

"We have to avoid almonds or anything using the extract, also heat, as you know, and there is a flower native to Iceland called Red Fang. It can be crushed, boiled, any manner of variations, and if administered to us through the skin, food, or drink, it will render us paralyzed."

She gasped. "Will it kill you?"

He shook his head. "In order for it to kill us, it would take a lot more than most people have on hand, but it will temporarily paralyze us, and then if we are left somewhere hot, *that* could kill us."

"Does that happen a lot? People running around dosing each other with Red Fang?"

He shook his head. "No, but we all carry the antidote on our person. It's like an EpiPen, and will counteract the drug."

"Good to know."

The waiter returned with their wine and Kaspar approved it before he poured Jesska a glass. Once they ordered, Jesska kept her connection to Kaspar as she sipped the gloriously rich and delicious red. "You have excellent taste in wine."

Kaspar tipped his glass towards her. "Thank you."

She glanced behind her and caught sight of Austri, smiling at him before facing Kaspar again. "Is he okay all alone?"

"Of course."

"Does he go everywhere with you?"

Kaspar nodded.

She looked at Austri again. "And he's okay with that?"

"Why wouldn't he be?" Kaspar asked. "It's his job."

Jesska smiled. "It's all so alien to me, I guess. Security."

"I've never really given it much thought. Someone has been at my back since I was little."

"What if you just wanted to be alone?"

"That's what my bedroom is for, I suppose," he said. "Although, there are always servants close at hand."

"What's your living situation like now?" she asked, and sipped her wine.

"I live in our ancestral home in Iceland. It's isolated enough that most people wouldn't be able to find it, even if they were looking for it."

"Do you live alone?"

He shook his head with a smile. "Not in the way you mean. I live without my brothers. However, I have a house full of servants. Although, they aren't seen until they need to be."

"Meaning, you forget they're there until you need them."

"I suppose, yes."

"Where does your family live? Your brothers and the like?"

"Ari lives in Reykjavik and Gunnar lives close to me. My parents are no longer living. We have a large clan, and for the most part, they are near me, although folks have spread out in other parts of Iceland."

"Wow. Mine all live close," she said. "My father's parents are long gone, but my mother's are still alive, and I see them as often as possible. And of course, you know my brother and sister."

"Are you close to your parents?"

She shook her head.

"Why not?"

Jesska pulled her hand from his and settled it on her lap. Her mind flashed back to her time in the psych ward.

"I'm sorry, sweetheart. I don't mean to upset you."

"No, it's okay." She took a deep breath. "Um, no. I'm not close to my parents. I am close to Cameron and Megan, but not them."

Kaspar smiled gently. "Let's change the subject, hmm?"

She nodded and took another sip of wine.

He set his wine down. "Tell me about your job. Do you like it?"

"No, not really." She grimaced. "Actually, I hate it."

"How come?"

"Because bitches be loco," she retorted.

He let out a quiet cough. "I'm sorry?"

Jesska smiled. "Don't get me wrong, I like the work. I'm naturally organized and enjoy that aspect of it, but I'm in the administrative field, which is dominated by women. And unfortunately, women are mean, horrible creatures who will do their best to drag you down if you rise above anything." She sighed. "If I could get away with doing my job and not having to deal with people, I'd love it."

Kaspar chuckled. "I quite like women."

"Well, that's because they probably grovel at your feet."

He tilted his head. "Perhaps you are onto something there."

She smiled. "What about you? Do you have a real job, or do you just sit atop your throne and order everyone about?"

"I have a real job," he said. "And I work a lot with animals. Horses and dogs mostly... I'm not a fan of cats."

Jesska shuddered. "Me neither. Horrible little devils."

Kaspar laughed. "They certainly can be."

"What do you mean by 'work' with them?"

"We have a number of charities run through our main company that rescue and rehabilitate animals. We partner with some human elements, but they don't know who we are."

"I would imagine that wouldn't be something to share."

"No," he agreed.

"What's your main company?"

"I own the third largest oil company in the world."

"Shut up."

He smiled. "From that umbrella, I'm able to do things that interest me personally."

"Do you want kids?"

"Absolutely."

"Please tell me you're not one of those people who think animals are more important than children."

Kaspar laughed. "Absolutely not. We consider having children a great honor. It's one of the reasons we don't deal with some of the same issues as humans."

"Like?" She raised an eyebrow. She thought it was cute he would lower his voice to a whisper anytime he said "human."

"No child is ever abandoned. If by some rare chance a child is orphaned, I meet with the child, other family members, and our Council to provide a new and safe place for them."

"You are responsible for that?"

He nodded. "Why?"

"I don't know. It just seems like a big burden."

He took her hand again. "Not a burden, sweetheart. A responsibility that I enjoy."

Jesska smiled. "You're sweet."

"Don't say that too loudly. It will ruin my carefully formed persona."

She giggled. "Oh, okay. Sorry."

Dinner was served, and Jesska concentrated on eating. She liked Kaspar. He wasn't at all what she expected, and she wondered how this was going to play out for her. She wasn't sure how far she should let it go. He was sweet and attentive, and they had a lot of things in common. He was also gorgeous. Sexier than any man she'd ever known, which wasn't saying much, since Brady was the extent of her experience, but Brady had been seriously gorgeous and she'd loved him completely.

Her thoughts turned to Kaspar and his "gifts." She wondered what it all meant. Was he able to time travel? Space travel? Like teleport, not get on a spaceship and fly into space, but turn into mist and just show up on another planet, *Star Trek* style? Could they shapeshift?

She wrinkled her nose. *Ew, did they drink blood?*

What about procreation? Did the women have children the normal way? Did the men carry the babies? How would they give birth?

"You okay?" he asked.

"Um, yep," she rushed to say. "All good. Um..."

He cocked his head. "Are you sure?"

"Hunh-huh. Yeppers."

He chuckled and gave her hand a squeeze. Jesska stared at her plate and focused back on her food.

At the end of the night, Kaspar took her home, kissed her sweetly on her doorstep, and waited for her to step inside and lock the door. Jesska watched him through her window until he drove away, her heart lighter than it had been in a long time. He'd promised to call her the next day to make plans for another date, and she looked forward to seeing him again.

* * *

Wednesday was Jesska's ride-share day and Kim's day to drive, but when Kim had to leave work to pick up a sick kid, Jesska planned to grab the MAX home. She had a dinner date with Kaspar and couldn't wait to shower and change. She hadn't seen him since he took her to dinner the Friday before, but they'd spoken on the phone every night, and the more they talked, the more she liked him.

At just after five o'clock, she walked out of her building to find Kaspar waiting for her, leaning up against the car, a bouquet of roses in his hand. He smiled, and her heart raced.

He closed the distance between them and kissed her cheek. "Hi, beautiful."

"Hi. What are you doing here?"

"You texted that you were going to take public transportation home, so I thought I could provide something a little more comfortable."

She grinned, her nose in the bouquet, sighing at the smell. "You didn't need to do that."

"It's my absolute pleasure, elskan."

He held the car door for her and she slid inside. "I planned to change before dinner, but maybe we can eat now and then head back to my place for a nightcap? I have an early meeting tomorrow that was sprung on me at the last minute."

"I would love that." Kaspar smiled as he secured his seatbelt. "Another option would be to grab some American fast-food and eat at your house."

"You'd eat greasy fast-food with me?"

"I have yet to experience a...what is it called? Driveway in?"

Jesska giggled. His accent was delicious. "Drive through."

"Yes, that."

"Burgerville it is."

"Burgerville?"

"Pacific Northwest staple, my friend. You might have to mortgage your house for a burger, but it's a damn good burger."

Kaspar grinned. "Direct the way, sweetheart."

Jesska gave Austri the address of the Burgerville closest to her, and they loaded up on burgers, fries, and smoothies. It had been ages since

Jesska had eaten so badly, but the lure of a Chocolate Monkey was too much to resist.

Arriving home, Jesska led Kaspar inside, flipping on the lights, toeing off her Jimmy Choos, and heading to the kitchen to open wine and put the roses in water. "I'm sorry I don't have beer to offer. Probably better with burgers, but I rarely drink it."

"Wine's fine, sweetheart." Kaspar said, and set the food on her dining table.

Jesska set glasses and the open bottle of red on the table. "I'm just going to get out of these clothes. I'll be right back."

At his nod, she dashed into her room and pulled on black yoga pants and a long-sleeved pink T-shirt, pulling her hair back into a loose bun on top of her head. She rejoined Kaspar and he smiled as he poured the wine.

"What?" she asked.

"You manage to go from sexy to sexier in a manner of seconds, sweetheart. I'm simply amazed."

Jesska giggled. "And you're obviously blind."

He waved a finger over his eyes. "Perfect eyesight. Better than twenty-twenty."

"Thank you."

Before sitting, he leaned down and kissed her. "I have missed that."

Jesska smiled. "I have too."

"I'm sorry the week has gotten away from us. After tomorrow, I'm yours for the weekend."

"Oh, Kaspar." She let out a dramatic sigh. "That doesn't work for me, I'm afraid."

"It doesn't?"

"No. I have plans."

"You do?"

"Yes." She grinned. "You see, there's this man I met recently, and he's extremely demanding of my time."

"Is he? That's all right, then." Kaspar smiled. "You had me worried for a minute."

"Just thought I'd keep you on your toes." She bit into her burger.

Kaspar chuckled. "Baby, you do that without thought."

Jesska chewed, choosing not to retort, although him calling her 'baby' made her shiver...in a very good way.

Once dinner was over, Jesska found herself sitting in the curve of Kaspar's body on her sofa as they talked. He stayed later than he planned to and she fell asleep on him, but he woke her with a sweet kiss and promised a weekend she would never forget.

* * *

Friday rolled around again, and Jesska and Kaspar were back on her porch after another fabulous and expensive dinner. She'd thought more than once in the last week that she could get used to his seemingly unending devotion and money.

"Do you want to come in?" she asked when Kaspar dropped her home and walked her to her door.

"Are you sure you're up to another late night?"

She giggled. "It's the weekend. I'll crash on Sunday."

"Then, yes, I'd love to come in."

Jesska grinned as she unlocked and pushed the door open, leading him inside. "Wine?"

"I'd love some," he said, and closed the door.

Jesska unzipped her boots and removed them, throwing them into her bedroom before heading to the kitchen to pour wine from the bottle she'd opened earlier.

She poured two glasses and joined Kaspar in the living room.

"First things first," he said, and took the glasses from her.

"What are you doing?"

He grinned, sliding his hand to the back of her neck and squeezing gently as he leaned down to kiss her. Jesska smiled against his lips and then wrapped her arms around his waist in an effort to get closer.

An urgent banging on her front door startled her and she broke the kiss with a groan of frustration. The banging came again and Jesska made her way to it, pulling it open to find Kaspar's driver.

He bowed. "I apologize, m'lady."

"Austri?" Kaspar asked, gently moving Jesska behind him. "What's the matter?"

Austri handed Kaspar an envelope. "Jesska Shane" was written on it.

"Hey, that's mine. Why are you giving it to him?" Jesska asked.

"I apologize," Austri said, glancing at Kaspar.

Jesska frowned. "Where was it?"

"A man left it on your doorstep," Austri said.

She tore open the envelope and read the first line, her eyes clouding with tears as she recognized Jason's handwriting. "No."

Jesska, you need to stop lying. You need to tell them I didn't do anything wrong and that I would never hurt you. I love you. I love your family and I know that you want me to be a part of it. I can drive your mother to her weekly nail appointment at Oasis Nails, or meet your father for his seven a.m. tee time on Tuesdays at the Portland Golf Club. And Sophia. She's growing up to be such a beautiful girl and Ms. Mills is a great cheerleading coach, but what if she was sick and Sophia was stranded at school without a car? Would Megan's court schedule really allow her to drop everything to pick her up? Please tell the police the truth...that this has all been a misunderstanding and that you were angry with me after a simple lover's quarrel. Forever yours, Jason.

"What's wrong?" Kaspar asked gently.

"Did you see who left this?" she demanded.

Austri pulled out his cell phone. "I got a photo of him."

She found herself grabbing for Kaspar as she looked at the photo of Jason. "I don't understand. He's supposed to be on house arrest. Cameron said he'd have to wear an ankle monitor. How did he know where I live?" She fell against Kaspar and closed her eyes.

CHAPTER TEN

KASPAR PULLED JESSKA close and nodded to his driver. "*Þakka þér Austri. Við erum alveg að koma.*" (Thank you, Austri. We'll be right there.)

Jesska stared up at Kaspar as he closed the door. "I don't know what to do."

He smiled, stroking her cheek. "I want you to pack a bag and come with me back to the hotel. We'll call your brother on the way."

"I can't let him run me out of my own home." She shook her head. "I have to work on Monday."

"Which gives us two days to figure this out." He raised an eyebrow. "Will you please come back to the hotel with me so I can keep you safe?"

She scoffed. "Jason Rogers is a coward, Kaspar. He won't publicly attack me."

"May I see the note?" She handed it to him and he read it, scowling as he did. "You're coming back to the hotel with me, Jesska. I'll brook no argument."

She snatched the note back. "I get that you're all alpha male and entitled, Kaspar, but I'm a grown-ass woman, and I'm not just going to run and hide because you say so. Let me call my brother, and if he feels as though I should leave, then I'll go stay with him."

Kaspar nodded, although he wasn't happy about it.

Jesska left him standing by the front door, but he heard her on the phone with Cameron. He took a moment to send a text to Austri, then joined her in the front room.

"Yep, that's all it says. Yes, it was Jason. Kaspar's driver got a picture of him." She glanced up at Kaspar. "I'm sure he can forward it to you."

Kaspar nodded and sent Austri the request, along with Cameron's number.

"But how did he get here, Cam? How did he even know where I live? Does his ankle monitor allow him to go wherever he wants? How does he know all that stuff about where everyone goes? It's creepy." She squeezed her eyes shut and sank to the couch. "No. Seriously? Why wasn't I told? Well, that's lame." She stared up at Kaspar again. "I guess. Yes, Kaspar offered. Fine." She nodded. "For how long?" She sighed. "I'll ask him. Yep. I'll figure it out. Okay. Thanks, Cam. Talk to you tomorrow." She hung up and rose to her feet. "Cameron thinks I should go with you. He has Megan and Sophia at his place, which makes it a bit crowded."

Kaspar smiled. "I feel more comfortable with you being with me anyway, sweetheart. It means I can protect you. Did your brother say how Jason managed to come here without notice?"

She rolled her eyes. "Jason's halfway house is only a few blocks from here, which is within his tether, so to speak. I am technically not a victim of his, so they don't need to fill me in when he moves. *So*, Cam also feels more comfortable with me being out of here and somewhere protected."

"It will give us a chance to get to know each other, eh?"

Jesska nodded. "I guess that's true."

"Go pack. I'll speak with Austri and return in a little while." Kaspar smiled. "Lock the door behind me."

Jesska nodded and walked him to the door. He leaned down and kissed her quickly and then stepped onto her porch.

* * *

Jesska grabbed a large suitcase from her hall closet and wheeled it into her bedroom. As she set it on the bed and unzipped it, she wondered about the strange direction her life was suddenly taking. She grabbed for Brady's ring, realizing she didn't feel as though she needed the talisman like she did before. Kaspar was worming his way into her heart, and she was surprisingly excited by that. Her attraction to him was unlike anything she'd ever experienced.

She packed enough clothes for a week, not sure if the situation with Jason would be resolved by then or not. She supposed that after the weekend, she'd have to figure something else out if coming home wasn't an option.

Jesska packed up her makeup and hair supplies and dragged her suitcase into the living room, pulling open the front door to head out to the car.

"Jess."

She tried to slam her door, but Jason shoved his foot against it.

"Don't," he warned.

"What do you want?" she asked.

He scowled. "I want you to make this right."

"Make what right?" Her heart was beating so fast, she thought it might jump out of her chest.

"You know I didn't kill him. And you need to tell the judge and the DA and anyone else who needs to hear it."

"I watched you stab him, Jason!"

"You lying little bitch," he spat out, raising a knife to her face. "You don't know what you saw."

Jesska didn't even have the chance to scream. Jason was yanked away from the door and slammed up against the wall. He let out a very feminine squeak as Kaspar lifted him off his feet, his hand wrapped around Jason's throat. "What the hell are you doing here?"

The knife dropped to the ground and Jason grabbed Kaspar's wrist, trying to loosen his grip.

Jesska dialed 9-1-1 as Kaspar continued to demand answers from Jason. The problem was, Jason couldn't answer, considering Kaspar was cutting off his air supply.

"9-1-1, what's your emergency?"

"Hi. Jason Rogers tried to break into my apartment. My friend is here, holding him at bay, but could you please send the police? He's on house arrest, awaiting a trial date. He killed my fiancé ten years ago."

"What's your name, ma'am?"

"Jesska Shane," she said. "Please hurry."

"I have dispatched officers to your home. Please stay on the line with me."

"Okay," she said, and focused back on Kaspar. "The police are on the way, Kaspar."

Jason was starting to turn blue, and she grabbed for Kaspar's arm. He glanced at her and she nodded toward her attacker. "The police are coming."

She was relieved that she didn't have to give another warning Kaspar eased up on Jason, who took several gasping breaths just as she heard the sirens. "They're here," she said to the operator.

"Okay, ma'am. If you need anything further, give us a call back."

"Thanks." She hung up and turned to Jason. "Jason, you will never get it, will you? You need serious help...or God. Maybe both, but all know is that I hope they lock you up and throw away the key. You disgust me."

"You always were a selfish little bitch."

Kaspar hissed at him and slammed him against the wall again. "You will never see her again. You will forget her name. You will only tell the truth about your actions when you killed Brady."

Jason appeared dazed as the officers arrived, and it took a few minutes for Kaspar to relinquish him to the authorities. Jesska was afraid they'd try to take Kaspar as well, but he finally let go of Jason's arms and stepped away from him.

"Ma'am? Will you please explain what happened?" one of the officers asked.

"Jason left a threatening note earlier and then came back to try and make me lie to get him released," she explained, and her voice hitched. "He had a knife. He's supposed to be at his halfway house, but I guess his ankle monitor allows him enough freedom to come here."

The officer took notes and nodded. "And who are you?" he asked Kaspar.

"He's my friend," Jesska said.

"I was speaking to him, ma'am."

"Sorry," she grumbled.

Kaspar pulled out his passport and handed it to the officer.

"His Majesty, huh?"

"Já...yes."

"How come I've never heard of you?" the officer asked.

"We are a small monarchy in Iceland. We don't travel much."

The officer eyed him for few seconds before handing him back his passport. "I think we have everything we need. Officer Jenkins has your contact information, so we'll call you should we need anything further."

"Thank you," Jesska said.

"Are you sure you don't need medical attention?"

Jesska shook her head and glanced at Kaspar. "No, Jason didn't get the chance to hurt me."

"Okay, we'll take it from here."

"Thanks," she said, and wrapped her arms around herself, suddenly freezing.

As the police officers led Jason away in handcuffs, Kaspar pulled her into the shelter of his body and guided her back into the house. "Are you all right?"

She shook her head, the sudden realization that Jason had been waiting at her front door, with a knife of all things, hitting her like a freight train. What if Kaspar hadn't been close? She shivered as she settled her cheek against Kaspar's chest and closed her eyes. He rubbed her back as she allowed his comfort to surround her.

"I know he's being locked up at the moment, but I would still like you to come back to the hotel with me," he said.

She glanced up at him. "But like you just said, Jason's not a threat anymore."

"Unless they let him out."

Jesska gasped. "Do you think they would?"

"I don't know, sweetheart, but I'd rather be safe than sorry."

She sighed and stepped away from him. "You just want me at your beck and call."

He raised an eyebrow. "For what purpose?"

"Because you feel the need to kiss me...*all* the freakin' time," she retorted.

Kaspar chuckled. "Perhaps you're not far from the truth."

"Perhaps?" she challenged.

He closed the distance between them again and pulled her into his arms, kissing her deeply. She looped her arms around his neck and slipped her fingers into his hair. "This is exactly what I was talking about," she said, smiling against his lips.

"Well, if you don't like it, sweetheart, I'll stop."

"Don't you dare."

Kaspar chuckled and kissed her again.

She broke the kiss and stared up at him as she continued to run her fingers through his hair. "Did you see Jason? Is that why you came?"

"First I felt your panic, then when I saw the man in the photo approach and... " He shook his head. "I'm sorry I wasn't here sooner."

"What are you talking about?" She wrinkled her nose. "Jason didn't stand a chance."

Kaspar ran his knuckles down her cheek. "If he'd done anything to you..."

"He didn't," she rushed to say. "Look, maybe I should go and stay with Amanda for a few days."

"Who's Amanda?"

"My best friend," Jesska said. "She would be happy to let me crash, and I could help with her daughter."

He frowned. "I'm not comfortable with that."

"Why not?"

"Because, what if the people who are after Megan and Sophie are watching you and they go after her?"

Jesska bit her lip. "I didn't think about that."

"Will you please come to the hotel with me so that I can protect you?"

She studied him for several tense seconds before nodding. "Yes, I'll come with you."

He kissed her again. "Thank you."

She smiled and pointed to her suitcase. "I'm ready whenever you are."

He pulled out his cell phone. "Austri will take your bag."

"I can take it."

Kaspar smiled as he opened the door to admit Austri, who grabbed her bag without comment.

"Or he can," she grumbled.

"If you need anything else, we'll buy it, or Austri will come back and pick it up this weekend."

"Okay," she said, and locked up, following him to the car.

Kaspar waited on the sidewalk while she slid inside and secured her seatbelt. He joined her, linking his fingers with hers as Austri started the car and pulled away from the curb. Kaspar lifted her hand to his lips and kissed her palm. "You okay?"

She nodded, offering up what she hoped was a genuine smile. "I'm fine."

Jesska turned her head and stared out the window as Austri drove to the hotel. She was thankful that Kaspar left her to her thoughts, as dark as they might be.

The car went over a bump and she looked up to see that they were driving into an underground parking lot.

Without speaking, Kaspar followed her out of the car and to the elevator bank. He wrapped an arm around her and guided her into the elevator, pushed the button, and kissed her temple as they rode up to his floor.

Jesska leaned against him, shutting down in an effort to control her emotions. As soon as she felt anything that might be considered unsettling, he'd calm her with a touch. He also seemed to pick up on her need for silence, and walked her to a non-descript door, using the key to open it and then guiding her inside. "This is your room, sweetheart."

She surveyed the space, unable to feel anything even in the midst of the room's warm décor. "It's nice."

"You can choose a different one if it's not acceptable."

"No, it's gorgeous." She smiled up at him. "I'm sorry, I'm just a little out of sorts."

"You be whatever you need to be." He stroked her cheek and smiled. "The bathroom has a large tub."

She raised an eyebrow. "Okay, you couldn't possibly know about my obsession with tubby time."

"Tubby time?"

She shook her head. "Never mind."

He chuckled. "I mention it because you've had a rough day and I thought you might want to relax."

"Stop being so sweet."

Kaspar leaned down and kissed her cheek. "No."

Jesska sighed. "So now that I've ruined your entire evening, shouldn't you get back to whatever it is kings do?"

He checked his watch. "I only need an hour. Then I'm all yours."

"No, don't worry about it. I don't think I'd be very good company tonight," she admitted. "I'll just take a bath and go to bed."

He cocked his head. "I will come see you in an hour."

She rolled her eyes. *Bossy britches.*

"Here's Austri with your bags," he said as Jesska's door opened and the driver arrived with her luggage. "I'll have Camilla unpack them for you."

"Um, *no.* I can do that."

"She will be happy to."

"No. I'm good. Go to your meeting or whatever you need to do. I'll talk to you in the morning."

"I'll come see you in an hour."

"Kaz," she droned. "I'm fine, really."

He leaned down and kissed her quickly. "I'll be back in an hour."

"Fine."

Kaspar studied her for a few seconds before disappearing out the door, and she was left blissfully alone.

As she went about unpacking her luggage and filling the bathtub, she realized the monotony of the work wasn't helping to divert her thoughts from the harrowing evening. She squeezed her eyes shut as fear slipped in, frustrated because Kaspar wasn't close to take it away. Shaking off the negative emotion, she closed her now empty suitcase and turned off the bath taps.

Fear pressed in again, and she did what she always did. She reached for her purse. Inside was the only relief she knew, and she needed that relief in a big way. Removing her clothes, she set the blade on the corner of the tub and slid into the warmth of the bath. When she felt the fear again, she grabbed for the razor, pressing it against the skin of her thigh. She'd barely gotten a nick when she heard her door smash open.

"Jesska!" Kaspar called, frantic worry in his voice.

She squeaked, standing in the tub and grabbing for her robe. She managed to pull it on and step out of the tub even though she was still wet.

"Jesska, baby, are you okay? Where are you?"

"I'm...I'm fine, Kaz. I'm in the bathroom," she called.

The door to the bathroom slid open and Kaspar's eyes went from her, to her leg, to the razor blade on the floor where it had fallen.

"What are you doing?" she snapped.

He frowned and made his way to her razor blade, picking it up and holding it between his index and middle fingers. "What's this, Jesska?"

"None of your business."

He pushed her robe open and knelt before her, surveying the small cut on her leg. With a touch, the wound closed and, other than a little staining from the blood, you'd never know she'd done anything to her leg. "How did you do that?"

"Baby."

"Kaz. How did you do that?"

"I can heal you, elskan."

"How?"

"I don't know how, sweetheart, it's just something between mates. Now," Kaspar kissed her knee and then rose to his feet, throwing the razor blade in the trash. "Tell me. What is this?"

She shook her head.

Kaspar pulled her close, cupping the back of her head and kissing her temple. "I felt your fear, baby. Why are you frightened?"

Jesska shook her head again. "It's dumb."

"Not to me it isn't."

Jesska burst into tears, angry with herself that he affected her so deeply.

"Elskan, shhh. Tell me."

"The note. He...he knew everything about us. He had a knife, Kaz, and he said I lied. But I didn't lie. I watched him kill Brady."

"Oh, baby, Jason can't hurt you anymore," Kaspar whispered. He lifted her face and wiped her tears away, kissing her forehead and smiling. "I'm here."

She nodded, her pain and fear gone as suddenly as it came.

"Where are the rest?" he asked.

"Rest of what?"

"Jesska." His voice dipped low in warning. "Where are they?"

She bit her lip. "In my purse."

"*And?*"

Big, fat, bossy king dude.

"In the pocket in my suitcase," she grumbled.

"You dry off and get dressed while I take care of this," he said, as he leaned down and grabbed the trash can. "I'll open some wine and we can watch a movie when you're done."

"What about your meeting?"

"My meeting's over."

Guilt slipped in. "Because of me?"

He wrapped his hand around the back of her neck and gave her a gentle squeeze. Her guilt slipped away and she licked her lips.

"My meeting was over because I said it was over." He leaned down and gave her another quick kiss before pulling the door closed behind her and leaving her alone.

Jesska sat on the edge of the tub and dropped her head in her hands. She studied her leg. The now white scars of many of her "relief sessions," slanted over her skin, but the place she'd just cut was perfect. No scar, no scab, no pain.

"Are you getting dressed?" Kaspar called through the door.

She frowned, but not in an I'm-mad-at-you, this-is-none-of-your-business kind of way, but in a how-will-I-ever-deserve-you kind of way.

"Yes, Kaz. I'm getting dressed."

She applied lotion and then pulled on her favorite pajamas. A dark blue camisole with white lace around the neckline and matching short-shorts. She slipped from the bathroom to her bedroom and peeked into the living room. Kaz stood by the sofa pouring red wine into a glass, his eyes focused on the television.

Some hockey game was on, but since she didn't follow hockey, she had no idea who was playing. He caught sight of her and dripped wine down the side of the glass.

"Skít," he hissed, and set the glass on the table, reaching for a napkin to clean up before turning to her again. "God, baby, you're stunning."

Her heart raced. "I am?"

"Yes." He closed the distance between them. "Maybe you should put on a robe."

"It's wet."

Kaspar groaned.

"You okay?" she asked.

He shook his head, leaning down to cover her lips with his. Jesska grasped his arms when he deepened the kiss, wrapping her legs around his waist as he lifted her and carried her into her bedroom.

He laid her on the mattress, his body covering her as he broke the kiss, dropping his head to her neck and taking several deep breaths. "I need you to put on more clothes, elskan."

She slid her hands into his hair to keep him from moving. "Or we could take more off."

He shook his head, his breathing shallow. "No. I will not do this until I bind you, but you make it very difficult to stay with my conviction."

"Bind me, then."

He looked up at her slowly, his expression difficult to read. "When you are ready, I will bind you, sweetheart, but not before."

"I'm ready."

"No, you're horny. We both are. There's a difference."

She huffed, slipping her hands under his shirt. "Not when the end result is the same."

Kaspar groaned again, kissing her neck and pushing himself up and off of her. "Please put some clothes on. I will wait for you in the living room."

She watched him leave, frustrated that he could so quickly gain control, unlike her. She dragged her hands down her face and then slid from the mattress. Reluctantly, she pulled on yoga pants and a long-sleeved T-shirt before joining him back out in the living room.

"That didn't help much," he snapped.

Jesska threw her hands in the air. "Well, what am I supposed to do about it? Apparently, everything I own drives you crazy."

"No, just the woman in the fabric." Kaspar smiled and held his hand out to her. "Sorry, elskan. I don't mean to snap. I will endeavor to control myself."

"Something I'm not asking you to do."

He stroked her cheek. "I know, baby, but something I'm going to do all the same."

"You're right about me needing time," she admitted.

"I know. You take as long as you need." Kaspar kissed her hair. "You're still dealing with a lot of confusion over your feelings, sweetheart, but we'll sort them out together."

She dropped her cheek to his chest, her favorite place to be of late, and closed her eyes. "I feel like when I'm with you, nothing bad can touch me."

"Nothing bad *can* touch you."

Jesska raised her head again. "I'm going to hold you to that. I will try to avoid my desire to stop myself from loving you, but you can't leave me. Whether it's death or otherwise. Deal?"

He grinned. "Deal. Now come and have some wine. You're going to show me your city tomorrow."

"Alone?" she challenged.

"Yes."

"No, I mean without Austri."

"Oh, then, no."

She wrinkled her nose. "Will we ever be alone?"

"We're alone now, elskan."

"You know what I mean."

He led her to the sofa and pulled her down beside him. "Outside of my home, my security is never far, but I will speak with them about being less conspicuous while we're touring tomorrow."

She grabbed her wine glass. "Thank you."

Kaspar grinned and picked up his own wine. "Now, relax."

"Yes, Mr. Bossy Pants."

"My pants are bossy?"

"Probably," she retorted.

He chuckled. "Kiss me, elskan."

"You kiss *me*."

Kaspar gave her a wolfish smile and did as he was commanded.

CHAPTER ELEVEN

SATURDAY MORNING ARRIVED and Jesska awoke before her alarm. She grabbed her cell phone and noted the time. Nine a.m. She closed her eyes and smiled at the memory of Kaspar kissing her awake after she'd fallen asleep pretty much on top of him, and carrying her to her room.

"Stay," she'd whispered, sleepily, and he'd stretched out beside her, pulling her close.

He must have waited until she fell asleep, because now she was awake and very much alone. She fired off a quick text to him and then headed for the shower. Her fear had been replaced with peace, which couldn't have come at a better time.

As she dressed, she peeked out the window and saw the day was gray, but no rain. Even so, she grabbed a warm sweater, knowing it would still be cold. Her phone rang, and she smiled to see Kaspar's number pop up. "Good morning."

"Good morning, sweetheart. How did you sleep?"

"Really well. You?"

"Same. Do you want to join me for breakfast, or shall I come to you?"

Jesska grinned. "Oh, no, mister, we're going to Voodoo and then the Saturday market."

"I'm not really into voodoo, baby."

She giggled. "Voodoo Doughnuts. If I'm going to show you Portland, we have to start there."

"I'm in your hands, then."

"Good. I'm ready if you are."

"I'll meet you in the hall."

"Race ya." She pulled open her door and found him standing on the threshold, grinning. "Sneaky."

He laughed, slipping his phone into his pocket and leaning down to kiss her. "Hi."

"Hi." Jesska placed her phone in her purse and smiled up at him. "You're going to love the Saturday market. So much food, great gift stuff, and tons of people to watch."

"Lead the way, baby."

They followed Austri downstairs to the awaiting car. Jóvin was driving this morning and Austri rode shotgun. Jóvin was tall with dark hair and deep-blue eyes, whereas Austri was blond like Kaspar. Either Kaspar didn't hire ugly people, or Iceland was a nation of beauty.

Arriving at Voodoo, Jesska tugged Kaspar to the back of the line, which was surprisingly short on a Saturday morning.

Jóvin drove away while Austri stood sentry, a look of displeasure on his face.

"I take it you've never had to wait in line, huh?" Jesska said.

Kaspar smiled, wrapping an arm around her shoulders. "Can't say that I have, no."

He said something to Austri in Icelandic and Austri backed away a bit, but not out of sight.

"Did you find out what he and Jóvin want?" she asked.

"They won't want anything."

"Kaz, it's Voodoo. They have to try it."

He pulled out his phone and fired off a text…Austri was no longer close enough to speak to without shouting.

"He doesn't want anything," Kaspar confirmed.

"I'll pick out something for them."

"Jess."

"What? It's my treat and I'd like to buy them donuts."

His response was a gentle squeeze. She grinned up at him, unable to hide her excitement. Finally making their way into the crowded bakery, she decided on a dozen doughnuts, varying flavors, picking the chocolate cream one for herself. Kaspar chose the one covered in Fruit Loops although he looked mildly concerned about eating it.

"Live a little, Kaz," she said, giggling as Kaspar handed the box with the rest of the doughnuts to Austri.

"Tell me again. Are any of these almond?"

Jesska smiled. "No almond. I promise."

She wondered what it would be like to live without almonds. She loved almost everything almondy.

Kaspar took a bite and grimaced as he chewed. She watched him swallow and grab for the bottle of water Austri handed to him.

"Not your thing?" she teased.

"We'll go with that," he said. "A little overwhelming on the palate."

Jesska laughed. "Suit yourself." She bit into her treat, humming in pleasure as she chewed.

Jóvin arrived with the car, and Austri set the box in the trunk before holding the back door open for them.

"We're close enough to walk," Jesska said. "Let's enjoy the little sliver of sunshine there is."

Austri shook his head.

"Seriously?" she complained.

"Let's just do as he asks, elskan. We'll enjoy the sunshine at the market."

"Fine." Jesska slid in first, difficult to do while holding her doughnut, but Kaspar helped her with her seatbelt and she finished off her breakfast, full of more sugar than she typically consumed in the morning.

They drove the half mile to where Jóvin could drop them off and Jesska followed Kaspar out of the car, Austri behind them.

Kaspar took his thumb and brushed the corner of her mouth, slipping his thumb into his mouth. "Chocolate."

"Hey." Jesska frowned. "I was saving that for later."

He chuckled and linked his fingers with hers. "Where do we begin?"

Jesska led Kaspar through the booths and vendor stores, stopping at a few of her favorites, including Lacework Jewelry, where they always had unique, filigree jewelry. She made him try the garlic fries and after he deemed them delicious, he bought his own paper basket full. They were standing in front of the main stage waiting to see who would be playing when the heavens opened up and the inevitable downpour began.

Kaspar pulled her through the small crowd to shelter, but by the time they were away from the rain, Jesska's fries were drenched and so was she.

Kaspar handed her a handkerchief. "We can always buy more, baby."

"If I keep eating like this, I'll gain a thousand pounds." She dumped the fries in the closest trash can and then blotted her face dry. "It's fine. It was a nice treat."

"Shall we head back to the hotel and get dry?"

Jesska raised an eyebrow. "But we're not done."

"Baby, it's pouring."

"And it will probably stop in the next twenty minutes." She smiled. "We Pacific Northwesterners are used to this. This is nothing."

Kaspar chuckled, pulling her close and kissing her as the rain continued around them. "If it's not over in twenty minutes, I'm taking you back to the hotel."

"Okay, fine." She gave his waist a gentle squeeze. "For now, give me another kiss."

Kaspar complied and they waited for the rain to stop. When it didn't, Kaspar insisted they head back to the hotel and "continue their day off." Jesska wasn't surprised to discover that translated into movies, wine, and a lot of making out.

* * *

The next morning Cameron was scheduled to arrive to pick Jesska up for church, and she was late. She'd wanted to blow him off again, but he wouldn't take no for an answer, so she was stuck. She pulled on jeans and a black turtleneck, finishing off the ensemble with knee-high black boots. As she slid her watch on, a knock came at her door.

"You're early," she said as she pulled open the door.

"Am I?" Kaspar asked.

She grinned. "Sorry. I thought you were my brother."

Kaspar walked inside and Jesska let the door close behind him. He gave a wolf whistle. "You look beautiful."

"Thank you," she said. "I'm late, though, so Cam's not going to be happy when he gets up here."

"Your brother won't be getting up here, baby."

Jesska paused in securing her earrings. "What? Why not?"

"It's a secure floor."

She frowned. "But Cam should be allowed up here. My family, too."

"Not how it works."

"Well, can you *make* it work that way?"

He shook his head. "But I will walk you downstairs when your brother arrives."

"Oh thank you so much, my liege," she droned.

Kaspar smiled, ignoring her snark. "Do you want me to come with you?"

"You'd come to church with me?" she asked in disbelief.

"I do have a belief system and a moral compass. It might not be in the form of evangelical Christianity like your brother's, but it's a strong Catholic one."

"No, I know." She grimaced. "I'm sorry, Kaz. I really didn't mean for that to sound like it did. I don't know what the Catholic church is like where you're from, so I have no reason to doubt it's any less genuine than my own beliefs. I guess I just have a tough time wrapping my head around praying to anyone other than God. You know, like Mary or the saints?"

Kaspar chuckled. "Which I understand."

"Anyway, I think I really need to go without you today. I can't explain it, I just feel like I need to."

"Okay, baby."

"Are you really okay?"

"Of course." He smiled. "I wouldn't say it if I wasn't."

"Thank you."

"For?"

"For always being honest with me."

He ran a knuckle down her cheek. "That's the easy part."

"So, so charming."

Kaspar chuckled, reaching for his phone in his pocket. "Austri. Hmm, mmm. Já. I'll walk her down." He slipped his phone back in his pocket. "Your brother is here."

Jesska rolled her eyes. "Yeah, picked up on that, thanks."

"Come on. He's waiting in the lobby."

She grabbed her purse, keys, and a jacket and followed Kaspar out the door. He took her hand, linking his fingers with hers as they went downstairs, Austri following.

Arriving in the lobby, Kaspar handed her off to Cameron, shook his hand, and then kissed her quickly before watching her leave. She gave him a little wave as they walked out the front door and to Cameron's awaiting car.

"You used your badge to park illegally," she observed as she sat in the passenger seat. Cameron's security badge sat on the dashboard.

"Membership has its privileges," Cameron said, and closed her door.

Jesska giggled.

Cameron slid into the driver's seat and started the car, pulling out onto the street and heading to the church on Ankeny. It didn't take long and the parking gods were watching out for them. Someone pulled out just as they arrived and they got a spot very close to the entrance.

"Your parking magic still works, I see," Cameron said.

Jesska laughed and they climbed from the car. Her brother wrapped an arm around her shoulders and gave her a squeeze, and they made their way inside.

Several of Jesska's friends were at the service and they rallied around her, pulling her...no, *dragging* her back into the fold. It was as though she'd never left. No judgment, no pity, just her friends happy to see her. She glanced at her brother and smiled. He gave her his told-you-so look and grinned. She took a few minutes to introduce him to a few of the people who hadn't met him yet and then it was time to head into the service.

There was a guest speaker rather than the regular pastor, and Jesska tried not to be disappointed. She'd hoped that Dan, the main teaching pastor, would be there, but Cameron smiled reassuringly and tapped her shoulder with his.

Worship was awesome; it always was, especially when it was possible to pull quality musicians from the huge pool of a mega church. The congregation sat down, and Jesska's world closed in around her.

The speaker walked up to the podium. "Good morning, everyone. Thanks for having me. Today I'm going to be speaking on my favorite verse. We'll look at it, dissect it, and, I trust, give you something to be hopeful for when you leave today.

"Please turn in your Bibles to Jeremiah 29:11, where the Lord tells Jeremiah, 'For I know the plans I have for you, plans to prosper you and not to harm you, plans to give you hope and a future.'"

Jesska stopped fidgeting, her focus now fully on the stage. This had once been her favorite verse. One she used to hold on to daily...until *that* happened and she'd abandoned it, along with her heart. By the end of the service, she'd used all the tissues in her purse—luckily, Cameron came prepared—and received a new perspective on heartache and God. She'd confessed in her heart, made her peace, and realized just how much she'd been protected, even in her choice to be angry. She leaned against her brother, felt him kiss her temple, and heard him praying quietly as they sat through the final song.

She managed to pull herself together enough to say her good-byes as she and Cameron filed out of the church with everyone else, and then they were on their way back to the hotel for Jesska to freshen up. Lunch needed to wait until she didn't have mascara caked on her face.

Cameron pulled up to the hotel and squeezed her hand. "I'll wait here, okay?"

"Thanks, Cam. I won't be long."

Jesska climbed from the car and rushed to the elevator, arriving at her floor slower than she would have liked. Nodding to Jóvin, she let herself into her room and headed to the bathroom. She'd just wiped the mascara from her cheeks when she heard a knock at the door. She wasn't surprised and knew who it was. Jóvin would have called Kaspar as soon as he saw her. She opened her door and smiled.

"Are you okay?" Kaspar asked as he walked inside. "I thought you were going to lunch." He tipped her chin gently. "Why have you been crying?"

"I'm fine, I *am* going to lunch after I freshen up, and I've been crying because I realized I've been angry for a really long time and I'm done being angry." He studied her for a few seconds before she pulled away from him and made her way back to the bathroom. "What's your plan today?"

Kaspar followed her. "I have a couple of meetings before dinner."

She smiled at him in the mirror. "Do you ever not work?"

He grinned. "I haven't worked much since I met you, baby. I have things to catch up on."

Jesska giggled, turning to face him. "Are you *blaming* me?"

"Absolutely," he said, settling his hands on her waist.

"I just wanted to be clear."

He leaned down and kissed her, and Jesska wove her fingers into his hair. Breaking the kiss, she wiped his lips with a sigh. "That shade of lipstick doesn't really suit you."

"Worth it, though," he retorted. "Do you want me to walk you down to your brother?"

"Code for: I'm forming my demand into a question, so Jesska thinks she has some say in the matter."

"Don't tell me you have me figured out already."

She tapped his cheek and sidled past him to grab her purse. "Come on, baby. Protect me from the monsters lurking in the elevator."

Kaspar laughed and took her hand. "I am but a lowly knight at your service."

* * *

Monday morning, Jesska slid from Austri's car and walked into the lobby of her office building. She couldn't believe she'd only been away from her job for two days. It felt like an eternity. After her lunch with Cameron the day before, she'd arrived back at the hotel to find Kaspar had booked her a massage in her room, and then spent the rest of the evening showing her how special he thought she was. He'd poured wine, served her ice cream, and watched *Ever After* with her, only complaining twice about Drew Barrymore's pseudo-British accent.

"Isn't he supposed to be a French prince?"

"Yes," she'd said.

"Then why do they have English accents, or I should say, very bad English accents?"

"I have no idea," she'd admitted with a giggle. "It always seems to me that American films portraying anyone European are done in an English accent."

"And this is your favorite movie?" he'd asked in disbelief.

"One of them, yes. Dougray Scott is gorgeous."

"So you watch it because you think he's gorgeous?"

She leaned back and smiled. "I'm not sure I should answer that."

"I'm not sure you should either."

Jesska ran a finger along his jaw. "He's nowhere near as gorgeous as you are."

Kaspar had smiled and kissed her, settling her closer to him as they returned to the movie. She'd fallen asleep on him again, and woke up to find she was in her bed, tucked in, and without Kaspar. He'd arrived that morning with breakfast, which she could only manage a bite or two of, and drove with her to work, kissing her quite thoroughly before she left the car. She hummed as she rode the elevator to the eleventh floor and then headed to her cubicle.

"Hey, Jess," Kim said, popping her head over the partition.

"Hi. You're here early."

"Yeah, no choice. You missed the drama Friday night."

"Night?"

"Yeah, got pulled into the conference room after you left."

"Oh, really?"

She nodded. "Yep, Tim's on the warpath. He fired a butt-load of people."

"Shut up. Seriously? Why?"

"Orders came down from corporate. Major cuts, I guess." Kim frowned. "I can't believe I'm still here, to be honest."

"You're the only one who does what you do, Kim. I can't imagine them ever getting rid of you."

"Jess," Tim said from his office door. "Can I speak with you for a bit?"

"Sure." Jesska stepped into Tim's office and sat in the chair facing his desk. She was surprised when Paula from HR arrived a few minutes later.

"We're going to have to let you go, Jesska," Tim said.

"I'm sorry? Did you just say you're firing me?"

Tim frowned and nodded.

"What? Why?"

"Budget cuts," he said, evasively. "I'm sorry, Jess. It's over my head."

"But I just had a glowing review. You said you couldn't live without me."

Tim sighed. "I know. I'm so sorry. You're amazing. I *don't* know what I'm going to do without you, but it's out of my control. I've spent the better part of a week trying to figure out how to keep you, but like I said, it's over my head."

Jesska forced back a laugh. Of course this was what her life had come to. Her fiancé was murdered, she gave up college because she couldn't hack it emotionally, she was threatened by the murderer of the love of her life, and now she was jobless. Just freakin' perfect.

She stood. "I'll pack up my office."

"You can come back and do that next week, if that helps," Tim offered. "We've paid you through the end of the month and given you an extra month of benefits."

Paula handed Jesska a file with her severance package.

"I'd rather just pack up my things and go now," Jesska said. "I'm not really interested in coming back again."

"Fair enough," Tim said, and stood. "Let me know if you need me to carry anything down."

"I'll grab you a box," Paula offered.

Jesska went back to her desk. A few of her coworkers came over to hug her good-bye once the word got out, and without any fanfare, she packed up her desk. She realized into her second box of crap that she didn't have her car and she'd have to call someone to pick her up, so she grabbed her phone and dialed her brother and then her sister. No one answered.

She really didn't want to call Austri so soon after him dropping her off, but didn't know what else to do, so she made the call. Austri was sympathetic to her plight.

"I'll call his majesty."

Jesska frowned. "No, Austri, please don't call him."

"I must, m'lady."

"Never mind. I'll just call my brother again. He can drop me at my car. Don't worry about it."

"Wait, m'lady." A moment of silence. "I'll be there in five minutes."

"Thanks, Austri," she said, and hung up.

Her phone rang and she answered it without looking at her screen. "Hello?"

"What's wrong?" Kaspar demanded.

"What do you mean?" She bit her lip. "Nothing."

"Don't lie to me, elskan. Tell me."

"Kaz, seriously. I'm okay."

"But you're upset. I can feel it."

Jesska took a deep breath. "I lost my job," she whispered.

"Oh, baby, I'm sorry. I'll be right there."

She shivered when he said 'baby.' She liked it far more than she was willing to admit.

"Kaz, it's okay," she said. "Really. I've already called Austri."

"I'd like to collect you."

"There's no point." She dumped a photo frame into the box. "You have stuff to do and I need to figure out a few things."

He sighed. "All right. I'll be at the hotel when you get back."

"I thought you were supposed to be in meetings all day."

"Já. But I'll be there when you get there."

"Kaz," she said.

"No arguments, sweetheart. I'll see you when you arrive."

She couldn't help a smile. "Bossy."

He chuckled. "You haven't begun to see bossy, sweetheart."

"You don't scare me."

"I have to go." She still heard his smile in his answer. "But I'll see you when you get there."

She nodded. "Okay."

"*Ég elska þig, fallega stúlka.*"

"What does that mean?" Jesska opened a drawer and grabbed a few personal files, laying them flat into the box.

"I'll tell you when you get here," he promised.

"Okay."

"Are you really all right?"

"Yes. I'm fine. Go back to your meeting," she said.

"Austri should be there now."

"He told you?"

"Já, elskan. He told me, but not until just now when he said he was at your building."

She wrinkled her nose. "I didn't want him to worry you."

"We can talk about it when you get here."

Jesska sighed. "Fine."

"Can I let you go?"

"Yes," she said. "'Bye."

She hung up and glanced around her cube. Empty. Just as she opened a drawer for one last check, her office phone rang and she answered it. "Jesska Shane."

"Hey, Jess," Tiffany, the receptionist said.

"Hi, Tiff."

"There's a really hot guy in the lobby for you. He said his name is Austri."

"Right. He's here to pick me up."

"Are you dating him?" she whispered.

"No. He's...um...a friend, I guess you could say."

"Cool. Is he taking you to lunch at nine o'clock in the morning?" Tiffany was bubbly, cute, and incredibly nosy.

"I just got fired, Tiff."

"Shut the front door. You?" she exclaimed.

"Yep. Me." Jesska glanced around and realized she needed an extra pair of hands to carry it all down. "Can you send him up, please? I need some help getting this stuff down to the car."

"Of course I can. Hey, if you guys aren't dating, give him my number, okay?"

"Sure, Tiffany." She rolled her eyes. "I'll do that."

"Thanks, lady. Okay, he's on his way up."

"Thanks." Jesska hung up and went to the elevator bank to await Austri.

CHAPTER TWELVE

THE DOORS OPENED and Austri walked out, his face blank, but his eyes concerned. "Hi, Austri."

"M'lady."

"Thanks for telling Kaspar," she droned sarcastically.

"That's out of my control, m'lady. In my defense, I only told him I was picking you up."

Jesska shook her head. "I'm not really mad, Austri. I'm just a little out of sorts this morning."

He looked grim.

"It's not the end of the world," she said, and forced a smile. "People lose their jobs all the time. Especially in this economy."

He nodded, his face now devoid of expression. "What can I carry down for you, m'lady?"

"I'll show you." She led him to her cube, and he picked up both boxes as though they weighed nothing. "I can take one," she protested.

"I have them, m'lady. Anything else?"

She shook her head and grabbed her purse.

"Jess?" Tim called.

"Sorry, Austri, just a sec," she said, and stepped into her boss...no, ex-boss's office. "I'm out of here."

"I'm really sorry, Jesska. Truly. I tried to keep you." He stood and reached out his hand.

She shook it, but didn't know what to say. She went with the higher road. "Good luck with everything, Tim."

Pulling her hand away, she turned and, noticing a hovering Austri led the driver out of the building, finding the car at the curb, Jóvin inside Austri popped open the trunk...how he did it, she wasn't sure...set he boxes inside, and then opened the door for her. She slid into the car and secured her seatbelt, dropping her head on the headrest and sighing. What the hell was she going to do now?

Her phone buzzed and she saw her brother's number pop up. "Hey, Cam."

"Hey. You called?"

"Yeah. But I'm good now. I just needed a ride."

"How come?" he asked.

"Got fired."

"*Right*," he said with a chuckle.

"No, I'm serious. I got laid off this morning." She stared at the roof of the car. "You know, I think this is why Monday's get a bad name."

"Don't companies usually fire folks on Fridays?" he countered.

Jesska glanced out the window. "Never been fired before, so I have no idea."

"Are you okay? Do you want me to come take you to lunch?"

"No, I'm okay. Austri picked me up and we're headed back to the hotel. I just want to eat a bag of Cheetos and drink a bottle of wine."

"Delicious."

Jesska chuckled. "Totes."

"Are you really okay?"

"Ask me tomorrow. Right now, I'm in shock and I need to process."

"I'm sorry, Messka. This sucks."

"Totes."

Cameron chuckled. "You still have your warped sense of humor, I see."

She smiled. "Totes."

"Okay, thirteen-year-old girl. I'm going to let you go, but I'll keep my phone on and close if you need me."

"Brother of year award, Cam."

"Aw, thanks, Messka. Love you too."

"'Bye."

"'Bye, sis."

She hung up and closed her eyes. A slight bump indicated they were heading into the garage, so Jesska sat up and set her phone in her purse. She was surprised to see Kaspar waiting for her as they drove in. Lordy, he was pretty. Austri pulled the car to a stop and Kaspar opened the door, holding his hand out to her. She took it and climbed out.

"Austri will handle your personal items," he said, reading her mind.

Jesska nodded. "Thanks for everything, Austri."

The driver nodded and then drove off to find a parking spot. Kaspar wrapped an arm around her and kissed her temple. "Are you all right?"

She nodded, giving him a gentle squeeze. "I think so. I'm a little numb right now, but I'm okay."

"Come upstairs and we'll talk."

"Don't you have meetings?"

He smiled. "Nothing I can't take a little time away from."

She sighed. "I think you're too good to be true."

Kaspar chuckled. "We'll see how long I can fool you."

They stepped into the elevator and Kaspar hit the button for the top floor, keeping his other arm firmly around her. Entering his suite, she laid her purse on the table and kicked off her shoes, flopping onto the sofa with a sigh. "What did you say earlier?"

"I love you, beautiful girl."

She smiled. "Say it in Icelandic again."

"Ég elska þig, fallega stúlka."

"So pretty."

He leaned down and kissed her. "As are you. Are you hungry?"

"Kaz, you fed me until I nearly burst this morning."

He frowned. "You had two bites of food."

"Three."

"Two," he corrected.

"You notice everything, don't you?" She caught his amused expression. "What? I almost never eat breakfast. Plus, I was way too tired to eat. *Someone* kept me up far past my bedtime."

"Regardless. Are you hungry?" he repeated.

She sighed. "Starved. But if you keep insisting I eat all the time, you can't complain when I gain a hundred pounds."

Kaspar laughed as he picked up the phone and she heard him order food, all her favorites, of course, then he headed back to her and joined her on the sofa. "You should never skip breakfast, elskan."

"See?" She poked him with her foot. "Bossy."

He grabbed her foot, grinning as he massaged it. "Perhaps this new development is a relief, hmm?"

Jesska sighed, and shifted to give him better access. "Well, yes, considering I didn't really like my job." She grimaced. "But I only have a few months of savings and a little money left over from my trust fund, so I'm going to have to look for something else pretty quick."

"Not if you don't want to."

"What do you mean by that?"

He paused in his attention to her feet. "I will take care of you."

Jesska snorted. "I have never—and I mean, *never*—wanted anyone to take care of me. Hence the reason I moved out of my parents' house the day I turned eighteen."

Kaspar cocked his head.

"What?" she challenged.

"Was that the real reason?"

She stared at him. "No. The real reason was they had me committed to the psych ward two days before I turned eighteen."

"Is that why your relationship is strained?"

Jesska frowned. "It's a little early in the morning to psychoanalyze my relationship with my parents, Kaz."

"Do you think they might have wanted to take care of you?" he continued.

She pulled her foot from his hands and sat up. "By putting me in the loony bin? I was restrained, Kaspar. Tied *down*. I wasn't allowed to pee."

He grabbed her hand, tugging her onto his lap. "I'm not saying that what they did was right, elskan, but I can sympathize with them. How frightened they must have been to find you passed out and losing blood."

She blinked back tears. "I was fine."

Kaspar linked his fingers with hers. "You were passed out in a pool of your own blood."

Jesska nodded. "So?"

"*So*. That's the very definition of not fine."

"Your point?" she snapped.

"When I saw you bleeding, I nearly lost my mind, Jesska, and that was a small nick. What your parents must have thought when they found you nearly dead…"

She slid her face into his neck. "You might be right."

"I will admit, I don't agree with the severity of their actions, sweetheart, but I can sympathize with their predicament. And I wonder, if they hadn't acted so rashly, would you be gone from this world?" He lifted her chin. "What then, hmm? I would have never found you."

"Perhaps I've been a bit too hard on them."

"I think you might have been, elskan. And I'd like to meet them before I take you home to Iceland. They must have done something right, because they made you."

She smiled through her tears. "You are ridiculously sweet sometimes."

"Just sometimes?"

"Yes. That's all I'm giving you. Otherwise your head won't fit through the door."

Kaspar laughed. "Well, in the spirit of being sweet, will you let me take care of you until you find something else?"

"Kaz," she said slowly, pushing herself from his lap. "In all reality, I don't know where this is going. I like where we're at, and I'm liking the way we are together, but let's be honest, we don't know how long this is going to last. I've worked really hard to be independent, and as much as I like the idea of being taken care of in theory, the reality is, I would probably rather chew my own arm off than ever have a man take care of me."

A knock at the door cut off Kaspar's response, and he rose to his feet to answer it. A young man from room service wheeled a cart in. Kaspar signed the check and then closed the door behind him. Jesska stood and rushed to the food, her stomach rumbling at the smell of deliciousness wafting from the covered trays. Before she could remove one of the lids, Kaspar took her hand and backed her up against the sofa.

"What are you doing?" she asked, and laid her hands on his chest.

He smiled, running his thumb along her pulse. "Although I am sympathetic to your quandary, sweetheart, and one of the things I love the most about you is your independence…"

She bit her lip. He said "love."

"…I am not particularly interested in whether or not you want me to take care of you. It's just going to happen." He leaned down and kissed her neck. "And *this*, baby, is going to last a lifetime, so you better get used to me caring about you." His lips moved to her jaw and then he smiled before covering her mouth with his.

Jesska closed her eyes and slid her hands up his chest and into his hair. She loved the way he called her baby. This could become a problem for her. But right now, she loved his lips on hers and his body close, heating her in more ways than one. She whimpered when he broke the kiss, settling his forehead against hers and trying to catch his breath.

"That backfired."

She giggled. "Now I'm hungry in a really different way."

"Me too." He kissed her nose and stepped away from her, focusing on the food. "Come and eat elskan."

Jesska took time to pull herself together as she sat at the table and scooped eggs onto a plate. Once she felt she could speak without drooling, she asked, "How is it you speak English so well?"

He shrugged. "I speak several languages fluently. I never really thought about the why or the how, it's just something I do. My entire clan does as well."

"Well, I couldn't even master pig-Latin as a kid, so I'm impressed. Languages are not really my thing."

He smiled. "Once we're bound, you'll speak and understand Icelandic."

"Shut up, really?"

Kaspar nodded and pulled a dome off a plate, setting it aside. "Our minds become linked, and we'll be able speak telepathically as well."

"Linked?" She gasped. "As in, we'll be able to read each other's thoughts?"

He popped a grape into his mouth and nodded.

"Um…" She shook her head. "Pass."

"What?"

"There is no way in hell I'm going to let you into my head. You're already taking up valuable real estate in there, and I'm not giving you anymore."

Kaspar grinned. "I'm in your head?"

"*That's* what you took from that?"

"I like that I'm in your head, elskan, but I'd love to be in your heart."

"Oh, don't you dare start getting all nice on me again, Kaz. I can't take it."

He stood and wrapped an arm around her from behind. Leaning down, he kissed the sensitive part just below her ear. "I love it when you call me Kaz."

She closed her eyes, a shiver running through her. "Do you?" she whispered.

He nodded, kissing her neck. "I do."

"Noted."

He released her and and took his seat again, and she spent the better part of their breakfast trying to figure out how to untangle Kaspar from her heart. He'd woven himself so completely into her life in such a short amount of time, she wasn't entirely sure how, or even if she wanted, to cut him loose.

"I have to go, sweetheart," he said, frowning at his phone.

"Go. I'm okay."

"Are you sure?"

She nodded. "I'll watch some bad soaps and maybe look for a job while you work."

He chuckled. "Easing your way into being taken care of?"

"Something like that."

"Do you want to go out for dinner, or stay in?"

She smiled. "Mmm, I don't know. Out?"

He rose to his feet and bent down to kiss her. "Tell Camilla where you want to go and she'll handle it."

Jesska snorted. "What kind of executive assistant would I be if I couldn't make a simple reservation?"

"Camilla will handle it."

"Jesska will handle it," she countered.

"Stubborn."

"Bossy."

He grinned and kissed her again. "If you need me, call me."

"I won't need you."

He gripped his chest and groaned. "You wound me."

Jesska giggled. "Oh, baby, how will I live without you for..." she looked at her watch, "...all of three hours until you figure you need to check on me?"

"It'll be closer to four."

She laid the back of her hand on her forehead and tipped her head back. "*No! Not* four. I can't live without you for *four*."

He stroked her cheek. "I love you, silly girl."

She nodded, not sure how to respond. He loved her? Was that even possible in such a short amount of time? She watched him leave and then finished her food before stacking things in the hallway for the staff to retrieve. Sitting down with her laptop, she went about finding a job. The problem was, she couldn't think about anything other than Kaspar's words of devotion.

The man was irresistible, and she realized that she was falling in love with him. It was different than what she had with Brady. It was mature and deeper, and much, much scarier. It was forever.

* * *

Jesska felt soft lips on her cheek and sat up, colliding with Kaspar's chin "Oh, sorry," she said.

"I didn't mean to startle you, elskan. You just looked so sweet lying there asleep."

She smiled and dragged her hands down her face. "What time is it?"

"Six."

"Crap. I didn't make a reservation." She grimaced. "I got busy with job searches and then I must have fallen asleep. I'm sorry, Kaz, I totally forgot."

Kaspar chuckled. "Camilla made one at Serratto for seven if you want to go there, or we can still stay in if you'd rather."

She blinked up at him. "Would it be horrible to stay in?"

"I'd prefer it."

"You would?"

He nodded. "It's been a long day, sweetheart, and my brother arrives in the morning, delayed as usual, so it means we can spend a little extra time together tonight if we stay in."

"Your brother's coming? Megan's...ah...boyfriend? What do I call him?"

Kaspar removed his watch, pulling his shirt from his trousers as he headed to the bedroom. "No, Ari's not coming. Gunnar is. As far as Ari and his title as it pertains to your sister, I suppose they are mates. As you and I are."

Jesska craned her neck to watch Kaspar as he unbuttoned his shirt and slipped it from his shoulders. His chest was like granite and when he turned to grab a T-shirt, the muscles on his back rippled with the motion. He caught her eye and she gasped, sitting back down on the sofa, hoping he hadn't seen her staring at him. He returned to the living room devoid of shoes, but in the same pants he wore that morning.

She smiled up at him and he leaned down, one hand on the armrest and one behind her head, his face within inches of hers. "Did you like what you saw?"

"Very much." Jesska took a deep breath. "Sorry."

"Don't be sorry, baby. I like you watching me."

She licked her lips. "I like it too."

He grinned and leaned closer, kissing her before sitting beside her. "What do you want for dinner?"

"Right now, I could eat the entire left side of a cow."

Kaspar raised an eyebrow. "Not the right?"

"Oh, I'll take the right too, but I don't want to be greedy."

He laughed. "I'll order two, then."

"This is you taking care of me, huh?"

"Part of it, yes," he said, and kissed her palm.

"Okay, brownie points for you. Cooking's not my strong suit."

He turned and reached behind him, grabbing his phone, texting who? Jesska could only guess. Setting his phone aside, he grabbed her hand again.

"Who was that?" she asked.

"Camilla. She will order our food."

"I could do that, you know. As could you."

Kaspar cocked his head. "But it's her job."

"Does she ever get a day off?" she asked.

"Sundays. Except when we're traveling."

"Kaz," she said in exasperation. "Are you seriously telling me she only gets one day off a week? And sometimes not even that?"

He rubbed the back of her neck. "Yes."

"What about dating or just doing girl things? Girls need more than one day off a week."

"We don't date."

She leaned away from his touch. "Well, what happens when she finds her true love or whatever?"

"Then he will bind her, and she will no longer work for me." He frowned. "Her assistant will take over, I suppose."

"What if she doesn't want her assistant to take the job? What if she *wants* to work for you?"

"She'll need to speak to her mate about that."

Jesska tugged her hand from his. "You're not serious."

"I don't understand."

"Obviously." She rose to her feet.

"What are you doing?"

"I think I should go back to my room."

Kasper stood. "Why?"

"Because if I don't, I'm going to get really pissed off."

"I'm guessing I said something really wrong, but I have no idea what it was." He crossed his arms. "Care to fill me in?"

She fisted her hands at her side. "You know, sometimes you're just the sweetest, most brilliant man on earth, and then you say something so…so…unbelievably chauvinistic and stupid."

Kaspar ran his hands through his hair. "I don't know what to tell you, Jess. It's my world. I've never known anything different."

"I know," she said.

He reached out his hand. "Stay."

"Is that an order, my liege?"

"Baby."

Jesska cocked her head. "I'll stay if you promise me you'll give Camilla another day off."

He sighed. "If she would like another day off, I will give it to her."

She took his hand and let him pull her back down on the sofa. His phone buzzed, so he grabbed it and then set it on the coffee table. "Our meal is being sent up."

"That was quick."

Kaspar smiled. "We have a chef at our disposal."

"We do?"

He nodded.

"That's awesome," she said.

A knock at the door sounded and Kaspar rose to his feet to open it.

"Sire," Camilla said, and followed the server into the room.

Kaspar nodded in greeting.

"Hi, Camilla," Jesska said.

The assistant smiled. "M'lady."

Jesska still wasn't used to being called "m'lady," but she didn't react quite so shocked anymore. Camilla organized their meal and then walked out of the room with the server.

"She really didn't need to come all the way up here," Jesska said.

Kaspar opened his mouth and then closed it again.

She raised an eyebrow. "What?"

"I'm choosing my words, and the words I thought about choosing were probably going to get me in trouble, so I am now choosing to stay quiet."

Jesska giggled, standing on her toes to kiss his cheek. "Smart man."

Kaspar grinned, holding her chair until she sat down.

CHAPTER THIRTEEN

DINNER PASSED QUICKLY, and Camilla returned to pick up the dishes, prompting Jesska to give Kaspar a reminding glance to speak with her.

"You know, I'm beat," she said. "I'm going to head to my room."

"Stay, baby," he said.

"I should leave you alone for this." She smiled. "Come find me later."

He frowned, but then shook his head and kissed her quickly. Jesska walked out the door, surprised by Jóvin, who was lurking.

"Hi, Jóvin," she said with a smile.

"M'lady."

"You're never going to call me Jesska are you?"

He smiled and used his keycard to open her door. "No, m'lady."

He held the door open for her and Jesska headed into her suite, relieved Jóvin didn't follow her. She walked into her bathroom, filled up the large soaker tub, and set her phone next to it while she removed her clothing. Pinning her hair on top of her head, she poured in the jasmine oil Kaspar had bought her, removed her makeup, and then slid into the heat of the water.

She'd almost fallen asleep again when her phone buzzed and without opening her eyes, she answered it. "Hello?"

"What are you doing?"

"Taking a bath." She heard Kaspar let out a long breath and she grinned. "Naked."

"Yes, it's generally a good idea to be naked while taking a bath."

She giggled. "Stop picturing me naked."

"No," he said, and Jesska heard the smile in his voice.

She sighed and sank lower in the tub. "Did you talk to Camilla?"

"I did."

"And?"

"And we have come to an agreement. How long are you going to be in the tub?"

She rolled her eyes. "Depends on how long it takes you to tell me about your agreement."

"She doesn't want another day off."

"What?" Jesska frowned. "Why not?"

"It's complicated, elskan."

"Did you get all kingy on her?" she accused.

"Kingy?" he asked.

"Yes. All condescending and *kingy*."

"I'm her king, sweetheart."

"Yes, but that doesn't mean you have be a jerk."

"Jesska, I'm not having this conversation with you," he said.

"Why not?"

"Because matters of the Crown do not concern you."

Jesska forced herself not to swear, her indignation coming out in the form of a hiss.

"Jesska," he said, sounding irritated.

"I'm sorry, Sire. I was out of line. Again, I apologize. I totally forgot my *place*."

"Elskan."

"I'm going to bed after my bath, Kaspar, so if you'll excuse me, I have some relaxing to do. Have a great night." She hung up and dropped the phone on the floor.

Jerk. Big fat jerky, jerk, jerk. Kingly, entitled, big fat jerky jerk, jerk.

Her phone buzzed again but she ignored it and closed her eyes in an effort to relax. She forced her mind to the moments when Kaspar had been an ass in an effort to drown out the many more moments he'd been sweet. There weren't very many instances where he'd been an ass, and her spiral lasted all of six minutes or so, when she heard a knock on her bathroom door. She squeaked, sitting up and attempting to cover herself, wishing she had bubbles for strategic coverage.

"It's me, baby. I won't come in," Kaspar said.

"What are you doing here?" She craned her neck to see if she could see him. Luckily, the door was still closed. "How did you get in?" she asked. "Never mind. Stupid question. Don't answer that."

"You finish your bath and we'll talk when you get out."

"Just go back to your room, Kaspar."

She heard him sigh. "We obviously need to talk, so I'll wait for you to finish."

"Well, too bad for you, I'm never getting out of this bath."

"You'll get cold and your skin will shrivel, elskan, so you'll need to dry off at some point."

"You don't know my obsession with tubby time, Kaz. I could be here all night."

He chuckled. "Baby, I've been waiting a thousand years for you. You don't think I can wait out your bath time?"

She tried to ignore the sexy way his voice sounded when he said "baby," especially accented. *And* she tried to ignore the fact he'd waited a thousand years for her...'cause that wasn't sexy as hell. But she couldn't ignore the shiver than ran down her spine as she heard him moving around her room. She heard the pop of a cork and the clink of glasses that meant wine.

It also meant making out on the sofa after drinking said wine and then cuddling until she fell asleep. Which then meant him carrying her to her bed and kissing her sweetly before leaving her, because he was a gentleman and he'd vowed they wouldn't make love until their bonding night, but that didn't stop him from whispering exactly what he planned to do when he did finally make love to her. Jesska groaned and turned the hot water on with her foot in an attempt to block out his words.

"Did you say something, baby?" he called.

Sexy, gorgeous, sweet, romantic, jerky jerk, jerk.

"Nope," she snapped.

"Do you want some wine?"

"Does a bear shit in the woods?" she grumbled to herself.

"Baby? Do you want wine?" he repeated.

"Nope," she called. "I'm good."

His chuckle penetrated the thin door and she closed her eyes again. She heard the click of the television and then heard Chris Harrison say, "It's time for the rose ceremony."

"Oh my *god*, Kaz. Not even the Bachelor's going to get me out of this tub," she said.

The volume increased and Manny called out "Rosa."

"Wait. What?" She frowned. "Did he just say Rosa?" she called.

"I'm sorry, baby. I can't hear you," Kaspar called.

"Will you accept this rose?" Manny asked.

"He better not have said Rosa! She's a total cow!" Jesska snapped.

The television got even louder. "Sorry, baby. I really can't hear you over the television."

She let out a frustrated growl and pulled the plug on the tub. *Big fat creative knows how to push my buttons, jerky jerk, jerk.*

Climbing from the tub, she wrapped the towel around her and stomped into the living room. "He did *not* just say Rosa."

Kaspar paused the television and turned his head, his gaze sweeping her body, then a slow, sexy, I-want-to-peel-that-towel-from-your-body smile formed on his face and he rose to his feet. "Yes, Manny picked Rosa, elskan."

"Well, he's an idiot," she said, and turned back toward the bedroom.

She'd made it all of four inches before she was pulled up against him, his mouth gently kissing her shoulder.

"Hi," he breathed.

She squeezed her eyes shut. "I should get dressed."

"Okay. You get dressed and we can talk."

"I hate you so much right now," she said.

"I know, baby. It's a good thing I love you enough for both of us."

She walked into her bedroom and closed the door with a satisfying slam. Pulling on undies, yoga pants, and a T-shirt, she took a deep breath and then another…and then another, still debating on whether or not she was going to hide in her bedroom or hash things out with Kaspar.

She continued to debate for several minutes before pulling her door open and finding him grinning at her from where he stood just against the door frame, his arms folded across his chest.

She frowned and pushed past him. "I'm just getting some wine and then I'm going to bed."

"No, Jesska, we're going to talk."

"There's no point in talking."

He caught up to her and grabbed her arm, turning her gently to face him. "Baby. We're going to talk. Whether you want to or not. Neither of us is going to sleep until this is resolved."

She frowned up at him. "Well, until you're no longer all kingy and crap, this can't be resolved."

Kaspar smiled, squeezing her arms. "I have been king for half a millennium. I don't know how to be anything less than kingy…" He laid a finger over her mouth to stop her retort. "But, I will try to be more sensitive to my staff and listen when you have important things to tell me."

She wrinkled her nose, pressing her lips together in a thin line.

"I will also try to listen even when you *don't* have important things to say."

She gasped. "Are you trying to tell me that you think my words aren't important?"

At his sarcastic smile, she huffed and bit back her own smile.

"I think everything you have to say is important, sweetheart. But sometimes, I need to hear what you have to say when we're alone...not in front of my staff."

"I have never contradicted you in front of anyone."

He raised an eyebrow.

"Okay, one time...maybe. And only in front of Austri." She played with a button on his soft Henley T-shirt. "But in fairness, he's always around."

Kaspar smiled. "And that will change, I promise. We need to find out who and what the threat is first."

"I know." She sighed. "I'm sorry I was a shrew. I know I have a lot to learn about your life and how you do things and that I can't expect to be part of every decision, it's just really weird for me. I'm a normal American girl, and we tend to speak our mind. Well, I do, at least."

He smiled. "And I love that about you, elskan. We'll figure it out, it'll just take some time."

"Okay," she said with a smile.

"I have news."

"That sounds ominous."

Kaspar led her to the sofa and pulled her down onto his lap. "Cameron and I have been discussing Jason."

"How long have you been 'discussing' him?"

"Since the day he showed up at your house," Kaspar said.

"Of course you have." Jesska narrowed her eyes. "So, what does Cameron say?"

"Jason is back in jail...not prison...county jail for now."

"Do I need to be a witness again?"

"I believe a statement will suffice, since he's confessed."

"What?" She gasped. "Confessed to what, exactly?"

"The letter and the threat when he came to your house. He also confessed to stabbing Brady."

"Out loud? Like, told them in words what he did?"

"Yes, baby."

She widened her eyes. "You made him do that."

"Excuse me?"

"When you had him against the wall. You hypnotized him or something."

Kaspar gave her a gentle squeeze. "I compelled him to tell the truth, sweetheart. I didn't make him do anything he shouldn't."

"I know." She blinked back tears. "He's never admitted what he did."

"And now he has."

Jesska pushed herself off of him and stood. "Will I have to see him again?"

"I don't know. Right now, the statement will do."

"Are they going to need me to testify at his new trial?"

"Cameron seems to think there may not be another trial," Kaspar said. "Unless he recants his confession."

Jesska wrinkled his nose. "Could he do that? Does your 'compelling' wear off?"

"I buried it deep in him, sweetheart. So, no, he will not be able to lie." Kaspar rose to his feet and took her hand. "And we are doing everything we can to make sure he doesn't."

"We?" she asked, staring up at him.

"I am taking on a few of the expenses in order for Dalton and Cameron to investigate things the DA was ill-equipped to do so before."

She shook her head. "Seriously?"

"Já, baby. Does this upset you?"

"*No!*" Jesska slid her arms around him. "It makes me think I might be falling in love with you."

"You are already in love with me."

"Am I?"

"Yes."

"You're right. I am. For ages." She sighed. "Thank you."

Kaspar chuckled, rubbing her back and kissing her hair. "I would do anything for you."

"Yeah, I'm picking up on that." She smiled up at him. "On a similar subject, I have something for you."

"You do?"

She nodded and pulled away from him, heading into her bedroom. She returned with a little wooden box she'd bought at the Saturday Market. "I was going to wait for the right time, but I think the right time's now."

"It's beautiful," he said.

"That part's not for you. I mean, it is if you want it, but it's what's inside that's significant." She opened the lid. Sitting inside were Brady's rings and the chain. "I realized on Sunday that I no longer need them."

He studied her and she bit her lip.

"Is that weird?" she asked.

"Is what weird?"

She closed the lid. "That I'm telling you this? It's weird. I'm sorry, Kaz. I just felt like it was important to tell you."

She turned away, but found herself pulled up against him and kissed until she couldn't breathe. Kaspar kept his mouth on hers as he pulled her on top of him on the sofa and slipped a hand into her hair, holding her closer.

Jesska dropped the box onto the floor, freeing her hands so she could hold on to him. When she was sure they were at the edge of the point of no return, he broke the kiss, settling his forehead against hers and taking several deep breaths.

She licked her lips and smiled. "So…not weird?"

He laughed, dropping his head back on the armrest and giving her a squeeze. "It's the most beautiful gift I've ever received."

"Really?"

He nodded, stroking her back. "Thank you."

"You're welcome," she said, and settled her cheek against his chest. She heard the steady beat of his heart and he held her for several minutes, words unnecessary in the quiet of the room.

"I love you," he whispered.

She set her chin in her hands so she could smile at him. "I love you too."

"Can I give you my gift now?"

She sat up. "You bought me a gift?"

He nodded, sitting up beside her and sliding his hand into his pocket. "The Kalt Einn don't typically do proposals, because the binding is usually somewhat immediate, but we absolutely do rings."

He slipped something on her finger and Jesska gasped. A large emerald-cut diamond sat proudly in the middle of four other diamonds, stepping down in size, in platinum. It fit her perfectly, and she blinked back tears.

"Is this you asking me to marry you?" she joked.

"Yes, Jesska. Will you marry me, even though we're going to be bound, so the question is somewhat rhetorical?"

"Wow. Romantic." She giggled. "Yes, love of my life forever and ever and ever. I will marry you."

Kaspar grinned. "If you don't like the ring, sweetheart, we can choose something else."

"Not like it?" She rolled her eyes. "Are you kidding me? If I would have designed the perfect ring, it would be this."

He smiled. "Are you sure?"

"Yes." She threw her arms around his neck. "Thank you. I love it."

Kaspar's phone interrupted their celebration. Jesska sat back and frowned.

"It's your brother." Kaspar answered the call. "Hello?"

He paced the room as he spoke to her brother. Maybe spoke wasn't the right word—shot off one-syllable words was more accurate. As Kaspar continued to grunt and give the occasional "yes" and "no" answers, Jesska studied her ring. She couldn't even begin to guess how much it cost. She was pretty sure the diamonds were perfect, and they sparkled even when the light was dim.

"Jess?"

"Hmm?" She glanced at Kaspar, who was now off the phone and grinning at her.

He chuckled. "I'm done."

"What did Cam want?"

"His team has been working to decode the flash drive. They're onto something, so it's possible they'll have answers in a day or two."

"Oh, wow. That's great," she said.

"I will pick my brother up tomorrow, and then you and I can go out if you like."

"Oh, I made plans with Amanda for a girls' day. I figured you'd be busy with your family."

"He's your family now."

"I know, but you have stuff you need to talk to him about without me. I wanted to give you time to do that."

He smiled. "Then dinner with everyone tomorrow."

"Sounds good," she said. "For now, though, I'd like to make out with my fiancé."

Kaspar chuckled as he sat on the sofa and pulled her on top of him. "Your wish is my command."

CHAPTER FOURTEEN

Having seen Jesska off to spend the day with her friend, Kaspar organized his morning in order to have time to retrieve his brother. He'd managed only a few stolen moments with Jesska that morning, having joined her for breakfast and then riling them both up by kissing her for far too long.

Climbing into the back of the car, Austri and Jóvin in the front, Kaspar responded to a few emails as they drove to the private airstrip. They arrived just as the plane was taxiing to the gate, and Kaspar climbed out of the car to await his brother, leaning against the car and watching as the plane came to a stop and the engines shut down.

Gunnar walked off the plane…followed by Ari. Kaspar quickened his stride to greet them both, knowing his shock was evident on his face.

"Surprise," Gunnar said with a laugh.

Kaspar pulled Ari in for a hug, slapping his back. "What are you doing here, brother?"

"Turns out, Kade has a soft spot for his mate."

Kaspar rolled his eyes. "Don't we all?"

Ari nodded. "Samantha wants me to make things right with Megan, so I had to agree to a few rules on the threat of death if I didn't comply and then they released me to Gunnar."

"You're very lucky," Kaspar said.

Ari nodded and grew serious. "I need to see them, Kaz. Now."

Kaspar grabbed his phone. "I'll call Cameron."

"Who's Cameron?" Gunnar asked.

Kaspar paused. "The brother."

"Of?"

"My mate and your mate," Kaspar said.

"I don't understand," Ari said.

"Siblings by marriage."

"Not blood."

"Já," Kaspar confirmed.

Ari nodded and the brothers filed into the car. Kaspar called Cameron, and Cameron promised he would speak to Megan, but that they should head to the hotel.

"I want to see her now, Kaz," Ari stressed. "I'm not willing to wait any longer."

"Well, that's apparently not an option. Megan is a lawyer, and she's probably in court."

Ari smiled.. "She's always been brilliant. A lawyer. Perfect for her. It doesn't surprise me that she chose that."

"She was good at arguing her case, eh?"

"Always." Ari swore. "I can't believe I have to wait."

Kaspar squeezed his shoulder. "It'll give you a chance to settle in. You can see her tonight."

Ari scowled, but said nothing as he faced the window. Kaspar felt and understood his frustration. The thought of being kept from Jesska wouldn't sit well with him, either, so he could imagine how Ari felt. He pulled out his phone and scrolled to Jesska's number.

Are you having fun?

It took a few minutes, but his heart leapt when his phone buzzed.

Code for: are you safe, right? I'm breaking the laws of movie-dom right now, Kaz. I'm fine and Channing Tatum is sexy as hell. Now leave me alone so I can concentrate on his six-pack.

He frowned.

But I love you, even though you worry too much. Megan says hi.

Kaspar stared at the phone and then typed, *You're with your sister?*

Yep, she surprised me and Amanda. How's your brother?

Both of them are here.

Ari's with you too?

Yes.

Gotta go, movie starting. Shutting down my phone, you won't be able to reach me. Love you.

I love you too. Kaspar smiled. *And stop looking at another man's six-pack.*

Her response was an emoticon sticking out its tongue and then radio silence. He slipped his phone into his pocket just as Austri pulled into the hotel parking lot.

Without conversation, the brothers made their way to the floor, Kaspar's staff waiting for them, their heads bowed as the brothers entered Kaspar's suite. Ari and Gunnar both had personal valets who unpacked for the them while the brothers showered, agreeing to meet with Kaspar when they were finished.

They arrived at his suite less than an hour later.

"Any word on Megan?" Ari asked as he sat in one of the chairs next to the sofa.

Kaspar debated whether or not to lie by omission.

"Kaz?" he pressed.

"She's with Jesska at the movies," he admitted.

Ari shot out of his seat. "Take me to her."

Kaspar shook his head. "I promised Jess I'd give her some time with her friend. I won't go back on my word."

Ari swore, advancing on his brother with a look that would have made most men cower. "I want to see my mate, Kaspar. You'll take me to her now."

"I can—"

His response was cut off when a knock came at his door. Kaspar pulled it open to Megan, who stormed inside and threw herself into Ari's arms before stepping away and slapping him...hard.

"I can't believe you lied to me!" she snapped.

Ari had a stupid grin on his face as he took in his mate. "*Þú hefur ekki breyst, fallega.*" (You haven't changed, beautiful.)

Jesska frowned up in question to Kaspar, but didn't say anything. He wrapped an arm around her and whispered the translation in her ear.

"*Reyndu ekki að kalla mig fallega!*" Megan snapped. (Don't you dare call me beautiful!)

"Sweetheart, English. We're being rude," Ari said, the stupid grin still on his face as he wrapped his arms around her and pulled her close.

"I swear to *god*, Ari. You haven't begun to see rude," she snapped, and burst into tears.

"Let's give them some privacy," Jesska whispered, and made her way to Kaspar's door, tugging on his hand.

Kaspar nodded to Gunnar, who followed them into the hallway. Kaspar guided Jesska forward. "Sweetheart, this is Gunnar."

Jesska shook his hand. "It's nice to meet you."

"You too," Gunnar said with a smile. "Well, I have a feeling this is going to take a while, so I'm going to do some work. Dinner tonight?"

"Perfect," Kaspar said, and turned to Jesska as Gunnar walked away. "You didn't finish your movie."

Jesska sighed. "I know. I stupidly told Megan that Ari was here, and she hightailed it out of the theater so fast, I could barely catch her. Good thing it was cheapie movie…we didn't stop to get a refund…then there was traffic, and Megan was yelling, a *lot*. Then we had to drop Amanda home, and Megan just kept getting more and more irritated. I probably should have driven."

"You let her *drive* in that state?" he snapped.

"I didn't have much of a choice, Kaz. I didn't have my car with me, remember?"

"Let's go to your room and discuss this privately," he said, and grabbed her hand, tugging her toward her suite. He used his keycard and pushed open the door, standing back so she could precede him.

Jesska walked into the room, dropped her purse on the side table, and, as was her habit, slipped off her shoes before flopping onto the sofa. "I'm not fighting with you."

He frowned and sat beside her. "I have no intention of fighting. I was momentarily concerned for your safety, but you're here now and safe, so no fighting."

"I don't want a lecture either."

He chuckled. "No lecture."

She reached over and lifted his T-shirt.

"What are you doing?" he asked.

"Well, I didn't get to see Channing Tatum's abs, so figured you could show me yours."

Kaspar laughed and shifted, pulling her on top of him while he settled his feet on the coffee table. "You can look at me anytime you like. In fact, I'd prefer it."

Jesska grinned, snuggling against his chest and kissing his neck. "You smell good. You always smell good. I missed you."

"You did?"

"I did. You're growing on me."

He chuckled. "I'm glad."

"Any news on the 'threat' front?" She glanced up at him. "You let me go to the movies without the muscle, so you must feel I'm safe."

"You weren't without the muscle, baby."

"I wasn't?"

"No. I have just instructed them to be less conspicuous."

"Oh." She smiled, burrowing against him again. "Thank you."

"And as far as the threat goes, Jason is still in jail, so he can't touch you for the moment. We have not located who is after Ása...ah...Sophia, so until we do, you'll stay here."

She pushed herself up, settling her chin on her hands splayed on his chest. "Why do I feel like this is going to be a more permanent situation than I originally thought?"

"Because you're extremely smart."

She settled her head back on his chest. "Well, my lease isn't up for another three months, so I'll have to go back there until then."

"I'll buy out your lease."

"No, you won't."

He gave her a gentle squeeze, not in the mood to argue. Jesska's phone pealed in the quiet and he reached for her purse behind him.

"Thanks," she said, and pulled out her phone. "Cam? Hey, you okay?" She sat up and crossed her legs. "Yes. Megan's here. Seriously?"

Kaspar sat up, feeling her worry. He texted his brothers and Austri.

"Yes, I'm with him. Okay, we'll stay put. Where's Sophia?"

She glanced at Kaspar as he got up and opened his door. Gunnar walked in.

"Okay, yes, bring her by," Jesska said.

Kaspar's phone buzzed, and he saw Dalton Moore's number come up. "Kaspar here."

"Hey, it's Dalton Moore. You need to close ranks."

"Okay," he said carefully.

"Megan and Sophia's accident wasn't an accident. We're closing in on the who, and then we'll figure out the why."

"Skít," he snapped. "Where am I meeting you?"

"You're not coming."

"I am."

"No, Kaspar, you're not," Moore stressed. "You're to stay in your royal compound and my men and I will take care of this."

Kaspar expressed his opinion in Icelandic, causing his brother to raise an eyebrow.

"I'll call you when I know something." Moore hung up.

A knock at his door brought Ari and Megan, and Kaspar didn't miss that Ari's shirt was on backwards and Megan's hair had been hastily put back into place.

"What's wrong?" Ari asked.

"Cameron's bringing Sophia here," Jesska explained.

"Why?" Megan asked.

"Because your accident wasn't an accident," Kaspar said.

"What?" Megan and Jesska said in stereo.

Ari wrapped his hand around the back of Megan's neck and squeezed. "We'll sort this out, sweetheart."

She smacked his arm away. "Don't you 'sweetheart' me. If you have put our daughter in danger, I'm going to castrate you."

"You're still mad, I see," Jesska observed.

Ari frowned. "What do you know?"

Kaspar shook his head. "Not much. Moore seems to think we're going to stay here while he figures it out. Austri is getting the car."

Jesska frowned, prompting Kaspar to pull her into the privacy of her bedroom, closing the door behind him. "Say what you need to say."

"It's dangerous." She settled her hands on her hips. "You need to let Dalton do his job."

"Jesska, I'm going to say this one time and then the conversation is done. My brothers and I are going to figure out who is threatening our family. I don't give a damn about what the lawman says, you are not his to worry about. You are mine. Megan and Sophia are Ari's. It's family business, period."

"I'm no one's but my own, Kaz."

He cupped her cheek. "You are mine, make no mistake about it. When one of my own is threatened, I deal with it."

"You're so freakin' bossy."

"Baby, what do you need me to say? I'll say it and then I have to go." He glanced at his phone and then answered it before she could respond to his question. "Austri."

"Mr. Shane is here."

"Does he have Ása?"

"Já."

"Send them up to Jesska's room, please." He hung up and found Jesska tapping her foot. "What?"

"Her name's Sophia."

"It's not actually."

"Whatever." Jesska yanked open her door and stormed back into the living room.

Kaspar followed just as Austri arrived with Cameron and Ása…and as Megan collapsed on the floor, groaning in pain.

"Mom!" Ása squeaked, kneeling beside her. "Someone call an ambulance."

Ari joined his daughter on the floor and laid a hand on Megan's forehead. "Your medicine can't help right now, daughter.

"*Ert þú bundinn henni?*" Kaspar bellowed. (You bound her?)

"What does 'bound' mean?" Ása asked.

"I'll explain later," Jesska said.

"*Það hjálpar ekki,*" (It couldn't be helped) Ari responded as he lifted Megan in his arms. She whimpered in pain, as he carried her to Jesska's bedroom, Ása worried and following behind.

"Yes, it could have been helped Ari, you selfish—" Kaspar snapped.

"I don't have time for you, brother," Ari said, and closed his family into the room.

"What happened?" Jesska asked, her hand going to her throat.

Her talisman was gone, and she realized it all too quickly as Kaspar scowled and pulled her hand down. "Don't," he said.

She fisted her hands at her side. "Then tell me what's happening."

"I don't have time to explain, elskan." He pulled out his phone and stepped into the hallway.

"What do you want now?" Kade answered, sounding irritated.

"What happens to a human woman when she is bound to a Kalt Einn?"

"Her body goes through a conversion and it's extremely painful."

"Skít," Kaspar hissed. "This is what I was afraid of."

"Who has been bound?"

"Ari bound Megan."

A shuffling sound and quiet arguing interrupted the conversation briefly.

"Hello? This is Samantha, I'm Kade's mate."

"I know who you are," Kaspar said. "Thank you for helping with my brother."

"You're welcome," she said, and he could sense her kindness. Perhaps it was the deep southern American accent, or the fact that she sounded like she was smiling. "If you have any questions during the conversion, would you or Ari please call me? I'd be happy to help.

"And how does Kade feel about that?"

"I plead the fifth." She chuckled. "I'm going to text you my phone number. Please call me. I can help walk you through it."

"I appreciate that," Kaspar said. "I should go now."

"Do you need to speak with Kade again?"

"Absolutely not."

She giggled. "Chicken."

Kaspar couldn't help a smile. "Thank you, Samantha. Truly."

"It's my pleasure. We'll talk soon."

He hung up and headed back into the suite. Stepping into the bedroom, he filled Ari in on what Samantha had said, gave him her phone number, and then focused back on Jesska.

"How did you know he bound her?" Jesska asked.

"When mates are bound we know. It's a vibration of sorts, I supposed."

"Oh."

"I have to go, elskan."

He could see she was trying not to cry. "Go, then," she ground out.

Kaspar kissed her quickly and then followed Gunnar out the door. Austri had the car waiting for them, and they managed to pick up Cameron's trail in relatively quick fashion. If Dalton Moore wasn't going to tell Kaspar where to go, he figured Cameron would be heading to the same place.

* * *

Jesska pushed open her bedroom door to find Megan writhing in pain on her bed. Sophia was inconsolable at the state of her mother, and Ari was carefully removing Megan's clothes, in an obvious attempt to make her more comfortable.

He glanced up at Jesska. "We'll need cold towels, and ice, if you have it."

Jesska nodded. "Soph, you want to help me?"

"Um…"

"Sophia, come on, honey, let's go get some stuff for your mom."

Ari stroked Sophia's face. "*Farðu og hjálpaðu frænku þinni, litla. Mamma þín þarf að kæla sig niður.*" (Go help your aunt, little one. Your mama needs to be cooled down.)

Sophia nodded and followed Jesska into the bathroom.

"You get some towels wet, okay?" Jesska said. "I'll go get ice."

"Is my mom going to die?"

"No, baby. She's going to be fine. I promise."

Sophia went about her duties, and Jesska stepped outside to find Jóvin hovering. "M'lady? You're to stay inside."

"I need ice, Jóvin."

"I'll get it for you, m'lady."

She shoved the bucket at him. "Fine. Hurry," she snapped, and stepped back inside, heading to her bedroom. Megan was naked from the waist up, as was Ari. He had his arms wrapped around her from behind, and she appeared to be calmer, although her skin was a blotchy red. Jesska gasped, making her way to the bed and covering them both with a sheet for privacy. "Do you really want Sophia to see this? It will scar her for life."

"I have to stay connected to her," Ari explained. "It helps with the conversion."

"What's conversion?"

"When a human is bound to a Kalt Einn, her body will change to be like ours."

"Pardon?"

"I'm sorry, sister, I don't have time to explain everything to you right now," Ari said. "Perhaps it would be better if you didn't watch."

"Are you saying I will go through this if Kaspar binds me?" Jesska asked, horrified.

"Já."

"Is she dying?" Sophia's small voice sounded from the threshold of the bathroom.

"No, baby," Ari answered, and waved his hand. "Come and lay the towel over your mama. Touch her as well. You can help."

Sophia rushed to do as he said and then she settled her hand on her mother's head. Megan sighed and shifted, turning towards Sophia. "That feels good, honey."

Jesska felt like she was intruding on a family moment, so she went back into the living room just as Jóvin arrived with the ice. He had three buckets full—where he got the other containers she wasn't sure, but she was glad for the help. "Thanks, Jóvin."

"M'lady," he said, and then left her again.

"Jess?" Sophia called from the bedroom. "Do you have the ice?"

"Yeah, honey. Right here."

Jesska didn't have time to obsess about what her body would go through when Kaspar bound her, because she was too focused on making sure Megan was as comfortable as possible. Once Megan was calm and sleeping, Ari pulled his shirt back on and left the suite. Sophia curled up next to her mother on Jesska's bed, and Jesska closed the door for privacy, fell onto her sofa, and curled up in a ball, bursting into quiet tears as the realization of what she would be subjected to sunk in. Megan's body had been wracked with pain and her skin had changed from milky white to a dark red in front of Jesska's eyes for several minutes before returning to normal. Jesska knew Megan was fighting the urge to scream for her and Sophia's sakes, but she couldn't hold back the occasional whimper which seemed to frighten Sophia. In the end, Ari had forced them out for a time before letting them back in when Megan was calmer.

Jesska didn't give herself much time to freak out, sitting up and wiping away her tears. She needed to do something, and she knew exactly what. She grabbed her cell phone, made a quick call, and then took her purse and keys and left the room.

CHAPTER FIFTEEN

JÓVIN STOOD IN the hallway and pushed away from the wall when Jesska walked out of her room. "M'lady."

"Jóvin," she said, and headed to the elevator.

"You can't leave, m'lady."

"I have something important to do," she said as she waited for the elevator.

"It doesn't matter. You are to stay here."

The elevator dinged and the door opened. She moved to step inside, but Jóvin grabbed her arm. "I can't let you leave."

She frowned. "Are you supposed to touch me?"

He released her immediately. She knew it was a low blow, but she was sick of being a prisoner, even if it was for her own good.

Jóvin swore and pushed his way inside. "I will take you where you need to go."

"I have my car."

"Jesska, I cannot let you leave here."

"You called me Jesska."

"I did, m'lady."

She grinned as the elevator doors closed. "I like that better than m'lady."

Jóvin chuckled. "I know, m'lady."

Without further discussion, he guided Jesska to one of the cars in the garage and then drove her to Brady's parents' home. While Jóvin awaited her in the car, she walked up to the house and rang the doorbell smiling nervously when Brady's mother answered the door.

"Hi, sweetie," she said, and hugged Jesska. "Are you okay? You sounded upset on the phone."

"I have to tell you and Brian something and I felt I should tell you face to face."

"Come into the kitchen."

Brady's father stood from his place at the kitchen peninsula and hugged Jesska. "How are you, honey?"

She bit her lip. "I've met someone."

"I'm sorry?" he said.

"I...I've met someone. Someone really special, and I think it might be serious."

Brian looked at his wife and then back at Jesska before letting out a holler. "It's about damn time."

"What?" she squeaked.

"Oh, honey, you've been so sad for far too long," Leslie said. "Brady wouldn't have wanted this for you. He would want you to be happy. And we do too."

Jesska let out a sigh of relief. "I thought you'd be mad or hurt."

"No way," Brian assured her. "This is a good thing, honey. You have our full blessing."

"Really?"

"Absolutely," he said. "And we'd love to meet him when you feel it's right."

"I'd really like that," she said.

"Can I get you something to drink?" Leslie asked.

"Actually, I should go. Kaspar's driver's waiting for me outside."

"Fancy," she said. "He must have money."

Jesska giggled. "Little bit, yes. But more than that, with the Jason thing in limbo, he's a little protective."

"I'm glad," Brian said.

"Thank you both. For being so kind to me. And patient. Especially that."

"We love you, Jess," Leslie said. "Always."

Jesska's heart floated as they walked her to the door. She hugged them and then stepped outside...to find a seething Kaspar stalking toward her.

"What are you doing here?" she asked.

He glanced at Brady's parents and then back at her. "Jóvin informed me you'd left the safety of the hotel," he said, carefully. A little too carefully.

"Yes. I needed to do something." She turned to the Kings. "Um, Brian and Leslie King, this is Kaspar Baldursson."

Kaspar shook their hands in greeting, his smile tight, his body locked. "It's lovely to meet you."

"You too, son," Brian said.

Jesska smiled at Brady's parents. "We should probably head back. Thanks for everything."

She hugged them once more and then Kaspar's hand was on the small of her back and guiding her to Austri's car. It appeared that Jóvin was gone, and she hoped he wasn't in trouble for doing her bidding.

Jesska slid inside and secured her seatbelt while Kaspar climbed in beside her. He pulled the door closed and raised the privacy glass. "If you ever do anything like that again, Jesska, I will take you over my knee."

She narrowed her eyes. "Excuse me?"

"We are in the middle of sorting out who's behind the attack on your sister and niece, and you leave the safety of the hotel?" he snapped. "I will have Jóvin's head for this."

"Um, no, you won't." She scowled. "For the record, Jóvin tried to stop me, but, a pretty glaring fact you seem to want to dismiss, is that I'm a grown-ass woman and I can make my own damn choices and go wherever the hell I want because I'm an *adult*. Jóvin drove me here, which apparently was the wrong thing for him to do, because you're obviously pissed at him, so next time I'll just drive myself."

"There won't be a next time."

"Screw you, Kaspar. I'm not your prisoner!"

He dragged his hands down his face and took several audible breaths. "You could have been hurt."

"Bullshit," she snapped. "Jóvin had me fully safe and protected. For the love of God, Kaspar, you have to trust your security detail to take care of me. It's what you pay them for, after all."

Austri pulled the car into the underground parking lot, and Jesska grimaced when she saw Jóvin waiting by the elevator bank.

Kaspar pushed open the door and stepped out, extending his hand to her. She ignored it and climbed from the car.

"I have to return to what I was doing," he said. "Go with Jóvin, and I'll see you as soon as I can."

"Oh, *now* Jóvin's on the approved list of jailors?"

"Jesska," he ground out. "Do as I say. We'll discuss this later."

"Fine."

He slid his hand behind her neck and gave her a gentle squeeze. "I love you, elskan."

"Good for you." She tried to pull away but he held firm.

"We'll talk later. I will come to your room."

"Don't bother," she whispered, dropping her chin. "I'd rather just go to bed."

He tipped her chin up. "We'll talk later."

She shrugged.

Kaspar smiled and stroked her cheek before kissing her gently. And then he was gone.

Jesska faced Jóvin and frowned. "I'm sorry if I got you in trouble."

"You didn't, m'lady."

"Thank you for driving me."

He held the elevator door for her. "'Twas my pleasure, m'lady."

"No more Jesska, huh?"

"No, m'lady."

They rode to the top floor without speaking. Jóvin let her into her room and she pushed open her bedroom door to see Megan and Sophia asleep, Megan's body molded around her daughter's.

Jesska closed the door and flopped onto the sofa. She was so angry, she wasn't sure how well she'd sleep, so she thought she'd use her time plotting revenge. Once again, laxative brownies popped into her head as a good option for Kaspar. Her last coherent image was of her placing a large chocolate treat in front of him as she rubbed her hands together in devilish glee.

* * *

Jesska awoke as strong arms wrapped around her and lifted her. She forced her eyes open to find Kaspar carrying her out of her suite and next door to his.

"What are you doing here?" she demanded, sleepily.

"Taking you to bed."

She pushed at his shoulders. "I'm not speaking to you."

"You can give me the silent treatment somewhere I can hold you."

She heard the exhaustion in his voice. "Are you okay?" she whispered.

"Yes, baby. Go back to sleep."

"Did you find the bad guy?"

"Go back to sleep." Kaspar laid her on his bed and kissed her forehead.

"Um…" She pushed his face away. "Hell, no."

"Jess."

"No," she snapped, and sat up. "Where have you been? What's going on?" The light from the bathroom illuminated him and she let out a horrified squeak. "Why are you bleeding?" She scrambled off the bed and lifted his shirt. "What happened?"

"It's not my blood, baby."

"Don't you dare 'baby' me right now, Kaspar. Tell me where you're hurt."

He stilled her hands. "Jesska. It's not my blood."

It took a minute for her to register his words, and then she grasped him around his waist and held him as hard as she could.

"Jess."

"Shut up right now, Kaz. I need to hold you for a minute before I let loose my rage."

He stroked her hair and she could feel his body shaking, which she tried to ignore, because as much as it pissed her off that he was laughing at her right now, it felt better to have him in her arms and to know he was okay.

"Why did you go to Brady's home?" he asked.

"Because I wanted to tell them about you."

"You did?"

She glanced up at him. "Yes. They were really happy and gave me their blessing."

"They did?"

"Yes. They said that I'd waited too long to let myself be happy and he wouldn't have wanted that." Jesska forced back tears as Kaspar pulled her close again. When she felt she could talk without blubbering, she pushed away from him. "Now tell me what happened."

"Let me shower first," he said.

"Are you stalling?"

"No, baby, I will tell you everything, but I want to wash off the blood." He pulled off his shirt and headed to the bathroom.

Jesska followed. "I'll listen while you wash."

"Jesska, do you really want to tempt this?"

"What?"

He frowned. "Ari said how frightened you were with Megan's conversion."

She shuddered at the memory. "What's that got to do with you talking to me while you shower?"

"I can't have you in here right now, sweetheart, unless I know I'm binding you. I'm too keyed up to control my reaction to you."

"I'm not leaving, Kaspar."

"You're certain about that?" he challenged.

"Definitely."

"Suit yourself," he retorted, and started the shower.

Jesska sat on the toilet lid while Kaspar undressed. When he removed his perfectly tailored kingy trousers, she bit her lip. Boxer briefs looked incredible on this man. Her heart sped up at the sight.

"Why don't you wait outside, Jesska?"

She shook her head.

"Baby." He leaned down and cupped her chin. "You do this, it means I shower and then I bind you."

Her breath hitched and she took a minute to think. "Will you tell me what happened while you shower?"

"Does that mean I'm binding you?"

She bit her lip, staring up at the man she hadn't expected, realizing she was no longer angry with him, and nodded.

His sexy smile was intoxicating as he leaned down and covered her mouth with his, kissing her slowly. He broke the kiss and stroked her cheek. "Last chance to change your mind."

"I'm not going to change my mind."

She'd never seen a man move so fast. Suddenly, he was naked in front of her and stepping into the shower. Good lord, he was gorgeous. Jesska took a moment to compose herself, gathering up Kaspar's discarded clothing and dropping it into the laundry bag. "Tell me."

"The blood was some Russian soldier who has ties to the same mob that kidnapped Vandi Whitmore a few months ago."

"Who's Vandi Whitmore?"

"She's Charlotte's sister. Charlotte is Megan's middle daughter who was taken from her. Vandi is the sister Charlotte was raised with."

"So, these people who took Vandi are the threat?" she asked.

"No."

"What do you mean, 'no'?"

"They are part of the threat, but the person, or *persons*, pulling the strings is someone different."

Jesska frowned, sitting back on the toilet lid. "So, what does that mean?"

"It means we have to go to Scotland."

"When?"

"Gunnar, Ari, Megan, and Sophia are going tomorrow. You and I will follow when the plane returns."

"I don't understand," she said. "Why aren't we all going together?"

The water stopped and Kaspar grabbed a towel. "As king, I have to travel separately."

He stepped from the shower, the towel around his waist, wet and sexy, and Jesska swallowed. She watched as he picked up his phone, sent a text, and then focused on her. "What do you want, baby?"

"I want to take a shower," she said.

"And then?"

She took a deep breath, staring up at him.

"Elskan?" he prodded.

"I want you to bind me, but on one condition."

"What's that?"

She frowned up at him. "If you *ever* threaten to put me over your knee again, I will make your life a living hell."

"I don't know about that, sweetheart." He bent down, face-to-face, and smiled. "I think you might enjoy it."

At her shiver, he leaned in and kissed her and then walked out of the room. Jesska stayed seated for several seconds, letting the weight of her decision sink in. She knew that she could change her mind if she wanted to. Kaspar would never force her. But she also knew she wanted this more than anything she'd ever wanted. She rose to her feet, removed her clothes, and took the fastest shower on earth before grabbing the hotel robe on the back of the door and sliding it on. She walked into Kaspar's room and stopped short. Candles were the only source of light, and she noted a bottle of champagne on top of the bureau. Kaspar wasn't in the bedroom, but she could hear him in the other part of the suite, talking low; whether he was on his phone or talking to someone in person, she wasn't sure.

A flat white box sat on the bed, and Jesska saw her name scrawled on an envelope on top of it. She slid the envelope out from behind the red ribbon and opened it.

> *Elskan, I love you more than you could ever know. Here is the first part of my bonding gift to you. Thank you for the gift of your love. Kaspar.*

Jesska set the note on the side table and untied the ribbon. She opened the box to find a black lace baby-doll with matching underwear. She smiled. This was really more a gift for him. She removed her robe and slid on the lingerie, noticing it fit as though it had been made for her.

"Elskan?" Kaspar called through the door as he knocked.

"Come in." She turned, not entirely sure what to do with her hands. She'd never been so exposed before. She took in a deep breath and stared up at him. He wore black satin pajama bottoms, his chest bare, and if there was a more beautiful man, she couldn't bring one to mind. "Hi."

"Hi." His gaze swept over her and he smiled. "You're stunning."

She dropped her head, heat creeping up her neck. "Thank you."

He lifted her chin and she stared up at him, her heart racing as he gently touched her face. She calmed, and leaned into his palm.

"Why do you tremble, elskan?" he asked.

She licked her lips. "Because you frighten me."

"I would never hurt you."

"No, I know. Not that way."

"What way?" he pressed.

"My heart." She took a deep breath and closed her eyes. "I couldn't take another…"

"You won't," he promised.

"How do you know?"

He smiled and ran his thumb across her lower lip. "Because I know."

Jesska rolled her eyes. "Cocky man."

"Confident," he corrected.

"Confident, cocky, kind of the same thing."

"You've forgotten something big, however."

"Have I?" She raised an eyebrow. "What's that?"

"I never break my promises."

Kaspar tilted her chin and covered her mouth with his. She sighed as he cupped the back of her head and held her tighter. Guilt crept in and she tried to pull away, but he wouldn't let her retreat. "Let it come, baby. We'll deal with it together."

"I haven't dealt with it in ten years. What makes you think we can deal with it together?"

"Because it's done, Jesska. There is nothing you can do to change it. But you can love me and let me love you, and remember your friend fondly."

She blinked. "He was far more than my friend."

"Perhaps I can't wrap my mind around that just yet."

"I feel like I'm forgetting him."

"You'll never forget him," Kaspar said. "He made an indelible mark."

"True." Jesska nodded and sighed. "But, honestly, I really wasn't expecting you."

He chuckled. "I wasn't expecting you either, but I'm very glad I found you."

"Me too," she admitted. "I never thought I'd feel again."

"What do you mean? You feel deeply. I can sense it."

"I loved Brady, but I love you very differently."

He swept her hair from her forehead, slipping it behind her ear. "Do you? How?"

"Deeper, I guess." She shook her head. "I'm not making sense."

"You're doing fine, sweetheart."

"When I lost Brady, I thought I'd never feel the same way about anyone the way I felt about him, and I don't. What I feel for you has surpassed him." She bit her lip. "I feel like I'm disrespecting his memory by saying it, but what I felt for him wasn't even close to what I feel for you."

"It's our way, elskan."

"I'm beginning to see that."

He grinned and stroked her cheek again. "Are you ready?"

"Do you know what to do?"

Kaspar raised an eyebrow. "Excuse me?"

She stroked his chest. "You said that your people had never bound a human before. How do you know what's going to happen? How did Ari?"

"Ah." He smiled. "I called Kade Gunnach."

"Why does that name sound familiar? I think Megan talked to him, right?"

"Yes. He's the one who gave the order to release Ari, but it was because his mate, Samantha convinced him to do so. She's a doctor and used to be human. I called him and she was kind enough to get on the phone and fill me in on a few things. She was also able to assist Ari tonight."

"I wondered who he was on the phone with."

He kissed her temple. "Are you ready, baby?"

She nodded.

"I will say the words first and then you will say them, já?"

She nodded again.

"And then together. Understand?"

"Yes."

He leaned close. "One more kiss and we'll begin."

She kissed him and he took her hands. "*Ég gef þér allt sem ég er, allt sem ég vil vera og allt sem ég get verið. Ég er þinn að eilífu. Einin okkar mun aldrei bresta. Ást mín er alger.*" (I give you everything I am, all I want to be and all I can be. I'm yours forever. Our bond will never be broken. My love is absolute.)

"Now me?" she asked.

He nodded. "I'll help you if you get stuck."

"Ég gef þér allt sem ég er, allt sem...um..."

"You're doing great. *Ég vil vera og allt sem ég get verið. Ég er þinn að eilífu. Eining okkar mun aldrei bresta. Ást mín er alger.*"

She nodded. "*Ég vil vera og allt sem ég get verið. Ég er þín að eilífu. Eining okkar mun aldrei bresta. Ást mín er alger.*"

"Well done, baby," he said. "Now together."

"*Ég gef þér allt sem ég er, allt sem ég vil vera og allt sem ég get verið. Ég er þinn að eilífu. Eining okkar mun aldrei bresta. Ást mín er alger,*" they said.

Jesska felt her legs give way beneath her, but Kaspar caught her and settled her on the bed. As he made love to her she couldn't stop a quiet sob as peace and all-encompassing love covered her. She'd never been loved like this.

"Shhh, elskan. Did I hurt you?"

She shook her head, her tears leaking down her temples.

"*Hvers vegna ertu að gráta*, elskan?" (Why are you crying, baby?)

"I'm crying because—wait, how can I understand you?" she asked.

He wiped her tears. "*Við erum bundin, elskan. Þú skilur... og munt brátt vera fær um að tala íslensku... reiprennandi.*" (We are bound, sweetheart. You can understand... and will soon be able to speak Icelandic... fluently.)

"Wow. I mean, I remember you saying that, but I didn't realize it would be so fast."

"Each person is different." He kissed her quickly. "Now, why are you crying?"

"Because I'm so happy."

"You're crying because you're happy?"

She nodded, slipping her fingers through his hair. "I didn't really think I'd ever be happy again."

Kaspar chuckled. "I love you, silly girl."

"Yeah, yeah, keep talking like that, buddy and I'll show you just how unhappy you'll be."

Kaspar laughed as he kissed her neck. "I apologize...little one."

Jesska couldn't stop a giggle, even though she tried to scowl... unsuccessfully. Within seconds, pain shot through her abdomen and she gripped Kaspar's arms as she groaned.

"*Allt í lagi, elskan, ég hef þig.*" (Okay, baby, I've got you.)

He reached over to where he'd put his phone, fired off a quick text to Camilla, and then pulled Jesska's back to his chest, sliding the sheet up to cover their lower bodies. He heard Camilla moving around in the other room and he prayed a quick prayer of thanks for his efficient and caring assistant.

CHAPTER SIXTEEN

KASPAR HELD JESSKA close, despite the fact she tried to push him away. He felt the heat and knew her skin burned, but he had no choice. "If I don't keep contact, baby, it will hurt more."

She hissed as she tried to scoot away again. He moved with her. It took a few minutes for him to calm her, but she finally stopped trying to fight him. "Good, baby. Breathe."

"Thirsty," she rasped.

"I know. Camilla will be here in a minute with water and ice."

As if on cue, his assistant knocked quietly on the door. "*Yðar hátign?*" (Your Majesty?)

"Come," he called.

Camilla pushed open the door. She had the ice sheets he'd asked her to retrieve from the plane. She laid them over the couple, averting her eyes as she did so.

Jesska whimpered as the sheets touched her, but she quieted quickly.

"Jesska's thirsty," Kaspar said, and Camilla nodded, holding up a bottled water.

She walked to Jesska's side of the bed, and Kaspar helped Jesska sit up to drink, keeping the sheet around her for modesty. Camilla placed a bowl on the side table next to Jesska and then walked back to the door. "I'll be right outside, Sire."

"Thank you," he said, and wrapped the ice sheet tighter around Jesska, relieved her body was starting to relax.

"When does this stop?"

"Soon, baby," he promised.

"That's not really an answer, Kaz," she complained.

He sighed. "I know."

Kaspar had no way of knowing exactly how any of this would go or how long it would last. He knew there were books on the subject of humans being converted to Kalt Einn, but he'd had no reason to read them up until now. He and his brothers—their entire clan—had been raised to believe it was impossible for a Kalt Einn to mate with a human, and it was one of the reasons Kade Gunnach's father had been exiled to Scotland. Or so he'd believed. Ari had said he'd discovered a few things Kaspar didn't know, and he would explain once he'd reunited Megan with their daughters. They would regroup in Scotland.

Jesska groaned, dragging Kaspar from his thoughts. "I think I'm going to be sick."

He grabbed the bowl Camilla had left and held it under Jesska's chin. When her stomach calmed, he gave her more water. She rolled over to face him, burrowing into his chest.

"I've got you, baby."

"My skin feels weird," she said, and glanced down, gasping. "The scars…"

Kaspar looked at her legs. Her scars were disappearing in front of them.

"They're going in order."

"What do you mean?" he asked.

She pointed to where one of the scars used to be on her arm. "This is where I made my first cut." Then she pointed to the scar on the inside of her thigh, already fading. "That was the cut that got me admitted to the psych ward." She blinked up at him. "They're all going away. Like whatever you did to heal my soul, is working to heal my body."

"I don't know that I had much to do with it."

"Okay, fine. God did it, but he gave me you to be my saving grace."

He grinned, kissing her nose. "I can live with that."

Jesska wrapped her arms around his waist and stroked his back. "I love you."

"I love you too, baby."

Another wave of pain hit her, but Kaspar wouldn't let her retreat from the shelter of his body. He pulled her closer and waited it out. The pain didn't last as long this time and within an hour, it seemed the worst was over.

"Can I sleep now?" she whispered.

"If you're tired, baby, sleep."

She nodded against his shoulder and closed her eyes. Kaspar held her for as long as it took for her breathing to even out and her body to com pletely relax, before sliding from the bed and pulling on clothing. He snuck out of the room and Camilla rose to her feet from her seat.

"Sire," she said. "How is she?"

"She's sleeping."

"Is she comfortable?"

"Já. Thank you for all your help."

"It's my pleasure, Your Majesty."

Kaspar glanced at the clock on the wall. "The plane will not be back until tomorrow afternoon and will need time to refuel, so we won't be able to leave until tomorrow evening."

"Yes, Sire."

"I think you should take the day tomorrow to explore."

"Excuse me?"

"Take Jóvin, if that is acceptable to you, and see Portland. You don't need to be back until five tomorrow afternoon to supervise packing."

"I...I don't really know what to say," she said.

"Would you rather not?"

"No," she rushed to say. "I'd love to. Thank you, Your Majesty."

"I will make sure Jóvin has everything you need. For now, please take the rest of the night off. I can take care of Jesska."

Camilla's eyes widened and then she nodded and lowered her head. He didn't miss her smile as she left the room, giving Kaspar much desired privacy.

Kaz?

He heard her voice in his head and turned to find Jesska standing in the bedroom doorway, the sheet draped around her and her hair a mess. He'd never seen a more beautiful sight. *Did I wake you?*

She gasped. "How did I hear you?"

We can speak telepathically now, baby.

That is so cool.

He smiled. "Was I too loud?"

She shook her head, tears sliding down her face.

He closed the distance between them. "What, baby? What's wrong?"

Jesska wrapped her arms around him. "You can just be so incredibly sweet sometimes."

"What did you hear?"

"All of it."

"Damn, my reputation is ruined," he complained.

Jesska giggled. "Well, if you gave Austri and Jens the day off too, then I'd be more concerned."

"I can't, baby."

She kissed his chest. "Why not? I plan to keep you busy all day tomorrow anyway, and that does not include Austri *or* Jens, so why do they even need to be here?"

"It's not done."

"Ooooh, it's not done," she retorted, and smiled up at him. "Aren't you like supreme ruler of all the land?"

He raised an eyebrow.

"Okay, maybe you just act like you're supreme ruler of all the land."

Kaspar chuckled. "What's your point, elskan?"

"My point is, that if you want them to take a day off, then you have all the power to *make* them take one, right?"

He sighed. "I suppose that's true."

She let the towel drop to the floor. "Then make it so."

Kaspar drew in a quick breath, the sight of his bonded mate irresistible. "I will make it so," he promised, picking her up and carrying her to the bed.

He spent the next hour making several more promises that he wasn't sure he'd remember in the morning, but he didn't care. He'd give her anything she wanted and do it with a smile on his face.

* * *

Charlotte MacMillan checked her appearance in the hallway mirror... again. Her biological mother was set to arrive in less than an hour, and she was beyond nervous. She ran her fingers through her long blonde hair and pinched her cheeks in an effort to give them a little more color.

Her husband grinned as he rounded the corner and slipped his arms around her from behind, laying his hands over her expanding middle. She still couldn't believe the direction her life was taking. Niall MacMillan was gorgeous and loved her more than she would ever deserve. Dark hair, blue eyes, tall, and the most incredible man she'd ever met.

"You look beautiful," he said.

She smoothed her hair. "Are you sure?"

"Beautiful girl, it's not going to matter to Megan what you look like. She's missed twenty-five years, she's going to be too excited to see you to care about your appearance."

"Are you telling me my appearance isn't good?"

"Yes, love. That's exactly what I'm telling you," Niall droned.

She turned to face him, laying her hands on his chest. "I'm actually more nervous about the dynamic of all of us. Pepper will be here in a few minutes, and we're just getting to know each other." She sighed, shaking her head. "I'm not good at this stuff."

Niall smiled, stroking her cheek. "Charlotte, you're perfect."

"What if I say something they don't like?" Charlotte frowned. "What if they hate me and I never know why? What if I offend them?"

"What could you possibly say that would offend anyone?"

She rolled her eyes. "You'd be surprised."

"One, if people misinterpret something you say and don't have the decency to talk to you about it, then they're not worth the trouble. And two, if they hate you for any reason, they'll deal with me."

Her heart raced. "I can fight my own battles, Nye."

"I know you can, but that doesn't mean they won't deal with me." He kissed her nose. "There will probably be several instances where they'll deal with both of us."

Charlotte laughed. "Anyone who has to deal with both of us, baby, might end up cowering in the corner. Perhaps we should make a deal not to tag team."

He shrugged. "No promises."

She slid her hand behind his neck and pulled his head down to kiss him. Niall ran his hands over her hips, cupping her bottom. "I just need five minutes."

Charlotte smiled against his lips. "When have you *ever* just needed five minutes?"

He slipped his hand under her shirt. "Ten then."

The doorbell rang and Niall swore as he removed his hand and smoothed her shirt. Charlotte stroked his face and smiled. "We'll resume this tonight."

"You're damn right we will," he vowed. "I'll get the door."

He jogged down the stairs and Charlotte heard him greet Connall and Pepper just as Charlotte's best friend and sister-in-law, Grace walked into the kitchen from the back patio. She and her husband, Max, were staying for a few days for moral support. Their regular home was in Inverness.

"Where's Max?" Charlotte asked.

"He's upstairs. He'll be down in a minute." Grace smiled. "How ya doin'?"

Niall, Connall, and Pepper walked into the room, cutting off whatever Charlotte might have said to Grace. Grace gave Charlotte a bolstering smile just as Pepper, who was holding Cody, grinned, and handed her baby off to Connall. She wrapped her arms around Charlotte. "Hi, little sister."

"Hi," Charlotte said with a giggle.

"How are you?" Pepper pulled away and cocked her head. "Nervous? I'm *so* nervous."

"I am too," Charlotte admitted while Pepper hugged Grace.

Connall hugged the women just as Max arrived, and Niall and Charlotte poured wine as everyone got comfortable.

Niall sat next to Charlotte on the sofa and wrapped an arm around her waist, pulling her close, bolstering her nerves.

"I'm dying to know what our sister is like," Pepper said.

"Me too." Charlotte widened her eyes. "I can't believe we lived so close to each other. I mean, Cameron was one of our worship leaders, and he's her uncle."

"Right?" Grace said.

"Did you ever meet her?" Max asked.

"I don't think so," Charlotte said. "I don't remember ever meeting any of Cameron's family. Did you, Grace?"

Grace shook her head. "I don't think so."

"How do you feel about Ari being here, Con?" Niall asked. Everyone in the room knew that Connall didn't exactly appreciate Ari's recent and very sudden appearance in Pepper's life.

Connall scowled and Pepper squeezed his knee. He glanced at her and she raised an eyebrow, giving him a gentle smile.

"Connall is fine with him being here," Pepper said. "Kade would have never let Ari out if he didn't feel it was safe."

"Kade would have never let him go had it not been for Samantha," Connall countered.

"Babe," Pepper said in warning. "Samantha's one of the smartest people I know. Tell me I'm wrong."

Connall pinched the bridge of his nose.

Charlotte gave Connall a sympathetic smile. "No messin' with the best friend and sister, Con. They kind of trump everything."

Grace snorted in an effort not to laugh, failing enough that within seconds the girls had dissolved into giggles. Charlotte was the first to recover. "Okay, I must be nervous. Giggling's not really my thing."

The doorbell rang and she grasped Niall's hand. He smiled, leaning over to kiss her cheek. "Do you and Pepper want to get it?"

Charlotte glanced at Pepper, who nodded as she rose to her feet. Charlotte stood as well and then led Pepper to the front door. "Ready?"

Pepper took her hand and nodded. "Ready."

Charlotte pulled open the door, her heart racing.

A gorgeous woman who didn't look old enough to be her mother pulled her in for a warm hug and then did the same for Pepper. She was blonde and looked quite a bit more like Pepper, although the resemblance to Charlotte was certainly there. Charlotte was a definite combination of her mother and father.

"I'm Megan," she said, and pulled a young girl forward. "This is Sophia."

"Ása," Ari corrected.

"Sophia, Papa," Sophia corrected.

Ari smiled, gripping her chin in fun. "All right, Sophia."

Sophia looked like the female version of Ari, which was saying something, because Ari was a very pretty man. Sophia was stunning. Long blonde hair, big blue eyes.

Charlotte stared up at her father. He'd come to her in her dreams for several years before she'd met him, and it was still strange for her to see him in person.

He reached out and stroked her face. "Don't be afraid of me."

"I'm not," she said, quickly.

He gave her a smile and then turned to Pepper, pulling her in for a hug. Charlotte could feel her sister's emotions as they swamped her. Connall appeared, seemingly out of nowhere, and pulled her away from Ari, wrapping her in his protective embrace.

"Come in," Niall said, and Charlotte grimaced up at him, realizing she was being rude.

Niall's eyes reassured her as she heard his thoughts. *You're not, baby. You're just overwhelmed.*

"Yes, come in," Charlotte said. "I wasn't sure if you'd be hungry, but we have food and drinks upstairs, if you'll follow me."

The small group made their way up to the family room. Charlotte was grateful that Megan took the initiative to introduce herself and Sophia to the rest of the family.

Nausea reared its ugly head and Charlotte gripped Niall's arm. Her newly pregnant body reacting all too normally and, she might add, inconveniently, to the baby girl growing inside of her. Niall laid his hand on her belly, calming her sickness and her nerves at the same time.

"Thank you," she whispered, and kissed him quickly, before joining the rest of the group.

Ari sat with Megan tucked into his side on the sofa. Sophia was on the other side of her mother, and Charlotte could see the closeness of the two. She felt sadness flood in at everything she and Pepper had missed through no fault of their own.

"Megan and Ari," Pepper said. "May I introduce you to your grandson? This is Cody."

Cody pitched himself toward Megan, who caught him with ease. Pepper laughed. "Well, I guess he likes you."

Megan blinked back tears as she settled the baby on her lap, facing her. "Well, hi there, little man. I can't believe I'm a grandma. I'm too young to be a grandma." Cody gurgled up at her. "Yes, I see you agree."

The group laughed as Niall pulled Charlotte down onto the sofa across from them. Max and Grace sat in one of the overstuffed chairs, Connall and Pepper in the other.

Ari leaned forward and smiled at Pepper. "First, I want to apologize for what I did at your home, elskan. I have no excuses other than a misguided effort to gain your help through force rather than asking."

Megan squeezed his knee. *"And."*

Ari shook his head. *"And...*I will never do anything to threaten you again. I am here to serve you until I die."

Megan rolled her eyes. "Okay, honey. A little melodramatic, but a good first start."

Cody smacked Ari's cheek, and Megan raised an eyebrow. "That's right, baby, you tell grandpa what you think of that."

Charlotte bit the inside of her cheek to keep from laughing. Megan had obviously read Ari the riot act, and his devotion to her was evident. Sophia still looked a bit like a deer in the headlights, but Charlotte chalked it up to the fact she was probably still processing.

"You look like Mom," Sophia said to Pepper.

Pepper smiled. "I know. It's a little weird, huh?"

Sophia turned to Charlotte. "I think you and I look the most alike. Even more than your pictures."

"You've seen pictures?" Charlotte asked.

"Sorry." Sophia glanced at Megan. "Wasn't I supposed to? Cam showed me a couple on Facebook."

"No, honey, I'm sorry," Charlotte rushed to say. "It's totally fine. I'm just surprised. I still can't believe Cameron's your uncle."

The sound of Megan's sudden sob drew their focus to her and she jumped to her feet, handing the baby to Ari, and rushed out of the room. Ari gave Cody to Connall, and followed her.

"She's been doing this a lot lately," Sophia said, her voice soft with sadness.

Pepper slid her arm around Sophia's shoulders. "Should we go see if we can help? Perhaps the men can stay here and we'll just go find Mom. Okay?"

Sophia nodded and Charlotte led her and Pepper out of the room. Ari stood in the hallway, his arms wrapped around a sobbing Megan, stroking her hair.

Sophia laid her hand on her mother's back and Charlotte felt a vibration of sorts. She glanced at Pepper, who cocked her head. She'd obviously felt it too.

Before they could ask about it, Megan stepped away from Ari, wiped her tears, and forced a smile. "I'm so sorry. That was rude."

"There's nothing to apologize for," Charlotte said. "This is all really overwhelming, so please feel free to cry or whatever if you need to."

Megan nodded. "I just really, really want to hold you both."

Without hesitation, Charlotte and Pepper gathered their mother in their arms, the three of them taking a moment to reconnect on a physical level, even as their emotions calmed in proximity to each other. Megan cupped Charlotte's cheeks and then Pepper's as she studied her daughters. "I missed out on so much. Can you ever forgive me?"

Ari sighed in frustration. "Stop apologizing for something that was not your fault."

Megan frowned. "I should have protected my babies, Ari. It *is* my fault."

He dragged his hands down his face, but didn't respond. At least not audibly.

"Well, I don't think any of this was your fault," Charlotte said.

"Me neither," Pepper agreed.

"You're both very gracious."

"Mom. I really would like to know the full story now," Sophia said.

Megan smiled. "You've been waiting a long time, honey, huh?"

"Ya think?"

"We wanted to tell the three of you together," Megan explained. "So, Sophia's feeling a little left out of the loop."

"Are you up to it?" Ari asked.

Megan took his hand. "Yes. I'm fine. I just needed a cry."

He lifted her fingers to his lips and kissed them.

"You know, we can talk privately, Megan," Charlotte offered. "It doesn't have to be done with everyone else. They will understand."

"Connall might not," Pepper countered. "But I can deal with him."

Megan smiled again. "This is family. I have no problem sharing what we know with them."

"Give us a moment, hmm?" Ari requested.

Charlotte held her hand out to Sophia who took it, and Pepper followed them back to the family room. The men stood as the ladies entered the room and Charlotte stepped into Niall's arms.

You okay?

She nodded, giving him a squeeze.

Ari and Megan returned a few minutes later, and Grace handed them both a glass of wine. She handed Charlotte a bottled water and then sat with Max again.

"Thanks, bestie," Charlotte said.

Grace just smiled.

"So, what we know…" Megan began. "We know that you were both taken from me right after I gave birth. We don't know exactly how or who, but we know that Ari was drugged with Red Fang each time, which is how they got past him. I was not well with either birth, so I was pretty much out of it."

"Can we backtrack a bit?" Charlotte asked. "How did you two get together in the first place? I can feel you're mates, but why weren't you bound back then?"

Megan and Ari tag-teamed the explanation of how they met and how they got together, filling in a few of the blanks surrounding Megan's choice to leave him and bring Sophia to America.

"Why didn't you look for her?" Pepper asked.

"I did," Ari said. "I never stopped."

"In his defense, I did everything I could to make sure he couldn't find me," Megan said. "I went back to my mother's maiden name, which isn't in any of my records. I changed Ása's name to Sophia, and Cameron helped me with the rest." She grimaced at Ari. "I felt you sometimes, and that was the toughest part…not reaching out to you."

"Why did you leave?" Charlotte asked.

"I believed he was the threat."

Connall shifted, and Pepper grabbed his arm. "Nope. Don't, Con. Let her explain."

Megan sighed. "Because I hadn't reached mating year, and because I was still human, Ari was able to manipulate my memories. Because of this, I didn't know what was true. Had he just let me keep my memories I would have known he'd been a victim in all of this as well, but he had a misguided need to protect me, so I was easily confused."

Charlotte wondered how that was possible, because Grace hadn't been manipulated by Max when they first met. He'd tried to use his gift on her, and failed miserably.

What Max has is the gift of suggestion, love. Megan would have been able to resist that as well. However, Ari has the gift of manipulation and that's something much more powerful. She may be able to resist it now that she is bound, but she would never have been able to as a human.

Charlotte nodded an "Ah" at Niall, and he gave her a gentle squeeze.

"How did you manage to find her?" Pepper asked.

"Kaspar actually did that," Ari admitted. "A woman came to him when I was…well, when I was in Inverness…and she told him what she knew of Megan. She gave him a flash drive with information on it. We are still weeding through it to sort out everything."

"What kind of information?" Charlotte asked.

"Much of it's encrypted, so it's taking some time. Whoever the threat is, they aren't revealing themselves easily."

"Do you know what they want?" Pepper asked.

"You," Connall guessed.

"What?"

"He's right," Ari confirmed. "You girls are what we call the Trifecta. Charlotte, you have the gift of ice; Pepper, you have fire; and Ása… sorry, Sophia, has earth. Individually, you have the ability to change your surroundings, but together, you have a power that's never been seen before."

"What kinds of things can you do, Sophia?" Charlotte asked.

"I can heal pretty much anyone," Sophia said. "I can also heal plants and animals. I didn't know that was what I was doing, but Papa told me. When Mom and I got into our accident, I had major internal bleeding, but it didn't last very long. Mom broke her leg, but I was able to touch her and heal her."

"How do you know about the plants?" Charlotte asked.

"Oh, that was so cool," Sophia said, her face brightening. "Grandpa had put one of Nana's plants out with the yard waste, and I was helping to sort everything. As soon as I touched one of the plants, it turned green and the leaves kind of raised up. Right in front of me. It was so weird. I thought maybe it just hadn't died and so did he, so we put it back in the house, and it still looks great." She glanced at Ari and then back at Charlotte. "Papa said it's part of my gift."

"That really is cool," Charlotte said.

"If this gets out," Ari said, growing serious, "you could all be in danger."

"It sounds like it's already gotten out."

"You have nothing to worry about," Niall said. "You will be protected."

Charlotte rolled her eyes. "I know that you and Connall will protect us, and obviously, Ari will protect Sophia, but if we don't know who these people are, we don't know who we're being protected against. What if their powers or gifts or whatever are way stronger than ours?"

Ari shook his head. "There's no way."

"I don't understand."

"There may be the occasional Cauld Ane or Kalt Einn who might have stronger powers than you do individually. For instance, Pepper, you could not defend yourself fully against me because I am your Papa, and your gift is partly from me. But no one would be able to defend themselves from two of you, and if the three of you work together...well, I pity the person who would be stupid enough to try."

Charlotte glanced at Pepper, and the girls laughed.

"Did you hear that, Con?" Pepper said. "You're gonna need to behave when my sisters and I are together."

Connall shook his head. "No monster creating, Ari."

"Sorry," Ari said with a smile.

"When will you know what we're up against?" Pepper asked.

"Kaspar and Jesska arrive tomorrow, and we'll regroup then. Don't worry, elskan. We'll take care of everything."

"Have you sorted out where you'll stay?" Charlotte asked.

Niall and Connall still weren't comfortable with Ari staying in their homes. Megan had assured Pepper and Charlotte she understood their reluctance, and she and Ari made other arrangements.

Megan nodded. "We have suites at the Caledonian."

Charlotte noticed Sophia frown at that. "Do you think Sophia could stay with us?"

Sophia perked up. "Please, Mom?"

Pepper and Charlotte grinned. "Please, Mom," they added in stereo.

Megan laughed, her eyes filling with joyous tears. "Okay, okay. If you would like her to stay, she can stay."

"We would like her to stay," Charlotte said.

Megan shook her head. "You have no idea how I've longed for my girls to call me Mom."

"Girls' day tomorrow," Pepper announced. "The men will all be trying to figure out what's going on anyway, so maybe we can tour the Mile and have lunch. Just the five of us."

"Our family will be here tomorrow as well, love," Connall pointed out.

"That's right." Pepper smiled. "So we'll take everyone."

"I love that idea," Charlotte said.

"I do too," Megan agreed.

"It's not too much?" Charlotte asked.

"No, honey," Megan assured. "I love the idea of getting to know the people you love the most." She glanced at Ari and then back at Charlotte

"I wanted to talk to you about something, actually, and we'll do whatever you want to do, but I'd like to spend some time in Scotland...an extended amount of time. With both of you. Pepper, we can come to Inverness...or just I can. I absolutely understand if it's too much too soon." She sighed. "Whatever you'd like to do."

Charlotte could see that Megan wanted to be sensitive in the wake of Ari's bad judgment, but she could also see the longing on her face. The longing of a mother for her children. "I would love that," Charlotte said.

"I would too," Pepper said. "And knowing how hard it is to be separated from your mate, I would never ask you to come alone." Charlotte saw her squeeze Connall's knee and figured he was probably objecting to something, albeit telepathically. "I think we can work something out where both of you can stay. Right, baby?"

Connall stared at Pepper for a few seconds and Charlotte wasn't sure what he'd do, but in the end, he nodded his agreement. Pepper grinned in victory. "I love you."

Connall rolled his eyes, but leaned over to kiss her with a smile.

"I say let's plan our day tomorrow," Megan suggested. "Over dinner perhaps?"

"Great idea," Charlotte agreed. "I'm starved. Max and Niall just happened to cook tonight."

"Shut up!" Pepper said. "I can't wait for this!"

Charlotte giggled and led everyone to the dining room before helping her family serve up a feast that should have been touted as award winning. She had to admit, she was disappointed that chicken alfredo wasn't on the menu, but petite game hens served on a bed of roasted vegetables, with garlic mashed potatoes were certainly much fancier. Luckily, the meal wasn't indicative of the relaxed conversation and casual atmosphere as the new family got to know each other. Charlotte found herself laughing often throughout the evening, and she smiled at Niall as she took in her new life. She was loving every minute of it.

CHAPTER SEVENTEEN

A FEW DAYS later, Jesska followed Kaspar onto the plane, awed by the size of it and the fact that it didn't look like any airplane she'd ever been on. "This is huge."

"That's what she said," he retorted.

Jesska giggled. "Well, that too, but admittedly, the plane's just a tad big larger."

Kaspar laughed. "It's the family plane. We have two others that are smaller, but with such a long trip, I thought you might be more comfortable on this one."

"As long as it's safe, I don't really care. I just like the idea of joining the mile-high club with you." She grinned. "We *will* get to do that, right?"

"Absolutely." He kissed her. "That's a promise."

Austri, Jens, and Camilla were already moving around the interior, making sure Kaspar and Jesska's every need was seen to. "*Yðar Hátign við erum í undirbúningi fyrir flugtak.*" (Majesty, we are preparing for takeoff.)

"I'll show you the bedroom when it's safe to move around," Kaspar promised, and led her to large captain's chairs near the windows. She chose the window seat and secured her seatbelt. He sat beside her linking his fingers with hers.

Jesska dropped her head on Kaspar's shoulder as the plane took off and closed her eyes, relishing the peace that enveloped her. The day before had been somewhat stressful, having to give a sworn statement to the police about Jason's threats, but she was glad she didn't have to see him or testify to anything, at least for the moment. Her statement was enough to get him thrown back in jail while he awaited a new trial. H appeared to be sticking to his story, but his lawyers were pushing for him to recant, so a new trial was still a possibility.

Her parents had surprised her by showing up at the police station and, after her task was done, Kaspar took everyone out to lunch. Her parents liked him, and Jesska could see the bridge she'd charred years ago was slowly being rebuilt.

Kaspar ran a knuckle down her cheek and kissed her forehead, smiling at her with his 'what-are-you-thinking' smile.

"I love you," she said.

"You do?"

She nodded. "Yep. A lot a bit."

Kaspar chuckled. "Back atya, baby."

"How long until we can…you know?"

Have I created a monster?

She nodded. *A really horny one.* "I'm not sure I'm going to get used to speaking this way."

Yes you will.

He tipped her chin up and kissed her. Jesska couldn't get close enough, especially strapped in. Curling her hand around his throat, she broke the kiss. "Not fair, Kaz."

Patience, sweetheart.

She narrowed her eyes at him. *Screw patience.*

The ding of the seatbelt sign going off had Kaspar out of his seat, unbuckling Jesska, and tugging her to the bedroom at the back within seconds. He kicked the door closed and divested her of her clothes with lightning speed.

She giggled when her bra flew across the room and ended up hanging on a knob on the dresser.

"That was planned," he quipped.

"You're amazing," she retorted and tugged on his shirt. "Off. Now."

Kaspar released her only long enough to remove his clothing and settle her on the bed.

Jesska's introduction to the mile-high club lasted most of the night and the next morning, she stretched with a groan. "I need a shower," she grumbled.

Kaspar chuckled, rolling over to pull her close. "You did get a workout last night, but we don't sweat, baby."

"Yeah, but that doesn't mean I don't need a shower," she said. "Bad dreams kind of do that to me."

He eyes grew concerned. "You had a bad dream?"

"Not a nightmare or anything." She smiled. "It's that moment when you're having a romantical dream and you smell something weird and you're pretty sure you've rolled into your own armpit."

"Romantical?"

"Definitely romantical," Jesska said.

Kaspar laughed, a deep, rumbling, belly laugh. "Are you hungry?"

She nodded and ran a finger down his chest. "Definitely."

"For *food*."

"Oh. No. Not really."

Kaspar kissed her and fed a different hunger before they took a break for sustenance.

* * *

Arriving in Edinburgh, Jesska tried to take in everything as they drove to Niall and Charlotte's house. "Have you been here before?" she asked.

Kaspar nodded. "A few times, yes."

"Will we have time to explore?"

"Absolutely," he promised.

"How long do we have?"

"A week, baby," he said. "Then I'll take you home."

"You can be away for a week?"

"Camilla has everything under control." He pulled her fingers to his lips and kissed them softly. "So, yes, I can be away for a week."

Jesska grinned, leaning into him. "I love you."

"Love you too, baby."

How long until I can get you naked again?

Kaspar chuckled. *A few hours.*

Too long.

I'll figure something out, then.

"Promise?"

He leaned down and kissed her. "Promise."

Austri pulled the car up to a medieval-looking Georgian townhouse.

"Wow," Jesska breathed as she stepped out. "It's stunning."

Kaspar nodded and took her hand, leading her to the front door. He kept his arm around her waist as he rang the doorbell, and then the door was open and Jesska was pulled into a bear hug by Sophia. "You're finally here!"

"Hi, honey," Jesska said, hugging her niece tighter. "How are you?"

"Good," Sophia said. "Come and meet everyone. Oh my gah, Jess, my sisters are so cool."

Jesska stepped inside and didn't have much time to appreciate her surroundings before she was dragged upstairs and into a large great room where Megan sat with a group of people Jesska didn't know. Megan stood and rushed to her for a hug and then introduced her and Kaspar to the family.

* * *

The next morning, Jesska smoothed her hands down the thighs of her jeans as she stared at herself in the mirror. She looked so different. Younger…better. Her skin was incredibly clear, not a blemish in sight. She still had a few freckles, but they looked less like sun damage now. And her hair was beginning to lighten. The dye she'd put in her hair two months ago was fading, and her hair was rapidly returning to its natural blonde.

"I don't think I'm going to miss the black," Kaspar said as he wrapped his arms around her from behind.

Jesska giggled. "I haven't seen my natural hair color in almost ten years, so this is going to be an adjustment for me."

"Why black?"

"Technically, it's called darkest brown."

Kaspar chuckled. "I stand corrected."

"It started as a rebellion, I guess. My soul felt black, so I wanted everything to match my mood, but then everyone began to know me like this…which meant I could forget my old life a little." She turned to face him and looped her hands around his neck. "But now, with this new part of our journey, I like the idea of going back to the real me."

"I love all parts of you," Kaspar said. "So, blonde, black, purple… no, perhaps not purple."

Jesska laughed. "I promise I will refrain from purple."

He leaned down and kissed her. "Thank you."

"Are you really not joining us this morning?"

"I have a few things to catch up on, but I will meet up with you at lunch. Along with the rest of the men."

Jesska sighed. "You are leaving all of your wives to shop alone. You do realize how unwise that is, right?"

"Which reminds me," he said, and pulled out his wallet, handing her a credit card. "Shop to your heart's content."

"Oh, really?" she asked. "What's the limit?"

"Limitless."

"All cards have limits, Kaz."

"That's not actually true, baby."

"Seriously?" she challenged. "So, I could, I don't know, buy a house for two-point-five-million dollars, outfit it with a million bucks worth of furniture, and then buy myself a hundred-thousand-dollar BMW, and do it all on this card?"

"Yes."

"Shut up!"

He chuckled. "It's limitless."

She shook her head and handed it back to him. "Um, no way am I carrying this around with me. What if I lose it?"

"Then I'll get you a new one."

"It's worth a lot of money."

"It's a piece of plastic," he countered.

"A piece of plastic that's worth a lot of money."

Kaspar laughed. "Baby, it's protected. It's yours to do with as you like."

"I really don't have a limit?"

"You really don't have a limit."

"Oh, okay." Jesska bit her lip. "But I won't really buy a house and a car."

"I know you won't, baby. They're difficult to fit on a plane."

"There is that," she conceded, and held her hand out. "Hand it over."

He shook his head. "Take it from me."

"I'm trying."

"No, I mean, try to take it."

Jesska frowned. "I don't get it…oh, wait. Without picking it up, you mean?"

"Yes."

She giggled. "How?"

"Imagine where you want the card to go and then use your hand to guide it."

"That easy?"

"That easy," he confirmed.

Jesska stared at the card in Kaspar's hand and waved her hand. It went skittering to the floor. Kaspar laughed and raised it back to his hand. Jesska tried again and again, only managing to get it out of his hand. Kaspar's phone buzzed and he pulled it from his pocket. "We'll work on it more," he promised, handing her the card and answering the call. "Austri. Já. We'll be right down."

Jesska grabbed her purse. "Is Austri coming with me?"

"Yes."

"But I thought Kade has his security, as do the Gunnachs…and Ar and—"

"You made your point," Kaspar said, cutting off her diatribe. "But don't know anyone other than Ari's men, so you will have Austri for the day."

"But what will you do without him? Jóvin would be fine." Kaspar frowned, and Jesska raised an eyebrow. "You can't seriously still be mad at him."

"I'm not discussing this with you, Jesska."

She crossed her arms. "You're punishing him for making sure I was safe. Does that sound right to you?"

"He was supposed to stop you from leaving."

"And he *tried*!" she snapped. "Outside of chaining me to the towel rail in the bathroom, he didn't really have a choice."

"Well, then he should have chained you."

"If he'd really done anything remotely close to that, you would have had his head...or stuck him in some dungeon somewhere!"

"I don't have a dungeon."

"You're being an ass." She threw her hands in the air.

"I'm an ass because I want you protected?"

"No, you're an ass because you refuse to see that even *you* wouldn't have been able to stop me from leaving that frickin' hotel room, and Jóvin made a judgment call—the same one you would have made, I might add—and he protected me from beginning to end. Case in point, I'm standing in front of you right now, and without a scratch on me."

Kaspar dragged his hands down his face.

"Let's go. We obviously need a little time away from each other."

Jesska stalked out of the hotel and to the elevator without waiting for Kaspar.

* * *

Kaspar reached for his phone, jostling Jesska, who was wrapped around him like ivy. He'd adjusted the security detail and sent Jóvin with her during their shopping excursion, which had earned him "brownie points," but had not gotten him entirely off the hook. Kaspar had to admit that she'd made a valid point and, once he wrapped his mind around said point, he was quick to tell her that she had been right, but he wouldn't go so far as to apologize to Jóvin. Jesska had responded by running his credit card up by almost ten-thousand dollars, somewhat disappointed that he hadn't reacted to the paltry amount.

In the end, they'd each said their piece, and spent the rest of the evening making up the way they enjoyed best, which meant she was now naked and burrowed into him.

Kaspar shifted again and Jesska groaned, but didn't fully awaken. "Kaz here."

"It's Kade. We have a problem."

Kaspar frowned. "What kind of problem?"

"We know who the threat is."

He sat up. "Who?"

"Not over the phone," Kade said. "We're on our way to Edinburgh. We'll be there in a few hours."

"Where do you want to meet?"

"We'll meet you at Connall's place. Niall has the address. Dinner."

"Okay," Kaspar said, and hung up.

"Who was that?" Jesska asked sleepily.

"No one, baby. Go back to sleep."

She curled her hand around his belly and sighed, her even breathing sounding within minutes. Kaspar's thoughts ran rampant with what Kade could possibly tell him. With their less than cordial relationship, Kaspar had a feeling it must be pretty extreme if Kade thought it was important to have a face-to-face meeting.

"What's extreme, baby?" Jesska asked, stroking his neck.

He sighed, rolling her gently to her back and kissing her neck. "Nothing."

She moved her head away from him and frowned. "Huh-uh. We don't play that game, Kaz. Something's wrong."

Kaspar shifted onto his back again and dragged his hands down his face. "Kade is on his way from Inverness. They know who the threat is."

Jesska gasped, sitting up on her knees. "Who?"

"He wouldn't tell me over the phone." He settled a hand on her hip. "We have to meet up with Niall at some point today, and he will direct us to Connall's home."

"Why Connall's home?"

"Probably because he's Kade's brother."

"Are you worried?"

He stared up at his mate, totally uninhibited in her nakedness, her hair falling around her shoulders, her face tight with concern. "I'm not sure what I am."

"Do you think we're in danger?"

"I wouldn't worry about that, baby. You will never be in danger."

"But will you?"

"I don't know," he said, honestly.

Jesska ran her hand across his abdomen. "But we're safe right now."

"Absolutely."

She smiled and straddled him, leaning down to kiss him. "Then a distraction is in order. We can worry when we need to worry."

Kaspar allowed her to distract him, resigning himself to worrying later.

CHAPTER EIGHTEEN

THREE HOURS LATER, Kaspar ushered Jesska into Austri's car and stamped down his concern as they drove to Connall's home.

Jesska squeezed his knee. "It's going to be okay."

"You shouldn't be here."

"Why not?" She faced him. "Babe, it's going to be fine. Austri and Jóvin are with us, as are all the men I'm sure the Gunnachs have around them. No one can touch me."

He forced a smile and kissed her palm.

When they arrived at the grand historical flat, Connall opened the door and welcomed the small group inside. Kaspar kept hold of Jesska's hand as they walked into the living room where Kade and Samantha waited with Pepper. Pepper held Cody, but he reached for Samantha so she took him onto her lap.

Ari, Megan, and Sophia sat on one of the sofas, while Niall, Charlotte, Max, and Grace were in chairs grouped close together. Gunnar stood by the window, staring out to the street. Kade and Kaspar hadn't officially met, so they took the time to greet one another and then Kade introduced Kaspar and Jesska to Brodie, Kade and Connall's brother, and Brodie's wife, Payton.

Pepper stood and gave them a small smile. "Can I get you something to drink? Food?"

"We're fine for now," Kaspar said.

Pepper returned to her seat and curled into Connall.

"So what do we know?" Kaspar asked.

"We recently exiled our mother to Pohnpei for reasons we don't need to get into presently," Kade began. "However, we are finding that she set up some dominoes, and they're still falling, so to speak."

"Meaning?" Kaspar urged.

"We believe that she may have had something to do with the threats against your family and the kidnapping of Charlotte and Pepper."

Jesska squeezed Kaspar's hand.

"How so?"

"That we're unclear about," Kade admitted. "Alice, that's our mother, told me recently that the reason our clan sailed to Scotland was because of her indiscretion."

"Which is not true," Kaspar said.

"I figured as much," Kade said.

"What's the real reason?" Samantha asked.

"The final straw," Kaspar said, looking at Brodie, "was that your father bound a human."

"The final straw?" Brodie asked.

Kaspar nodded. "He bound a human woman, which was seen as an immoral act because our lore says it's impossible." He smiled at Jesska. "We know now that it's not. But it was when he attempted a coup, that my father took such severe action. Erik was stopped before he managed to get enough people together. Those people who had been part of the planning were sent with him to Scotland."

"What do you mean, immoral act?" Pepper asked.

"It was a different time, and my father was defending himself against people who were hell-bent on destroying his allies at the time. When your father-in-law rose up against our clan, my father was done."

"As king, shouldn't Kade's father have had immunity or something?" Samantha asked.

"He wasn't king," Kaspar answered.

Samantha gasped and looked at Kade. "What does that mean?"

"Honestly, it doesn't mean much now," Kaspar said. "The Gunnachs are royalty in Scotland, regardless of what happened in Iceland centuries ago. What it meant at the time, however, was that my father, who was king, exiled him. When he arrived in Scotland, he changed his name from Gunnar to Erik Gunnach, made himself king, and started his own empire, made up of the people who were exiled with him."

"Tangled web," Samantha said.

"Aye, love," Kade agreed.

Kaspar nodded to Kade. "What I'm unclear about is how you mother fits in this. She would have had no motive to steal Ari's children. Also, there's no evidence she was in Iceland at the time."

"She has reach," Kade said. "But you're right, there's no glaring motive."

The doorbell pealed, and Connall frowned. "Are we expecting anyone else?"

Jesska gasped. "Something's wrong."

"Babe?" Kaspar said, turning to her.

"Don't answer the door," she said. "Something's not right."

Kaspar pulled his phone from his pocket and texted Austri and Jóvin. There was no response. "My men aren't answering."

"Shite," Kade snapped, and rose to his feet.

"Upstairs," Connall demanded Pepper.

She took Cody from Samantha with a nod. "Ladies, if you'll come with me."

"Maybe we should stay," Charlotte said. "The three of us together are impossible to beat." She looked at Ari. "Right?"

Ari nodded. "Já, elskan, but—"

"Hell no," Niall snapped. "You're going upstairs where it's safe."

"But the three of us together are stronger than all of you, Nye," Charlotte said.

"No," Connall stressed. "I'm with Niall on this."

"As am I," Ari said.

"But you said we were strong, Papa," Sophia challenged.

Ari gave Megan a look of controlled irritation and she grabbed Sophia's hand and rose to her feet. "Come on, baby. If Papa says he wants us where we're safe, then we go where we're safe."

"But that's so...so lame," Sophia complained.

Without warning, Jesska couldn't catch her breath, her panic was so intense. She grabbed for Kaspar.

"Baby, what?"

She shook her head. She was suffocating.

"Skít," he snapped, forcing her down onto the sofa and rolling her onto her side.

Jesska, talk to me.

I can't breathe.

"Upstairs!" Connall snapped. "All of you, now."

Kaspar laid his hand on Jesska's chest. "You can calm this, baby. Try. Take a breath."

I can't.

"You can, sweetheart. I'm here. No one can hurt you. Breathe, baby."

Jesska shook her head, her panic overwhelming her.

"Breathe, baby."

She sucked in a short breath.

"That's it. Again," Kaspar encouraged.

Jesska took another breath, then another, until she was able to take in a deep one and let out a sigh of relief.

"Good, baby."

"What was that?" she whispered.

"You have the gift of prophetic empathy, elskan," Kaspar explained. "You can feel physically what will happen in the future."

"Then it's gonna be bad."

"That's how it seems." He stroked her hair. "Can you sit up?"

She nodded and pushed up from the couch. The doorbell pealed again.

"I need you to go upstairs, baby," Kaspar said.

Jesska nodded and rose to her feet. She headed out of the front room towards the stairs, but didn't quite make it. The front door exploded around her and she was dragged into the arms of someone incredibly strong. She let out a scream, but it was cut off by an arm around her neck. She was choking and gasping for breath as Kaspar ran toward her.

"I will kill her," the man snarled at Kaspar.

"Holy shite!" Kade snapped.

Kaspar focused on the man and swore.

"Father?" Kade asked.

"You're supposed to be dead," Brodie said.

Their father smiled. "Boys. It's wonderful to see you."

"Please let Jesska go," Connall said.

"No, Con. I need something from Kaspar, and she's going to help me get it."

Kaz?

It's okay, baby. I've got you.

Technically, he's *got me.*

"Release her," Kaspar demanded.

"What are you doing here?" Kade asked. "Where have you been for the last hundred and fifty years?"

"I will explain," Erik Gunnach said. "But for now, I need the girls."

"You will not get anywhere near my girls," Ari said with a scowl.

"I had them once," he said. "Alice stole them from me."

A feminine gasp was heard from upstairs, and then the temperature in the room dropped. Erik's arms were pried from Jesska's throat, and he was thrown to the ground. Jesska didn't take any time to be shocked or wonder what had just happened; she rushed for Kaspar. He pulled her into his arms and held her.

Erik writhed on the ground, his hands stretched out and his face turning red.

"Girls!" Ari bellowed up the stairs. "Enough!"

"How are they doing that?" Jesska asked.

"When they are together, they can do things we can't even fathom. This is apparently a quick and easy one."

Kade's head of security, Alasdair, rushed from the back of the house, Austri and Jóvin following, and secured Erik with handcuffs, sitting him in a metal chair Alasdair had dragged in from outside.

"Those won't hold, Ali," Kade said.

Alasdair held up his gloved hands. "They are covered in Red Fang."

"Good thinking."

Alasdair gave Kade a "ya think?" look as he carefully removed the gloves and pulled a syringe out of his pocket. "Backup if we need more."

Sophia came running down the stairs.

"Sophia, get back here," Megan called.

Sophia ignored her mother and rushed to Ari. "Did it work, Papa?"

He wrapped an arm around her shoulders and pulled her close, kissing the top of her head. "We'll discuss this later, elskan."

"But it worked, huh?" she pressed.

"Já, baby, it worked, but that doesn't mean you should have done it."

She ignored him, clapping her hands. "That's so awesome."

"Sophia," Megan hissed as she joined them. "Not cool."

The rest of the women filed in and Connall threw his hands up in frustration. "I did *not* say it was safe for you to come down!"

Pepper smiled, pushing up on her tiptoes to kiss his cheek, Cody firmly in her arms. "We just saved Jesska from possible death without even being in the room. No one's gonna be able to touch us if we're all together."

Connall scowled at his mate, and Jesska could see they were having some form of internal dialogue. Connall's face reddened as they continued to stare at each other. Finally, Pepper grinned and handed Cody to him. "Give your son a kiss."

"Austri, take Jesska back to the hotel," Kaspar directed.

"What? No. I want to stay here."

"We have work to do," he said. "And I want you safe."

Jesska pushed away from him. "I'm safer here with everyone."

"Kaspar, we'll take my father to our facility," Kade said. "You may come if you like."

Kaspar nodded. "Very well."

"I'd like some answers as well," Ari said.

Kade studied Ari for a few tense seconds before nodding.

"We'll load him," Alasdair said, and Kade nodded again.

"How long will you be gone?" Samantha asked Kade.

"I don't know, baby," he said and laid his hand on her expanding belly. "I'll come back as soon as I can."

She nodded and raised her head for a kiss.

After it was determined that Max, Niall, and Gunnar would stay behind, the rest of the men followed Kade from the house. Jóvin worked with one of Brodie's men to board up the broken front door.

Jesska sat with Megan and Sophia, while Pepper, Grace, Charlotte, and Samantha went about preparing food for the masses. Payton looked a little peaked, so with Brodie gone, Niall took on the role of fussing over her.

"Pay?" Niall said, and all focus turned to the pretty redhead.

She groaned and doubled over in pain.

"Contraction?" Fiona asked.

Payton nodded.

"Okay, love, let's get you upstairs," Fiona said. "Nye, can you take her?"

"What's wrong?" Sophia asked.

"She's in labor, honey," Megan said.

Niall helped Payton stand. "My water just broke," Payton said.

"Charlotte," he called, and scooped Payton into his arms and moved to the stairs.

"What's wrong?" Charlotte asked as she rushed from the kitchen.

"Payton's water broke. I'm going to get her comfortable, but I would imagine Brodie will be back shortly." He shifted Payton when she groaned. "Boil water and get towels or something."

Charlotte giggled. "Okay, babe, I'll get right on that."

"Nye, you jostlin' me is worse than walking. Put me down, Nye,' Payton demanded.

"No. I'm carrying you."

Payton groaned again and Fiona laid her hand on Niall's back, giving him a push up the stairs.

"Ladies, please let your mates know what's happening, and if Sam and Pepper could join me upstairs, that would be appreciated," Fiona said.

The threesome continued upstairs, and Pepper and Samantha followed shortly afterwards with ice sheets and towels.

"I feel like we're intruding," Jesska said.

"Don't worry," Grace assured her. "Seriously. You're part of the family. It's totally okay."

"What can we do to help?"

Grace rose to her feet. "Why don't we finish up with the food and watch for Brodie. He's going to be frantic when he can't get in the front door."

Grace wasn't kidding about Brodie. Jesska heard his yell all the way from the street and then he slammed the back door open, his face contorted in panic. "Where?" he bellowed.

"Upstairs, Brodie," Grace answered calmly. "Second door on the right."

Jesska had never seen a man move so quickly. She heard his footsteps pounding all the way up the stairs.

* * *

Brodie shoved the door open and he rushed to Payton's side. "Baby."

Payton smiled up at him. "I'm okay, love."

"You're in pain."

"I'm in labor, sweetheart. This is all normal."

He set his forehead against hers and stroked her cheek. Payton dropped her head back and whimpered as a contraction shot through her.

"Shite," he said.

"Brodie, we need to get her undressed," Pepper said. "But don't let go of her hand. You'll be able to help with the pain, okay?"

"I'll be outside," Niall said, and let himself out of the room, closing the door behind him.

Payton squeezed Brodie's hand when the contraction calmed. 'Brodie, love. Listen to Pepper."

He nodded and focused on Pepper.

"Okay, brother, we're going to get her undressed, okay?" Pepper said.

Brodie nodded and slipped Payton's shirt off over her head and then removed her bra, grasping her hand again as Samantha and Pepper took care of the rest.

"Let's get these pads under her," Samantha said, and Brodie helped lift her.

"We should get you to the hospital," Brodie said.

"She won't make it," Samantha said. "I've called Gillian, but if she doesn't make it in time, I'm quite capable to deliver the baby, hon. Don't worry."

Gillian was Payton's sister and one of the best OB/GYNs in the country.

Payton cried out again and Brodie scowled. "Do something! She's in pain!"

Pepper smiled. "Brodie, she's in labor. She's okay. Samantha's monitoring her. The baby's heartbeat is fine, right, Sam?"

Samantha slid her stethoscope back around her neck and nodded. "Perfect, Brod. They're both perfect."

Payton relaxed and licked her lips. "I'm okay, love."

"I'm going to check you, Payton," Samantha said, and leaned across the bed. "Aw, honey, you're ready. Next contraction, let's get ready to push."

"Is that too fast?" Brodie asked.

"No, she's doing great," Samantha assured him.

Payton giggled. "Baby, do I need to kick you out so us women can do the hard work?"

Brodie couldn't answer because another contraction hit.

"Okay, Payton, it's time to have this baby." Samantha smiled. "I need you to scoot to the edge of the bed. Can you do that?"

Payton shook her head.

"I'll help, love," Brodie said, and climbed onto the bed behind her, pushing her down the bed and settling her between his legs. He wrapped his arms around her and helped her sit up, bracing so that she could push against him.

"I can't," she rasped.

"Aye, you can, love. Come on. I've got you," he crooned.

The contraction hit and Payton cried out, but Brodie took the pain from her as she pushed.

"Good girl," Brodie said. "You're beautiful, sweetheart. Again."

"Head's crowning," Samantha said. "Push, Payton."

Three more pushes and Brodie and Payton's baby boy was born. Samantha settled him on Payton's chest and Payton leaned back against Brodie.

"Well done, beautiful girl," he said, his eyes filled with tears as he stroked his son's cheek. "I'm so amazed by you."

She smiled and kissed his chin.

"I'm going to check him really quick and clean him up," Samantha said, and took the baby from Payton. Once done, she handed him back and grinned. "He's perfect. You're already healing, so I'll get some scales and we'll see what your baby weighs. We'll give you some time, okay?"

"Thanks Sam," Payton said. "And you too, Pepper. I appreciate everything."

"Pepper leaned down and kissed her cheek. "Love you, sis."

"Love you too."

Samantha and Pepper left the couple to get to know their son.

* * *

Jesska pulled glasses from the cupboard and then opened the fridge and gathered various drinks. *You okay?*

Jesska smiled. *Yes. Some excitement here with Payton's water breaking.*

Can't wait until it's you.

Me too, baby. Everything okay with you?

Right now I'm waiting for Kade to finish. Lots of questions.

Jesska bit her lip. *Yeah, I bet.*

Plus, I need to beat the shit out of Erik for grabbing you.

She paused at the refrigerator. *Kaz. You don't. I'm fine.*

He put his hands on you, baby. No excuse for that.

Jesska sighed. *Okay, baby. Just don't kill him.*

No promises. Where's Gunnar?

Somewhere on the phone, I think. He's been there most of the time you've been gone.

He's sorting a few things out.

Jesska smiled. *Well, hopefully, he'll join us for dinner.*

He will. I have to go. I love you.

Love you too.

"Everything okay?" Grace asked.

Jesska rolled her eyes. "Yes. My hubby just seems to think that defending my honor is of the utmost importance."

Grace giggled. "Oh, yeah. They do. But that man did put his hands on you, so I don't blame Kaspar."

"I see you've drunk the Kool-Aid too, huh?"

Grace nodded. "Definitely."

Samantha and Pepper breezed into the kitchen, as did the group that had been waiting in the living room. "Well?" Grace prompted.

"Baby boy!" Pepper said, and clapped her hands.

"Aw, so sweet," Charlotte said, running her hands over her belly. "Perhaps I should start a marriage contract now."

"It's what royalty used to do, right?" Samantha said with a giggle.

"I get dibs on your first daughter, Grace," Pepper said.

"You got it," Grace said.

Charlotte grinned. "Well, the beauty of all of this is that we don't really have a say, huh? They will be with whoever is perfect for them."

"That's the most incredible part," Megan said. "With how much Ari and I lost, I'm amazed how quickly we have gotten back on track."

"What about me, Mom?" Sophia asked. "Will I have a forever mate?"

Jesska gasped. "Ooh, I wonder."

"I say yes," Charlotte said. "You're half Kalt Einn, sissy. I think it's likely."

Sophia blushed. "I love it when you call me sissy."

"Really? Vandi hates it! Which only makes me want to do it more." Charlotte giggled. "Gimme a hug, sissy."

Sophia laughed and wrapped her arms around Charlotte's waist.

"Let's eat," Grace said.

"I'll take something up to Brodie and Payton," Pepper said. "Sam, can you please check on Cody?"

"Of course."

Before anyone could move, Jesska saw two women walk by the back window.

"It's Kenna," Grace said. She set down the knife she was using to slice fruit and opened the back door.

Kenna McFadden was gorgeous, with a head full of glorious red curls, porcelain skin, and a smattering of freckles across her nose. She reminded Jesska of a live-action version of Merida from *Brave*.

Gillian resembled Kenna, but her hair was straight and cut into a bob that skimmed her jawline. She smiled, but Jesska got the impression that Gillian wasn't quite as easygoing as Kenna.

As the ladies walked from the kitchen into the front room, Gunnar emerged from a side door. Jesska watched his expression go from tight and irritated, to confused within a manner of seconds. "You okay?" Jesska asked.

"My mate is close."

"Seriously?"

He nodded and headed out of the kitchen. Jesska followed.

When Kenna saw Gunnar, her face went pink, and she gasped.

Grace turned to Jesska and Gunnar. "Gunnar, this is Kenna and Gillian. Payton's sisters."

Jesska shook their hands, as did Gunnar, however, he kept hold of Kenna's and she gave him a shy smile. "Hold that thought, love. I have to see my sister, but then you and I can talk."

Gunnar stared at her and nodded, releasing her hand.

Kenna followed Gillian upstairs, and Gunnar paced the foyer. Jesska watched him, fascinated by the change in his demeanor. He was settled somehow. He pulled his phone out of his pocket and appeared to text something, but then he slid it away and didn't reach for it again. Strange, considering it had been fused to his ear for the past three hours.

I feel your confusion. You okay?

Jesska smiled. *Fine. Just fascinated with watching your brother.*

Yes, he texted me. His mate has arrived.

That's what he said. This is so weird, Kaz. He's totally focused on her. Nothing else seems to matter.

Kaspar's chuckle sounded in her mind. *Nothing else* does *matter, elskan. Our mates are everything to us, baby.*

I'm beginning to see that. Jesska bit her lip. *I love you, Kaspar. In case I don't tell you enough.*

I love you too, baby. I'll show you how much later.

A shiver stole down her spine. *Can't wait.*

Kenna walked back down the stairs, pausing on the last step as Gunnar closed the distance between them. Jesska was transfixed by their interaction, but when he pulled Kenna in for a kiss, she had to turn away, voyeur not really her style.

She scurried back to the kitchen and helped Grace and the rest of the group finish up with food prep, making enough to feed a football team.

The group sat at the large dining table and spent the next hour getting to know one another. Jesska loved this new tribe of family. Gillian declared that Payton and the baby, Killian James, were perfectly healthy and would see everyone the next day. He'd weighed in at eleven pounds eleven ounces and was twenty-four inches long. In Payton's words, a moose. Jesska shuddered at the thought of giving birth to a baby so big, especially when she was informed that this was typical for the Kalt Einn.

Kenna and Gunnar had disappeared, and since the men had not returned, the rest of the group played a heated game of charades.

Jesska had never felt so connected and accepted and was a little saddened to think she'd be leaving them all in a few days for a whole new country. At least she'd have her sister and Sophia…that was a wonderful thought.

CHAPTER NINETEEN

JESSKA AWOKE TO warm, soft lips on her shoulder. "*Channing,* I told you my husband would be back soon and you were to disappear."

Kaspar chuckled, pulling her against him. She had fallen asleep in one of Pepper's many guest rooms because she didn't want to return to the hotel without Kaspar, and Pepper had offered a place for the night.

Jesska rolled to face him, checking for injuries.

"I'm fine, elskan," he said, leaning down to kiss her with a smile. "Do you want to know the details now, or can I sleep?"

"Neither."

"Oh?"

She smiled, pushing him onto his back and straddling him. "I will wait for details, but you're not going to sleep."

"We're in Connall's home."

"So?" she challenged.

Kaspar ran his hands along her thighs. "They will hear."

She leaned down and kissed his chest. "We'll be very quiet," she whispered.

"When are you ever quiet?"

Jesska lifted her head and raised an eyebrow. "Excuse me?"

He grinned. "I'm not complaining, baby. I'm simply pointing out that you're very vocal about what you enjoy."

"Well then you need to take care of me *and* figure out a way to keep me quiet."

"Challenge accepted," he quipped, and kissed her.

Once Kaspar succeeded in making love to his wife and keeping her from shouting the house down, he pulled her into his arms and ran his fingers along her naked hip.

"How did everything go?" she asked.

"Very tense, but I got several of the answers I wanted. Not so sure the brothers Gunnach did, however."

"What does their father want?"

"He wants to take down his wife."

"Why?"

"This whole mess started back in Iceland before Erik's clan was exiled. Erik and Alice, although married in the traditional human sense, were not mates. Before he was sent to Scotland, Erik found his true mate, a human. He bound her, and she gave birth to Brodie. Instead of telling anyone about his mate, he hid her because she was human, but took Brodie to be raised by their clan."

Jesska gasped. "How did he explain that?"

"He said Brodie was an orphan, but Alice knew the truth. Her response to his betrayal was to have an affair with a human man, and this produced Fiona."

"Oh, my word, it's like a soap opera."

Kaspar chuckled. "Very much so."

She settled her chin on his chest. "Is that why they were exiled?"

"Partly. Erik broke our laws by binding a human—"

"Which you have as well, may I point out—"

Kaspar grinned as he gave her bottom a gentle smack. "Let me finish."

Jesska giggled. "Sorry. Carry on."

"Erik had been planning a coup for a long time. He'd been watching and waiting and preparing, but what he didn't realize was that our people were far more loyal to my father than Erik knew. Even folks who told Erik they were with him continued to report back to my father about Erik's movements. In the end, my father had had enough, and Erik and anyone loyal to him were sent here. Erik arrived and claimed himself king, changed his name, and the Cauld Ane were born."

She scooted further up his body, kissing his neck. "Didn't Kade say something about his father being dead?"

Kaspar nodded. "Alice had him 'killed,' however, she didn't realize how loyal the people were to him. The ones she hired to commit the murder concocted this plan to fake his death until he could put an alternative plan into action. It took a little longer than he expected."

"How long?" she asked.

"Erik Gunnach's death certificate was issued in 1847."

Jesska sat up. "Shut up. Seriously?"

He pulled her back down. "Yes."

"Why did she want him dead?"

"Payback. From what I understand, Alice is a nasty, bitter woman, driven by her desire for revenge against the man who cheated on her."

"Well, I can kind of understand that," Jesska countered, her irritation rising. "I mean, not the actual going through with murder part, but *wanting* to, for sure. Can't you?"

"I'm not excusing him, baby. Personally, I've never understood someone marrying for any reason other than forever love, and joining with someone who isn't your mate is idiotic, but from all accounts, he was forced to marry."

"How could that happen with a race of people who know they're expected to mate to someone specifically?"

"Different time, sweetheart," he said. "I don't understand it either, and I don't think the order came from my father. Kade implied that his father may have been repaying a debt, but I'm not privy to exactly what happened."

"So many lies," she mused.

"Yes. He is not a good man." He kissed her forehead.

"So, what does he want with Sophia?"

"Erik's plan was to use the girls to take out Alice and her cohorts, believing Kade would have his back."

"And Kade didn't," she deduced.

"No. He didn't. Kade rules by honor, and he's been king for a long time. He's his own man and not someone to be manipulated."

Jesska raised her head. "Don't tell me you're growing fond of Kade Gunnach, Kaz."

He chuckled. "I have come to respect him, despite our beginning."

She kissed his chest. "I won't tell a soul."

"Thank you." He smiled.

"Was he the one who kidnapped Charlotte and Pepper?"

"No. But he knows who did."

"Who?"

"He won't tell us. His plan came together after he discovered their gifts. But he has a wide reach and managed to find enough people who were sympathetic to his cause, so someone within Erik's sphere of influence knows something. We just aren't sure what."

Jesska wrinkled her nose. "That's a little disconcerting."

"Yes," he agreed.

"How did you know to look for Megan and Sophia?" she asked.

"A woman came to warn me that they were in danger. I have since discovered she is Alice's sister, but they are estranged."

"Not so estranged that she didn't know what Alice did, it would appear."

Kaspar shook his head. "Edith only found out when Alice called for assistance after the Council had made the decision to incarcerate her. Apparently, Alice confessed part of the plan, which is why Edith felt the need to warn me. I am, after all, her king. She stayed in Iceland when Alice was exiled with Erik."

"And where's Edith now?"

"Safe."

"Safe where?"

"I have no idea. Austri took care of it so that I would have plausible deniability."

"It's that serious?" Jesska pressed. "That you can't know where she is?"

"It's that serious," he said. "But enough of this, baby. Home tomorrow."

Jesska bit her lip. "So soon?"

"We need to get back and deal with those who partnered with Erik," he said. "But we can return to Edinburgh as soon as these issues are taken care of."

"You just said you didn't know who partnered with Erik."

"I *don't* know."

"But you suspect," she said. "Kaz, what aren't you telling me?"

Kaspar shook his head.

"You're really not going to tell me?"

"I'm really not going to tell you," he confirmed. "I'm done with this touching you. I want to take you home. Ari and Megan will join us and stay until this is sorted, and then we are free to do whatever we like."

She sat up on her knees again and crossed her arms. "Are you getting all kingy on me?"

He sighed. "Jesska, this has nothing to do with my status as king. Outside of the fact you wouldn't know these people even if I told you who they were, I want you protected, and that includes protecting you from knowing things that might concern you or cause you worry."

"Kaz, I'm not a child. You don't have to protect me from worrying. You don't have too much control over that anyway."

"I know you're not a child, baby."

"Code for: I'm still not going to tell you anything."

He smiled.

"Will you tell me the story when it's done?"

Kaspar tugged on her arms, pulling her forward and on top of him. "I will tell you when it's done."

"This doesn't get you off the hook."

He rolled her onto her back, kissing her neck and running his hand over her hip. "It doesn't?"

"No, it doesn't."

He cupped her breast and she sucked in a deep breath.

"But maybe *that* does," she whispered.

Kaspar chuckled and distracted her from feeling slighted by keeping her extremely satisfied in other areas.

CHAPTER TWENTY

JESSKA'S FOCUS WAS on the view out the window of the family jet as they started their descent into Bíldudalur. For the most part, it looked like a dinky little town next to water. Very pretty, but quite sparse.

Kaspar's hand squeezing her thigh had her turning to face him. He smiled and linked his fingers with hers. "You wait."

"Hmm?"

"Our home is hidden, sweetheart. Just wait."

"I said nothing," she argued.

"I can read your thoughts."

"Dang it!" she ground out. "I forgot. I'm sorry, honey. I don't want to sound negative about your home. I'm sure it's lovely. I just don't see much in the way of...well...people. Lots of water and beautiful fjord-type water, but no people."

Kaspar laughed. "Our home."

"What's so funny over there?" Megan asked.

Megan, Sophia, and Ari were with them this time around. Gunnar chose to stay in Edinburgh with Kenna for a time.

"Jesska hates *our* home," Kaspar said.

She punched his arm. "I do not! Don't listen to him, Megan."

"Just wait, sister," Ari said. "You will be awed."

"See?" Kaspar said, and smiled.

"For the record," she said, squeezing his bicep, "I never said anything about hating anything."

Kaspar grinned as he kissed her. "I'm just busting your pork, baby."

Jesska laughed. "Chops, honey. You're busting my chops."

"*Yðar hátign, vinsamlegast undurbúðu þig fyrir lendingu,*" the captain said over the loudspeaker. (Your Majesty, please prepare for landing.)

Kaspar reached over to make sure Jesska was buckled and then kissed her before the plane landed smoothly and taxied to the tiny gate at the airstrip. Jesska's heart raced in excitement as they departed the plane and climbed into two awaiting SUVs. She and Kaspar in one; Ari, Megan, and Sophia in the other.

"Aren't they coming with us?" she asked.

"Yes, baby," Kaspar assured her. "They will be staying with us for a little while. Don't worry."

Jesska smiled and relaxed. The tiny fishing town really wasn't much to speak of, but she kept an open mind as the car pulled up to what looked like one-hundred-foot, solid-wood gates in the middle of a giant rock wall. The doors slowly slid open, and Jesska squeezed Kaspar's arm.

"I feel like I'm heading into *Jurassic Park* right now." She raised an eyebrow. "Please tell me you don't live on an island surrounded by dinosaurs. Those velociraptors were mean little suckers."

Kaspar laughed. "I don't know what *Jurassic Park* is or how it pertains, but we don't have any dinosaurs anywhere near our home."

Jesska's mouth dropped open. "You haven't seen *Jurassic Park*?"

"No. I don't know what it is."

She cocked her head. "It's a movie."

"Ah. I don't really watch movies. I suppose I enjoy the ones I see, but I haven't really considered it a priority."

"Not a priority?" She shook her head and tsked. "What about *Star Wars* or *Terminator? E.T.? Ghost? Saving Private Ryan?* Work with me here."

"I have seen *Star Wars* and *Terminator*, but the others I'm unfamiliar with."

"Oh, my word, baby, you and I are going to have to have the movie marathon to end all movie marathons."

He leaned over and kissed her cheek. "As long as said marathon happens while we're naked, I'm in."

"Well, duh," she retorted, and Kaspar laughed.

The car moved again, sliding through the gates and onto a paved road between sheer rock walls. The road was just wide enough for two cars to pass one another, but had no room for a shoulder. They arrived at another pair of gates, matching the first, and they opened to allow entry.

"No dinosaurs, right?" she joked.

Kaspar chuckled. "No dinosaurs."

The car traveled up, up, up, and the rock wall on her right slowly disappeared, and Jesska could see the water. A two-foot barrier kept the car from traveling over the edge of the cliff, while on the left, more rock wall was visible as they wound their way to what she was sure was a completely different hemisphere.

She shivered and scooted closer to Kaspar.

"You okay?" he asked.

She giggled. "Yes...my feet just feel nervous."

He chuckled and wrapped an arm around her waist, kissing her temple.

The car paused as a giant metal bridge lowered in front of them, and then they were moving again. She glanced behind her to see the bridge rise once the car with the rest of her family inside cleared it. Jesska faced forward again and her jaw dropped open at the magnificence of what she was seeing. A giant stone house appeared before her as though it had been built into the cliff. Four white-washed pillars sat proudly in front, obscuring a porch that ran the entire length of the house.

"Kaspar, it's gorgeous."

He beamed. "I'm glad you think so, elskan. I want you to be very happy here."

She stroked his cheek. "If you're here, I'll be happy."

Servants filed out of the house and stood side by side in front of the pillars.

"They are standing in order of rank," Kaspar explained, and smiled. "It will more than likely be overwhelming to figure out who everyone is at first, but they will help you."

Jesska nodded. "Is it okay to ask questions?"

"Of course." He raised an eyebrow. "Why would you think otherwise?"

She shrugged. "Too much *Downton Abbey*, I guess. They don't converse with their staff."

Kaspar chuckled. "You feel free to converse with anyone you wish."

"Thank you, my liege."

Austri pulled the car to a stop and then he and Jóvin jumped out of the front and opened the back doors for them. Jesska smiled as she slid from the car and waited for Kaspar to catch up to her. She gripped his hand and he lifted her fingers to his lips.

The line of staff members bowed or curtsied toward their king, and Kaspar greeted each of them by name. He settled his hand on Jesska's back and guided her toward each person.

A tall, thick-middled man with a receding gray hairline smiled kindly at Jesska as Kaspar guided her forward. "This is Eberg, sweetheart."

The man bowed, and Kaspar introduced her to the housekeeper, Elna. After that, Jesska couldn't keep all the names straight, but figured she'd learn them all eventually.

Ari introduced his family to a few of the servants he remembered and then the group moved into the large foyer of the mansion. The stone from the porch carried into the foyer, however it was intermixed with river rock. Staircases up each side of the wall met in the middle and created a landing overlooking the open space. To the left were tall double doors, and a matching pair to the right. She could see a music room behind the doors on the right—at least she assumed it was, as there was a grand piano inside. The room on the left had a few antique-looking sofas and chairs that she could see from her vantage point. She couldn't wait to explore the house.

Do you play?

I do. He smiled down at her. *However, Ari is far better than I am.*

Will he play for us later?

Kaspar wrapped an arm around her waist. *I'm sure he will if you desire it.*

"Please put my brother and his family in the West rooms," he said to Elna.

She curtsied and nodded, and Jesska watched as four housemaids scurried up the stairs.

Kaspar faced his brother. "We'll join you for dinner. Please make yourselves at home."

Shouldn't we spend time with them?

Kaspar gave her a gentle squeeze. *I have other plans, presently.*

Jesska grinned up at him before hugging her sister and her niece and following Kaspar up the east staircase and to the opposite side of the house from the rest of her family.

Kaspar showed her a few key rooms as they made their way to their suite of rooms. Jesska shook her head. "Babe, how big is this house?"

"Thirty-five thousand square feet, give or take."

"I'm going to need a map."

He pointed to antique knobs strategically placed along hallways and in rooms. "If you get turned around, press these, and someone will assist you."

"I'm sure that'll look really great. Your new wife calling for help because she's lost."

He stopped walking and cupped her cheeks. "They are here to help elskan. You don't have to feel weird about asking."

"Are you sure?"

Kaspar grinned and kissed her nose. "I'm sure, baby. Not that it matters, but they will love you."

"Why doesn't it matter?"

"Because you are their queen. I don't care if they like you, love you, are indifferent to you, but they will serve you and do it with a smile on their faces, or they will answer to me."

Jesska shivered. "Okay, baby, no need to go all alpha on me. I doubt there will be any issues."

He smiled and kissed her quickly. "Now, back to business. We have some christening to do."

She giggled and followed him through a set double doors—mahogany if she had to guess—and into a large sitting room with a flat-screen television above an ornate fireplace. Two overstuffed chairs and ottomans flanked a large window that looked out to manicured gardens, and she could see in the distance water of some kind. A sofa faced the television and fireplace, while a love seat sat against the wall, with a coffee table in front of it. The room was bigger than her living room at home, but just as cozy.

Through another set of mahogany doors was their bedroom. Possibly bigger than her entire duplex, it held a king-sized bed with a padded ice-blue, satin headboard that sat proudly between two windows. The down comforter, white and crisp against the blue, the sheets the same ice-blue as the headboard, and more pillows than she had on her own bed at home. "Kaz, this is amazing."

"You like it?"

She glanced up at him. "I love it." He relaxed, and she realized she hadn't noticed he'd been tense. "Were you worried?"

He smiled. "Not worried, per se. Just wondering if we were going to have to change everything again."

"You did this for me?"

"Of course, baby. I took photos of your home and sent them to Camilla, and she made a few suggestions."

Jesska slid her arms around his waist. "You must give that woman a hefty raise."

He chuckled. "If you love it, then I will."

"I *love* it."

Kaspar lifted her to his height and she wrapped her legs around him, kissing him as he carried her to the bed. He unbuttoned her blouse and spread it in order to kiss her belly, but before things could get interesting, her phone pealed in the silence. She slid it from the back pocket of her jeans.

"Hold that thought. It's my brother," she said, and answered. "Hi, Cam."

"Are you sitting down?" he asked.

She smiled. "In a manner of speaking."

"Jason's back in prison."

Jesska sat up, inadvertently shoving Kaspar off of her. "What?"

"Despite his lawyer's efforts, he refused to retract his confession. He admitted to everything, even that he'd planned the murder."

"What?" she snapped.

"He'd planned to kill Brady, but he'd had something else in mind. The stabbing part *wasn't* premeditated, but the murder was."

Jesska's eyes filled with tears as she slid off the bed. "What was the plan?"

"No."

"*Cameron*, what was the plan?"

"Put Kaspar on the phone."

"No! Damn it, Cameron, I swear to all that is holy, you better start talking, or I'm going to murder you in the face."

Before she could react, Kaspar pulled her phone from her hand and put it to his ear. "Cameron?"

Jesska slid to the floor, swallowing the bile that threatened to spill.

"You should have called me directly," Kaspar said into the phone.

Jesska tried to listen to Kaspar's thoughts, but either she was too upset and distracted to concentrate, or he was a master at blocking her.

"I understand," Kaspar continued. "No. Okay, thanks, that's some good news, I suppose. Yes. We'll talk later. 'Bye." Kaspar sat beside Jesska and pulled her onto his lap. "It's okay, elskan."

She buried her face in his neck and let a new wave of sadness wash over her. "I had no idea Jason hated Brady that much."

Kaspar slipped his hands into her hair and kissed her forehead.

"What was the plan?" she whispered.

"I think we should wait to discuss this."

"What was the plan, Kaz?"

He didn't say anything for several minutes. Just held her as he stroked her back.

"Tell me," she pressed.

"He had purchased a stun gun to incapacitate him, and had his father's rifle stowed in the trunk of his car. He'd planned to take him out to somewhere in a gorge—"

"*The* Gorge. It's beautiful, and somewhat remote."

Kaspar nodded. "That was the plan."

Jesska started to shake, but Kaspar pulled her closer and her shaking subsided. She tried to push away, but he just held her tighter. "We're going to stay right here, baby, until you're less shell-shocked."

"I'm okay."

He lifted her chin and frowned. "No, you're being brave. There's a difference."

She slid her arms around his waist and squeezed. "I can't get close enough."

"I know, baby."

"I need to be closer."

"I've got you, elskan," he pressed.

"You're not understanding," she said, and slid her hands under his shirt. "Make love to me. I need to be closer."

He stood with her in his arms and settled her back on the bed. "Are you sure?"

"Just shut up already and distract me," she demanded.

He obliged.

* * *

Jesska's body went rigid. She couldn't move, couldn't even blink. *Kaz?*

He didn't answer. She tried not to panic, but she felt like her body was in cement. She was paralyzed. *Kaz?*

And then yelling distracted her, particularly because it was a voice she recognized.

"What the hell are you doing, man?" Brady demanded.

"What do you mean?" Jason asked.

"You said you needed me to help you move the pool table to the basement. Why are we in the garage, and why do you have your dad's gun?"

"You were supposed to make this easy for me," Jason ground out.

"What was I supposed to make easy?" Brady asked.

Jason lifted the gun, but before he pulled the trigger, his face morphed into the face of a demon, and he laughed like the devil himself.

Then the deafening sound of a shot—

Jesska woke with a blood-curdling scream. One that even frightened herself. She kicked at her covers and tried to scramble off the bed. Kaspar was faster. He grabbed her around the waist and pulled her to him. "Shh, elskan, I've got you. It was a bad dream."

It took her a minute to realize where she was and then she turned and wrapped her arms around him, burying her face into his chest. "I was frozen, Kaspar. Couldn't move. Couldn't blink, and then Jason shot Brady. That's what the dream was about."

He stroked her hair. "I know, baby. It's over. He's never getting out. He can't hurt you anymore. And he can't hurt Brady."

"But if this is this empathy thing you told me I have, why would I be paralyzed?"

"I don't know, baby. But I'm here. No one can harm you."

She let Kaspar take the pain away and hold her until she could no longer keep her eyes open. Before she fully succumbed to sleep, though, she kissed his chin and whispered, "I love you."

"I love you too, baby."

CHAPTER TWENTY-ONE

JESSKA AWOKE TO an empty bed and sat up, her heart racing.

I'm downstairs, baby.

Why?

Because I have work to do.

Why didn't you wake me?

Because you needed to sleep.

"Next time, don't be so sweet," she said aloud.

He chuckled. *Take your time, baby. I'll have someone bring you breakfast.*

Where do you normally eat breakfast?

Typically in my office, unless I have guests. Ari and I ate together in the library this morning. Megan and Sophia were still sleeping.

Jesska climbed out of bed. *Maybe I should eat with them.*

Have you checked the time?

She grabbed her phone. Two p.m. *Babe, seriously, why didn't you wake me?*

Because you needed to sleep. Your body's getting used to the time difference.

Jesska smiled. *I'll shower and then I'll find my sister.*

What are you in the mood for?

She made her way into the bathroom. *Bacon, eggs, hash browns, orange juice, waffles, and coffee.*

It will be there when you get out of the shower.

I was kidding. She turned on the shower. *I can wait to eat.*

It will be there when you're done, baby. I have a conference call, gotta go.

Okay.

I love you.

Love you too. She undressed and slid into the shower, lingering because the cool water was far too delicious to interrupt.

She wrapped a towel around her head and then her body, applied lotion to her face and made her way back into the bedroom, letting out a surprised squeak to find a young woman standing by the bed. She was tall and thin, with dark-blonde hair pulled back into a tight bun at the nape of her neck, her dark blue uniform and crisp white apron something truly out of *Downton Abbey*, in Jesska's opinion.

"Your Majesty, I apologize," the woman said with a curtsy. "I didn't mean to startle you. I brought your meal."

Jesska saw that the table by the window had been moved from between the chairs, covered with a tablecloth, and was laden with covered plates.

"Wow, that's a lot of food."

"Yes, Your Majesty."

"What's your name?" Jesska asked.

"Gíta, your majesty."

Jesska smiled. "What a beautiful name."

"Thank you, Your Majesty."

"Would you feel comfortable calling me Jesska?"

Gíta met her eyes and shook her head.

Jesska sighed. "I didn't think so."

"I apologize." Gíta's face dropped, and Jesska internally berated herself.

"No. I'm sorry, Gíta," she rushed to say. "Ah, you feel free to call me whatever you feel comfortable with. It's just going to take me a little getting used to."

"Yes, Your Majesty."

"Okay, I'm just going to get dressed. I'm sure you have things you need to do, right?"

Gíta shook her head. "I'm your lady's maid, Your Majesty. I'm to serve you."

Kaspar, help.

What's wrong?

Gíta is in our room telling me she's supposed to serve me. What do I do?

His chuckled sounded. *You let her serve you.*

"Your Majesty?" Gíta said.

Kaz?

Baby, I'm on my call. I'll come up when I'm done.
No, I'll figure it out.

"Sorry, Gíta. Um, I'll just get dressed and then we'll talk about duties, okay?"

"Yes, Your Majesty. What would you like to wear today?"

"I can take care of that."

"It would be my pleasure, Your Majesty."

Jesska bit the inside of her cheek to keep from groaning out loud. "Jeans, the ones with the *s* on the back pockets, and the long-sleeved blue T-shirt."

"Anything else?"

Jesska felt the heat creep up her neck. "The underwear I'll handle."

"Yes, Your Majesty."

Jesska let out the quiet breath she didn't realize she was holding. The thought of someone choosing undies for her was a bit much. She figured Gíta probably picked up on that.

Jesska grabbed her unmentionables and slipped back into the bathroom. She brushed out her hair and then wrapped her towel back around her, even though she wasn't entirely naked, before heading back into the bedroom. She found Kaspar sitting at the table and pouring a cup of coffee. "Hi," she said.

"Hi." He rose to his feet and grinned. "Why are you in a towel?"

"Because I'm not an exhibitionist."

He laughed as she glanced around the room. "Gíta's gone?"

"Yes. I let her know we'd talk with her later," he said. "I'll also speak to the staff."

Jesska slipped the towel off. "I don't want to hurt her feelings, Kaz. But I have been dressing myself for as long as I can remember, and I like the idea of our room being just for us."

"You won't hurt her feelings, elskan." He pulled her into his arms and kissed her. "And I agree with keeping our suites private. Unless we're not in here or want room service. Deal?"

Jesska giggled. "Deal."

"Come and eat, sweetheart, and then we'll plan our day."

"Don't you have to work?"

"My work is done for now," he said. "I'm all yours."

"Yay." She grinned. "Okay, I'm starving. I'm assuming you'll be joining me, since there appears to be two of everything?"

"You're incredibly smart, elskan."

Jesska patted his bottom as she walked by him and sat at the table. He joined her and they took their time before joining Megan, Sophia, and Ari downstairs.

* * *

Jesska sat in the library with her laptop and signed off a Skipper call to Amanda. They'd talked for almost an hour, and it had been a much needed catch-up with her best friend. Ari had taken Megan and Sophia into "town"—the Kalt Einn town hidden in plain view behind Kaspar's home, not the tiny town they'd flown into.

Jesska had been surprised to find out that there were tunnels that led from their house to the fjord where they could travel by ferry—or boat if you had one, which Kaspar did—to the Kalt Einn village on an island not far from them. Outside of helicopters, there was no other air travel onto the island and, once on the island, there were no cars allowed. The most popular mode of transport was by horse and buggy. Megan, being a horse lover, jumped at the chance to visit, so Ari took them over early that morning. They planned to stay in the village all day, not returning until after dinner. Jesska had chosen to stay behind, wanting to experience it with Kaspar.

A knock at the door brought Camilla. "M'lady?"

"Hi, Camilla. Is everything okay?"

"Yes, m'lady. Elna was wondering if she might have a word with you."

Jesska stood and bit her lip. "Elna is the housekeeper, right?" she whispered.

Camilla smiled. "Yes, m'lady. His Highness asked me to assist you with a few logistics, if you are open to that."

"You mean helping me with what I'm supposed to do as Kaspar's mate?"

"Yes, m'lady."

Jesska let out a sigh of relief. "Oh, yes, please. That would be amazing. I have no idea what I'm doing."

"Follow me, m'lady, and I'll walk you through the basics."

Jesska grinned and flanked Camilla as they left the library.

"You have Eberg, who, as butler, is head of hiring and firing all staff. Then there's Elna, who is head of the female house staff, so in a sense she is Eberg's equal." Camilla smiled. "But don't tell him that. He likes to think he's in charge of everyone, including me."

Jesska giggled. "I won't tell a soul."

Camilla pushed a door to the side patio open and Jesska frowned. "Aren't we going to the kitchen?"

"No, m'lady."

Jesska felt a prick, and then she registered excruciating pain as her body crumpled to the ground.

Camilla knelt beside her and smiled. "I'm sure you're wondering what's going on, m'lady, so I'll give you an overview. As we speak, your sister and your niece are being taken to a secure facility in order to assist with our objective. You are needed to keep His Majesty in line. I apologize in advance, as the pain you're feeling isn't even the beginning, but be assured it will all be over shortly."

Kaz?

"And by the way, don't bother trying to contact His Majesty. He's dealing with something of the greatest importance. Far more important than you." Camilla glanced up and smiled again. "Jóvin, love. You're just in time."

Jesska felt tears leak down her face. Jóvin? The man she'd gone to bat for? The man she had trusted with her life and had fought with Kaspar over? Her heart broke. In a weird and naïve way, she had believed him to be her friend.

"What...what are you doing?" Camilla squeaked, and then Jesska heard nothing.

Jóvin appeared over her and gave her a sympathetic smile. "This is going to hurt, m'lady, I'm sorry."

Jesska's heart raced as he moved a pen-like device toward her. An EpiPen. That's what Kaspar had said. The antidote. Jóvin was helping her. She didn't get much further with her thoughts of relief. Fire swept her body as it contorted, and she cried out. Jóvin rolled her gently to her side, and she gasped for breath.

"I'm sorry, Jesska. You won't be in pain for long," Jóvin promised, and rubbed her back.

"Kaspar," she rasped.

"He'll be okay, m'lady. I felt it imperative to help you first."

"Where is he?" She pushed herself up.

"Austri has him." Jóvin made his way to Camilla, who was lying face up a few feet from Jesska, her body rigid.

"What do you mean Austri has him?" Jesska demanded. "What's going on?"

Before Jóvin could respond, Kaspar's bellow sounded as the side door slammed open, the glass in the windows shattering as the door hit the side of the house. Austri followed close behind.

Jesska was scooped up into Kaspar's arms and she pulled him close. I'm okay."

He kissed her hair before laying his hands on her face and studying her. "How much pain are you in?"

"Not much, Kaz. I'm okay."

"It's the Red Fang wearing off."

"I know, baby. Jóvin warned me." She cupped his chin. "Hey, I'm okay."

Kaspar glanced over at Jóvin. "Thank you."

"No time for that, Your Majesty," Jóvin said. "We need to find your brother."

Austri lifted Camilla from the ground, her body a floppy mess, and carried her inside. Much to Jesska's irritation, Kaspar wouldn't let her walk back inside, and insisted on carrying her. Arriving at the library, Austri set Camilla on one of the sofas and sat by her feet.

"Put me down, Kaspar. This is ridiculous," Jesska said.

He did, but he kept hold of her and pulled her close. She felt him waver, and gripped his waist. "Are you okay?"

He nodded.

"Sit down, Sire," Austri ordered. "I had to give you twice the antidote, and it's making you weak."

"I'm fine."

"Twice?" Jesska snapped. "You were dosed too?" At Kaspar's nod, she tugged him to one of the chairs and pushed him down. "Sit."

Kaspar frowned, but sat down, pulling Jesska onto his lap.

"Why did you have to give him twice the antidote, Austri?" Jesska asked.

He glanced at Kaspar and then back at her. "Because whoever dosed him, tried to kill him."

She gasped, her eyes filling with tears. "Why? Who are these people, and why do they want to hurt us?"

Kaspar's phone buzzed in his pocket, and he shifted so he could slide it out of his pocket to answer it. "Kade. Já. Já. We have her contained, but I don't know where my brother is currently. Skít. That's the connection. She's worked for me for fifty years. No, there was no warning. And Pepper and Charlotte? Okay. Thanks."

"What?" Jesska demanded.

"The woman who stole Ari's girls was Camilla's mother."

"What?" she said with a gasp. "Why?"

"If I'm correct, she was one of Alice's friends and supporters in the attempt on Erik's life. That's all I know at the moment."

"Are Pepper and Charlotte okay?"

"Yes, baby. Connall and Niall have them safely ensconced at home."

"Where is Camilla's mother?" Jesska asked.

"Kade has her."

"And what is he going to do with her?"

"Baby, please, just give me a minute to think," Kaspar snapped.

"Don't get all pissy with me," she snapped back, and rose to her feet. "I'm just trying to figure this out."

Dizziness washed over her, but before Kaspar could grab for her, Jóvin grasped her arms and steadied her. "Easy, m'lady. The antidote's still working its way through your system. You need to sit down."

Kaspar held his hand out to her. "I'm sorry, sweetheart."

Jesska took his hand and let him pull her back down, but she shifted so her bottom was on the cushion, rather than his lap. He wrapped his arm around her and settled her against him, kissing her temple.

"This is what I dreamed," she whispered.

"Yes, elskan."

"I don't think I like this gift."

Kaspar gave her a gentle smile. "I don't think I do either."

"Kaspar!" Ari called, his voice frantic.

"I'll get him," Jóvin said, and stepped out of the library.

Ari, Megan, and Sophia rushed into the room, and Jesska stood to give her sister and niece a hug. Kaspar pushed out of his seat as well, but Jesska insisted he sit back down. His face was ashen, and he didn't look steady.

"You're okay?" Ari said.

"Yes, fine. How did you know to come back?" Kaspar asked.

"Sophia picked up on something on the boat," Ari said.

Jesska looked at her niece, who blushed.

"It was nothing, Papa," she said.

"It wasn't nothing, elskan. You listened to your gift and told me. I'm very proud of you."

Sophia lowered her head, but not before she grinned.

"What's her gift?" Jesska asked.

"She can tell just by looking at someone, their intention. Whether it be good, bad, or neutral," Ari said.

"Well, that's kind of a nifty trick."

Sophia giggled.

"Sophia got a weird vibe from one of the crew," Megan explained. "She came to us right away, and as Ari will be less than willing to tell you, he listened to Sophia, something not a lot of people would have done. When the woman was detained, they found several doses of Red Fang on her. What she was trying to do or how she expected to get away with any of it is still a mystery."

"Where's the woman now?" Kaspar asked.

"Dreki has her under control," Ari said, referring to his head guard. He stepped over to Kaspar and frowned. "You don't look well, brother."

"I'm fine."

"You're hot, babe," Jesska said, and felt his forehead. "And you're so pale."

"Get him on the floor," Ari demanded.

Jesska jumped up. "What's going on?"

"Red Fang poisoning," Austri said. "The antidote's working against his body now, instead of helping."

Ari and Austri positioned Kaspar on the floor as Jóvin pushed one of the buttons for the staff. Eberg arrived, his face falling at the sight of his king on the ground.

"We need ice sheets, buckets of ice, and towels, Eberg," Jóvin demanded. "Quickly."

Jesska knelt beside Kaspar and forced her worry aside. "What can I do?"

Ari knelt on the opposite side of Kaspar and motioned to Sophia. "I need you to push the poison from his body, elskan."

"How?" Sophia asked.

"This has to be a group effort," Ari said as he positioned Sophia at Kaspar's head. "Jesska, your hand over his heart."

Jesska nodded and slipped her hand under his shirt, flattening her palm over Kaspar's heart. Ari took one of Kaspar's hands and held it between his.

"Sophia, you will need to lay your fingers on his temples. You need to imagine yourself forcing the poison down, does that make sense?"

"Yes, Papa," she said.

"Good girl." He glanced up at Megan. "I need you to wrap your arms around my waist."

Megan frowned. "I thought I couldn't help without a blood bond."

"That part's for me," he admitted. "But you will be able to help a little, sweetheart, because we are bonded, so you aren't without power."

Megan did as she was instructed and Jesska watched in amazement at her young niece, who inherently seemed to know exactly what to do. Sophia's eyes were closed and her fingers were still at first, and then they began to move gently against Kaspar's temples. His color was returning, the ashy gray turning to flesh color again. Jesska felt his heartbeat change from labored to steady under her hand. She leaned down and kissed his cheek, whispering, "That's it, baby. Please be okay."

"Perfect, angel," Ari encouraged. "You're almost there."

"She doesn't look good," Megan said.

"It's okay, baby. She's taking in some of the poison, but it won't stay."

Megan swore. "You said *nothing* about her taking in poison!"

"Mom, shush," Sophia demanded. "I can't do this and worry about you melting down at the same time."

Jesska glanced at Megan, her sister's face contorted in worry towards her daughter, and pure, unadulterated rage toward Ari. This was going to be a fun evening.

Kaspar coughed, then again, then continued to cough as Ari rolled him on his side. "Stay connected, elskan," he directed Sophia, who set her fingers back on Kaspar's temples.

"I'm okay," Kaspar rasped. He reached for Jesska's hand, pulling it from his chest and kissing her palm. "I'm fine, baby."

Sophia sat back and Kaspar rose to his feet, Ari standing with him, his hand on his shoulder. "You look better."

"I'm fine," Kaspar assured him, and then turned to Sophia and pulled her against him, kissing her crown. "Thank you, sweetheart."

She wrapped her arms around his waist. "You're welcome."

Kaspar cupped her cheeks. "Are you weak?"

Sophia shook her head. "No, I'm fine."

He smiled, stroking her face. "You rest, elskan. Sit down."

Sophia rolled her eyes. "I'm totally fine."

"No arguments," Megan demanded, reaching for her daughter. "Upstairs."

"*Mom.*"

"Now, young lady."

"Go, angel," Ari said. "I'll be up in a bit."

"You." Megan jabbed a finger toward him. "I will deal with later."

Ari grinned. "I look forward to it."

With one last scowl, Megan ushered Sophia from the library. Camilla appeared to be coming out of her paralyzed state, but Austri and Jóvin were quick to cover her with a blanket of some form. Jesska noticed the men had gloves on and were careful not to touch the fabric with any other part of their bodies.

"The blanket is covered in Red Fang," Kaspar explained. "It will keep her still, but won't take her ability to speak away."

Jesska nodded with a yawn.

"Why don't you rest, baby," Kaspar said. "Ari and I need to deal with this for now, but you're still working out the antidote, which will make you sleepy for a time."

"What about you?"

"I'm fine, sweetheart."

"I don't want to be alone," she whispered. "What if there are others?"

"There aren't," Jóvin said immediately. "I have been watching her, m'lady. She thought I was her ally, but as you can see, I wasn't. Austri and I have eliminated the threat."

Kaspar nodded. "Jóvin will walk you to our room. Lock the door, sweetheart, and I'll be there soon."

She forced back tears. "Are you sure?"

He smiled, leaning down to kiss her gently. "I'm sure."

"Can I please stay?"

"I'd feel more comfortable if you rested."

"M'lady, I will take you to your rooms and stay close," Jóvin said. "You'll be safe."

"What about Kaspar?"

"I have his back, m'lady," Austri answered.

She stared up at Kaspar. "Are you sure?"

He smiled. "Baby, I'm sure."

Kaspar kissed her again, and Jesska reluctantly followed Jóvin from the library and up the stairs. She made it to the halfway point and had to stop. "My legs feel like jelly."

"That's the antidote," Jóvin said. "You'll feel fine in a few hours."

She slid to her bottom, keeping hold of the handrail. "I just need a minute."

Jóvin hunkered down beside her. "Will you allow me to help?"

"How?"

"I will act as a crutch."

Jesska bit her lip. "Okay. Yes. Thank you."

He wrapped an arm around her waist, guiding her arm around his neck. "Ready?"

Jesska nodded and forced herself to her feet. In the end, Jóvin had to carry her to her suite, setting her on the sofa in the sitting room. Kaspar had given strict instructions that their bedroom was off-limits to anyone but them. Apparently, that meant his security as well.

Jesska couldn't keep her eyes open.

"Rest, m'lady. I'll stay here with you."

She nodded and curled into the sofa.

CHAPTER TWENTY-TWO

STRONG ARMS PULLED Jesska close as she was lifted and her cheek was kissed. "It's me, baby," Kaspar whispered.

Jesska sighed, forcing her eyes open and smiling. "I was a little concerned that Jóvin might have decided to take a few liberties."

"If he had, he'd be dead."

"I was joking."

Kaspar closed his eyes for a second after he set her on their mattress.

"Are you okay?" she asked.

"Yes."

"Why am I not convinced?"

Kaspar pulled his shirt over his head and walked into the bathroom. "Everything is dealt with, sweetheart."

She slid from the bed and headed to the bathroom. "What does that mean?"

"Come take a shower with me and then we'll talk in bed."

"Or we could talk in the tub," she suggested.

Kaspar gave her a tired smile. "Even better."

Jesska plugged the bath and started the water before staring at her mate. "You look exhausted, baby."

He sighed. "I am."

"Because of the Red Fang?"

"All of it, baby." He dragged his hands through his hair. "It's just been a skit day."

"Kaz." She slid her hands up his chest and looped them behind his neck. "Are. You. Okay?"

He smiled again. "I'm fine now, baby. All is done."

She rubbed her forehead.

"What?" Kaspar asked.

"I think I need to tell you something."

"What?" he pressed, his tone one of suspicion.

"It's your birthday in a week."

"I'm aware."

She sighed. "I kind of planned a party."

He raised an eyebrow. "You did?"

She nodded. "We have thirty people descending on our home in two days. Gunnar helped me organize it."

Kaspar laughed. "Are you serious?"

"Yes. I'm sorry, babe. I'll call everyone and cancel. It's just not a good time."

He shook his head. "No. I'll be fine. I just need a little time to process everything. It won't take long."

"Good. You can start your processing by telling me about everything that happened, and then we can christen the tub."

Kaspar chuckled. "I don't know if I have the energy to talk and christen, honestly."

Jesska gasped. "Don't tell me my virile, albeit, very old man, is fading on me."

"I just need to get my second wind."

She grinned. "I can help with that."

"Oh, really?"

"Yep. Consider me the wind beneath your wings."

Kaspar laughed. "If I were a bird, I would be grateful."

Jesska giggled. "It's an old song. Bette Midler did a cover. How and why I know that, I haven't got a clue."

"Your mind is like a steel trap, elskan. You never cease to amaze me." Kaspar removed the rest of his clothes and stepped into the bath, holding his hand out to her.

Jesska undressed and climbed in with him, settling herself between his legs, her back to his chest. "So, what happened?"

"Camilla was loyal to Alice, and Camilla was the one who found someone to hide the girls when they were taken."

Jesska stretched her neck to look at him. "But no one seemed to know where they were."

Kaspar nodded. "That's because the woman who warned me was the one who stopped Sophia being taken, and apparently, there was another nurse before her who had stepped in on behalf of Pepper. After that, the information gets fuzzy, because the original nurse is dead. But it would seem she was able to use her gift of manipulation to get Pepper out of Iceland at about the time Charlotte was born. She brought them to the States, and Pepper was given to a childless couple, while Charlotte was given to the Whitmores, who'd lost their child at birth."

Jesska whistled. "The logistics of all of that."

"I know. And it all started because two people were at war with one another. All those lives destroyed and interrupted for revenge."

"Total *War of the Roses* kind of thing."

"Yes."

"What will happen with Camilla?"

"She will be exiled somewhere she can't hurt anyone ever again. Along with anyone else attached to her and this scheme. Erik is being dealt with on Kade's end, and I have a sneaky suspicion he'll be sent to wherever Alice is."

Jesska giggled. "Poetic justice, considering they were each just as bad as the other. Cheating to get back at someone for cheating is stupid."

"Yes." He sighed. "I will have to find a new assistant, which will take some time."

"What about Camilla's assistant?"

He shook his head. "She knew what Camilla was doing and didn't say a word."

"See? Bitches be loco," Jesska said.

Kaspar grimaced. "Perhaps I should hire a man next."

Jesska smiled. "I could do it."

"I'm sorry?"

"I've been an administrative assistant for several types of executives for a while now." She looked up at him. "And who better than someone you know will always be loyal? 'Hire for attitude, train for skill' is my motto."

"You would want to do that? Work for me? It's a demanding job, and not without stress."

She shrugged. "Why not? You can help me figure things out, and I can yell at you if you're mean."

He chuckled. "I'll think about it."

"You'll *think* about it?" Jesska turned to face him. "What's there to think about?"

"Well, for one, my new assistant is going to need a certain skill set that I've never taken advantage of before."

"Oh, really? And what would that entail?"

He followed a drop of water with his finger as it trailed between her breasts. "She may be required to partake in meetings while in the nude."

"Why, sir, that is sexual harassment," she said in a deep, southern voice.

"If you're lucky," he retorted, shifting her so she straddled him.

"I will need to discuss your conduct with human resources."

He kissed her neck, running his hands down her back. "I *am* human resources."

She licked her lips and hummed in bliss. "I take it you've gotten your second wind."

"And third," he said, and proceeded to show her just how awake he was.

* * *

Jesska curled herself closer to Kaspar as he slept beside her, his even breathing finally indicating he was relaxed. She couldn't believe how quickly her life had gone from sadness to joy. The man who'd changed everything for her was more than she could have ever asked for or imagined.

She smiled, kissing his chest and wrapping an arm around his waist. Before she succumbed to sleep, she sent up a quick prayer of thanks for the man who'd helped her live again.

I was born and raised in New Zealand. With an American father, Scottish grandmother, and Kiwi mother, it's no doubt I have a unique personality.

After pursuing my American roots and disappearing into my time travel series, The Civil War Brides, I thought I'd explore the Scottish side of my family. I have loved delving into the Cauld Ane's and all their abilities…I hope you do too.

I've been happily married and gooey in love with my husband for twenty years. We live in the Pacific Northwest with our two sons.

I hope you've enjoyed **Bound by Tears**
For other titles in the Cauld Ane Series,
or to learn about The Civil War Brides Series, please visit:
www.traceyjanejackson.com

Find me on Facebook, too!
www.facebook.com/traceyjanejackson

Made in the USA
Middletown, DE
30 July 2016